Wu's Byte

A Mary Jo Thibodaux Novel

Thomas R. Lawrence

Also by Thomas R. Lawrence:

Delta Days, Tales of the Mississippi Delta

Cow College, Tales of Mississippi State College

will d...a life in science

My Magic Year

Jake's Revenge

The Queen's Captain

A Good Tale Well Told

Front Porch Press, LLC
Publishers
4881 Canada Road
Lakeland, Tennessee 38002

Library of Congress Cataloging-in-Publication Data
ISBN Print 978-0-9978114-1-4
E-Book 978-0-9978114-2-1

ACKNOWLEDGMENTS

Special Thanks to the Following:

My companion, Clista Haley, for providing her support, encouragement, and honest feedback throughout my writing.

My copy editor, Maggie Lee, for her final edits of the book.

My business partner, Deborah Fagan Carpenter, for performing the first edits, designing the cover, formatting the book, and executing all production.

For my grandchildren,

Jackson, Virginia, Ava, and Abby

INTRODUCTION

Tom Lawrence was a man whose essence was built on complexities. He was brilliant on multiple levels, outspoken and argumentative on most topics, humane to a fault, quietly generous, and a loyal friend to many. He was an avid reader who spent most of his adult life wanting to turn the wealth of information he had accumulated into engaging fiction.

Before his passing in March of 2017, Tom devoted every available moment to his passion for writing. He got his feet wet producing occasionally outrageous autobiographical short stories chronicling his childhood and college life, but all of his early writing led to his ultimate goal of creating fiction. It was fascinating to watch his literary growth, and intriguing to see how he was able to weave seven decades of information gathered through education and personal experience into entertaining narrative. Tom loved a good tête-à-tête, and he channeled that knack into delivering credible dialogue.

Tom had a deep respect for the military, a great regard for strong-willed women, and a predilection toward good overcoming evil. Not surprisingly, he conceived a protagonist for three of his novels who is a beautiful, smart, female ex-military intelligence officer who can, and often does, confront and annihilate the bad guys. Mary Jo Thibodaux, well-regarded by her peers, both male and female, is not only brilliant, able, and willing to take on any challenge, but she also suffers no idiots or bullies. She lives a life that anyone reading her escapades will find enviable. I have little doubt that Tom would have enjoyed being her male equivalent.

— Deborah Fagan Carpenter

ONE

ALAN BROOKS SLOUCHED on an uncomfortable wooden chair in the corridor of Tant Hall, the administration building at West Texas State University. Floor-to-ceiling windows allowed the superheated summer air in, and, along with the heat, came a variety of flying insects, the smell of smoldering vegetation, and baked dirt. There was a heap of baked dirt and damn little vegetation — smoldering or otherwise — in West Texas.

The heat didn't much bother Alan. He was a fifth-generation Texan, born and raised on his family's ranch, 15 miles west of Pecos Springs. He had also served two tours in Iraq and one in Afghanistan as an officer in the Marine Corps, and later as a Navy SEAL. Both places reminded him of home. Today, he was waiting to be summoned into the holiest of holies by the West Texas State University Tenure Committee. His future as a professor of Electrical Engineering would be decided by three of his peers.

"Peers, my ass. I hope to *God* these misfits aren't my peers."

The tenure committee was chaired by the university's Provost, who held a Ph.D. in abnormal psychology, which may have been the perfect field of study to deal with the zoo that was disguised as a university faculty. The Provost kept his job by making sure he avoided any unpleasantness or controversy. Alan knew he'd check out the way the wind was blowing and cast his vote accordingly.

The second member of the committee was the Dean of Women's Studies — whatever in the hell that was supposed to be. Alan had a suspicion that at one time it had been called Home Economics but had wisely kept that observation to himself. Dr. Marge Kemp was known to believe that all men were Neanderthals and would love to have them all exterminated. Her concept of procreation could not quite work with the idea of the male's participation. Alan couldn't imagine that she'd support his request.

The final member was Dr. Phinias Millsap, Dean of Academics, who was head of the faculty antiwar coalition, and an outspoken advocate of abolishing R.O.T.C. His would be the deciding vote. All in all, it didn't look good.

Alan was ambivalent himself. On one hand, he hated to lose any contest and would try to sway the committee's decision in his direction, but, in truth, the life of an academic didn't really appeal to him. He had a project that had captured his interest and fired up his imagination, and he'd like to spend full time working on it. A traditional teaching, writing, and research load would make that impossible.

In the end, he decided to go through the motions, out of respect and affection for his old teacher and mentor, Dr. Ellis Fields, Dean of Engineering. Dr. Fields had written a recommendation, which, had it been a military efficiency report, would probably have resulted in instant flag rank.

Dr. Fields had lured Alan into Electrical Engineering in his freshman year at WTSU and had nurtured his progress to his masters from Stanford and his Ph.D. from M.I.T. It was Field's plan for Alan to succeed him as Dean of Engineering. For Alan's part, it was a chance to return to West Texas to take over the family ranch, after the death of his parents.

The door opposite Alan's chair creaked open, and the bird-like figure of the Provost signaled that he should enter the inner sanctum to ascertain his fate. The large room had been set up for oral exams, with a long table sitting on a foot-high raised platform. The three members of the tenure committee sat behind the table, and Alan was guided to a lone wooden chair that faced them.

The Provost opened the discussion. "Please state your whole name for the record."

"Alan Prescott Brooks," Alan replied.

The Provost continued, "Dr. Brooks, what business do you have before this committee today?"

"Good Lord, don't you people have an agenda in front of you? Why do you think I'm here...to apply for a parking permit?" Alan's not-so-well-hidden hostility had overcome him, and the words had just slipped out.

"Yes, we have an agenda, and you are the last item to be dealt with. Incidentally, you might want to answer our questions in a civil manner, no matter how inane they may seem to be."

"I'll certainly try, no matter how inane."

"Very well, with your permission, we shall continue this meeting of the West Texas State University Tenure Committee. The last item on today's agenda is to rule on a request for tenure by Dr. Alan Brooks of the School of Engineering. The floor is now open for the members to examine Dr. Brooks."

Dr. Kemp asked, "Dr. Brooks, would you please give us a short summation of your academic credentials?"

"I have a B.S. in Electrical Engineering from West Texas State University, 1986; an M.S. in Electronics, Stanford University, 2003; and a Ph.D. in Applied Engineering, Massachusetts Institute of Technology, 2005."

Dr. Millsap asked, "I notice there is quite a gap between your bachelor's degree and your master's. Were you teaching during this period?"

"No, I was on active duty as an officer in the United States Marine Corps."

Millsap followed up: "Were you assigned as an engineering officer during your active service?"

"No, I was an infantry officer for both tours in Iraq, first as a platoon leader, and finally as a company commander. In Afghanistan, I served as a special operations officer with the SEALs."

"Did your duties in either capacity put you in the position of killing and maiming innocent civilians?"

"The rules of engagement imposed almost impossible restrictions to prevent civilian casualties, but there were occasions of collateral damage suffered by the local population."

"So, you admit to killing innocent Iraqis and Afghans?"

"Dr. Millsap, this line of questioning seems totally irrelevant to the issue of my academic tenure. Not one of the three of you has any concept of military operations, and I have no intention of answering further questions of this nature."

13

"Further questions will not be necessary; I believe we've established the truth," replied Millsap.

"Since the previous line of questioning seems to have made you both uncomfortable and hostile, I'd like to move on to your academic qualifications," said Kemp. "Have you acquired any academic credits in the area of female exploitation and mistreatment?"

"To my knowledge, these topics were never part of the Engineering curriculum at this or any other university. So, the answer is no; I have not. However, as part of my training in the Marine Corps, I completed the necessary courses in gender sensitivity and workplace behavior. I served successfully with women, both as superior officers and as subordinates. I have nothing but the greatest respect for women, particularly those who are defending this country."

"I believe this type of woman to be a traitor to her gender, and, as such, I hold them in abject contempt," Kemp muttered.

"Thanks for sharing your opinion," Alan snapped.

Aware that an explosive atmosphere was building, the Provost immediately sought to defuse it. "Dr. Brooks, we have a complete record of your academic and publishing history, and, if there are no more questions from the committee, I move that we retire into executive session for the next 15 minutes. We'll ask you, Dr. Brooks, to resume your seat outside this room, and you'll be informed of our decision shortly. Thank you for your cooperation and candor."

Alan returned to the corridor and reoccupied his seat in the uncomfortable, wooden chair. His contempt for the panel and the procedure had certainly not been masked, and it had been all he could do to keep his tongue during the preceding farce. Now, removed from the inquisition, he was boiling with anger. The thought of working in this atmosphere for the rest of his career sickened him, and his course of action was suddenly clear as day. He was lost in thought when the door opened, and the Provost invited him back into the room. He returned to the lone seat and looked intently at the committee.

"This committee has carefully reviewed your qualifications for a grant of tenure. There is no question regarding your academic qualifications. However, there has been serious concern raised about your ability to impart a modern and politically correct attitude to the young minds to be placed in your care." There were nods of agreement from the other two members, and the Provost continued. "Is there anything that you would like to say in rebuttal, Dr. Brooks?"

With no hesitation, Alan replied, "Tenure is the Holy Grail of an academic career and, as such, is much desired. At this moment I am reminded of something a great academic leader told me. Dr. Henry Britt, President of M.I.T., once asked a group of graduate students if they understood why faculty politics were so vicious. We all said that we didn't know the answer, and he replied, 'Because so little is at stake.'"

A look of puzzled concern swept the panel, and Alan continued. "I do not want to spend the rest of my productive years in a profession that is focused on the inane and pointless. I do not want to end up like the members of this panel: twisted, bitter, and living with so little at stake. After due consideration, I've decided to withdraw my application for tenure and also to resign my position with this university. I intend to spend the rest of my life in a more productive manner, but I thank you for your time and attention." With that, he stood, stepped off the platform, and left the room without looking behind him.

In the light of day outside the building, the question of what in the hell Alan would tell Dr. Fields hit him. He knew Fields would be disappointed, but the deed was done now, and the outcome was final. On his walk across the green irrigated lawns of the campus, Alan once again marveled at the miracle that took place when West Texas scrubland was given just a little moisture. By the time he arrived at his third-floor office in the Engineering building, he had made two decisions. He would be honest with Dr. Fields, and he would immediately begin work on his project — let the chips fall where they may.

The first thing Alan did was pick up the phone and call Fields' office. When Fields answered, Alan said, "Dr. Fields, this is Alan."

"Great, Alan. How'd it go?"

"Well, I guess there's good news and bad news. The bad news is that I turned down tenure, and the good news is that I've decided to tender my resignation."

There was a long, silent pause in the conversation, and, finally, Fields said, "It's interesting that you chose those particular words. Don't you move! I'm coming up to get this firsthand. DO NOT LEAVE! I'M ON MY WAY!"

In record time, Ellis Fields burst through Alan's office door like he'd been fired from a cannon. He was a tall, thin man, with a wispy halo of gray hair. When excited, he tended to pace the floor and speak in a staccato burst of words, accented by vigorous gestures with his arms and hands. He was clearly overwrought today, and he launched into his soliloquy without preamble. "Alan, I've known you long enough to be aware that you think before you act. Ergo, I assume that you've given this decision careful consideration and have arrived at this turning point in your career with confidence and certainty. That said, *what in the hell were you thinking*?"

"*Thinking* may not be the exact word I'd choose. It was more like what in the hell was I *feeling*. The truth is, I've been *suffocating* while pondering the whole concept of spending the rest of my life teaching and doing research, and the jury just happened to come in this morning."

Fields asked curtly, "You know my stance here, so I'm not going to try to change your mind, but can I safely assume that you have an alternative career path plotted?"

Alan thought for a moment before deciding to share at least the basic outline of the scheme he had planned. "Well, sir, it may be a little early to say that I've exactly plotted it out, but, yes, I have a firm *idea* of what I want to do. You may or may not remember, but I've always been an active securities trader, and, frankly, I've done rather well at it. For the last few years, I've been working persistently on a trading theory, which I believe I can turn into a full-time, *highly* profitable endeavor. I want to spend the next few months testing and perfecting the concept, and then get it into action as soon as possible."

Fields had calmed down considerably, and he'd finally taken a seat. At Alan's mention of a securities trading model, he sat up straight, and it was clear his interest had been piqued. "Yes, I knew you had traded some over the years. There's obviously money to be made in securities, but what makes you think you're proficient and knowledgeable enough to make it worthwhile long-term?"

"Well, I believe I've stumbled on something no one else ever has," Alan replied decisively, although the response was not entirely factual. He watched as Fields raised a surprised, if not skeptical, eyebrow after hearing this bold declaration. "Look, Dr. Fields, ultimately, I want to contribute something *positive* to society. If I'm successful in putting this strategy into action, I'll be in a position to do just that. If this system proves to be half as lucrative as I think it will, then I'll be able to create enough *free* capital to support research in the areas of clean, cheap energy, *and* abundant, clean water."

"That's a pretty ambitious agenda, Alan. An achievement of that magnitude would shake the very foundations of the world. Were you to achieve either, it would have game-changing effects in multiple areas: business, science, politics — at the very least. That's quite an order for a humble electrical engineer in the backwaters of West Texas. Don't get me wrong...I have great respect for your technical and intellectual gifts, but I think you've taken complete leave of your senses!"

"Probably so, but, as of this morning, I've burned my boats on the beach, and I don't have a way to retreat, so I guess I'd better get about making this plan work. One thing's for sure: I'll have to get my (yet to be proven) trading method up and running because there's no other way I can afford the research."

"Do you actually think you have a technique that can consistently provide that kind of revenue? Implementing a plan to tackle any *one* of the enormous problems you're considering will be financially astronomical. I don't have any idea what you think this is going to cost, but a *ton* might be low-balling it. Maybe you should consider taking in some investors as a backup plan. As your friend, I might be willing to take a small flyer with you."

"Your confidence and support mean the world to me, sir, but I'm well aware of the risks of what I'm proposing. I couldn't, in good conscience, allow anyone else to gamble their hard-earned capital on such an unproven and complicated long shot. This is something I'll have to finance with my own funds...in which event, if it doesn't work, then it'll only harm me."

"Very well, but my offer's there if you need it. I won't kid you or myself, Alan. I'm *enormously* disappointed that you've chosen to abandon your teaching career. I think that, in time, you would have been one of the best in our field, and, God knows, we need people like you. I also know, however, that you need to put your energy into something about which you're passionate. Look, I need to get back to my office to prepare for my next class, so I'll leave you to think through your scheme."

Fields turned, started walking toward the door, paused, and looked back. *"I hope the hell you know what you're doing!"*

TWO

NOT ONLY WAS ALAN NOT SURE he knew what the hell he was doing, but he was doubtful about its legality, as well. He hadn't come completely clean with Dr. Fields, and he was left alone in his office with the feeling that he had betrayed a friend and mentor. He hadn't lied to him, but he'd failed to be entirely truthful. A sin of omission, not commission, but a sin nevertheless, and Ellis deserved better.

Alan's sin of omission, as the lawyers would say, was substantive; he failed to mention that his trading system was very likely illegal, and, at best, borderline immoral. He took what little solace there was in the notion that he was protecting Fields from complicity.

Alan sat back in his chair, propped his feet on an open desk drawer, and stared at the ceiling. The muted sounds of the campus drifted in through his open window, and, somewhere, the dull rumble of a lawnmower was fading in and out as it moved back and forth across the distant quadrangle. The laughter and taunts of a volleyball game joined with the chatter of students coming and going to classes.

Not only was he uneasy about the encounter with Fields, but the project itself was causing Alan, at least momentarily, ethical and legal heartburn. He'd been so wrapped up in the theory and technical aspects of his plan that he hadn't spent much time on its long-term consequences. One thing the Marine Corps had taught him was to anticipate the unintended consequences of any action. This was certainly of strategic concern. He also knew that there was very little ethical and legal wiggle room. If he deployed his system, then he would cross a line, and there would be no turning back. Once you were a pickle, you could never be a cucumber again.

The program Alan had been perfecting had its origin in the work of an obscure Stanford graduate student, Stephen Wu, a citizen of the People's Republic of China, who had studied in the U.S. under a student visa. Wu had written a research paper hypothesizing the possibility of writing a computer algorithm that would allow him to harvest the excess decimal fractions of any financial transaction that crossed the myriad of governmental and commercial wire systems.

Stephen Wu was, at the time, a virtual nobody, and his work had been treated with the academic ho-hum reserved for those without a reputation. No one paid the least bit of attention to the paper. It was never peer-reviewed and never published. It was hiding securely in the archives of Stanford University. Wu eventually gained his Ph.D. and returned to China, disappearing into the morass of Chinese academia and bureaucracy.

Alan had serendipitously stumbled onto the paper while googling an entirely different subject. Typically, he would have paid no mind to the work of such a junior researcher, but something caught his interest, and he read the paper. He not only read it, but he studied the algorithm until he was convinced that the underlying theory/concept was valid. "There's no reason this damn thing shouldn't work!" The problem was that, at the time of Wu's discovery in 1982, there wasn't enough computational horsepower to put it to an actual test. Today, with the right computer framework, that would likely not be the case.

Alan had spent well over a year fine-tuning Wu's system, and he was nearing the point of hooking it up and giving it a beta test. However, his hastily tendered resignation this morning threw an operational wrench into the finely meshing gears of the plan. He depended on the university's mainframe to host his system, and, as of the end of the month, he would no longer have access to the big blue monster. This meant he would have to come up with a fairly powerful data-processing alternative.

Alan leaned back in his desk chair and stared at the ceiling. He had been in this little office for a couple of years, and this was the first time he had ever seen his ceiling. There were several water stains on the acoustical tiles, a host of spider webs, mold spots, and at least one dirt-dauber nest. He grinned to himself and thought, "Men are truly oblivious to their surroundings. I've been living in a micro-ecosystem of West Texas flora and fauna and never even noticed it. The only reason I'm noticing it now is that I don't want to deal with the problems concerning this hypothesis. Well, hell, they ain't going away, so I might as well get on with it."

The ethical issue was pretty straightforward; capturing any portion of the trailing decimal values from someone else's financial transaction was stealing. The fact that contemporary transfer systems dealt with only two decimal points and automatically rounded down sums to the nearest cent just happened to be coincidental. For instance, the amount $415.233391 would be rounded to $415.23, and the remaining $.003391 just disappeared, lost in the ether of cyberspace for all time.

So, whom did the $.003391 belong to? There was no case law that Alan could find dealing with this. Apparently, it just dropped off the grid once the transaction had been completed. It would belong to anyone who could harvest the minute bits of value and convert them back into dollars or euros or francs. No harm, no foul. Wu had figured out how to reap the excess, and Alan thought he knew how to implement Wu's system.

Alan's research had found that on an average day, worldwide, there were close to four-billion financial transactions executed. If one were to set the system to reap everything exceeding .000001, then one might expect to collect about $4,000 per day, more or less. Over time, this could be a consistent source of income that would provide financial security, as well as investment capital, that could support some new and innovative alternative-energy projects. If there are 252 business days in a year, then the system could bring in over a million dollars.

Alan had debated the ethical and moral implications at length and was leaning toward accepting the consequences of moving forward with his test. The money was disappearing into cyberspace, and no one would be hurt. The capital would allow him to invest in the research for the projects about which he was passionate: plentiful, safe energy, sufficient nutrition, clean water, and affordable health care. He could live with the trade-offs. He felt it was an acceptable rationalization of his moral dilemma.

Alan was not one to second-guess his decisions. Typically, once he decided a course of action, he moved ahead full speed, and this would be no exception. He would begin working to finish the necessary arrangements to support his upcoming test.

The first thing that would be needed was a base of operations. Alan needed an office. In order to rent an office, he needed a legal entity to serve as a foundation from which to do business, and, for this, he would need to see an attorney. Other than the issues surrounding his inheritance of the ranch when his parents died, he had never needed legal advice. His old high-school friend Randy Larson had handled the probate of his parent's will, so Alan figured he could set up a simple corporation and draw up a lease.

"Well, it's a fine mess you've got us in now, Ollie," Alan mused. "All those years of graduate school tossed away in a knee-jerk moment of pique. If I'm honest with myself, then I'll have to admit that I've known for a couple of months that I would have to give this a try, so I need to figure out how to go about doing it. Oh shit! I'd better give Pete a call before he hears it through the jungle drums."

Alan picked up the phone on his desk and dialed Pete Corelli's cell. After several rings, Pete picked up. "Corelli here!"

"Pete, it's Alan. What are you doing?"

"I've been putting together a plan to solve world hunger — just as soon as I finish brokering peace in the Middle East. Other than that, I'm not doing very much. How about you?"

"Want to go over to the Union and grab a cup of coffee? I've got something to share with you."

"You talking about telling the university to stick the job up their asses? That's old news by now."

"Damn! This place has more leaks than the men's room at Grand Central Station."

"I'll meet you, even though you've been scooped. See you at the Union in 30 minutes. I still want to hear it firsthand — exactly as it happened. I hear Millsap nearly had a stroke when you turned them down."

"I'll fill you in completely. See you at the Union."

Alan had a couple of things to attend to before he left to meet Pete. He quickly graded several of the final exams he'd given to his summer-school students and decided to take the rest of them home to look over during the weekend. Finally, he faced the task of writing a letter of resignation to Dr. Fields, formally surrendering his professorship, thus severing his ties with WTSU. He'd drop it in the university's internal mail system on his way out. He'd come back to clean out his office on Saturday.

After closing the big window in his office, Alan gathered his briefcase and locked his door as he left. As he walked down the three flights of old wooden stairs, he felt that he was leaving a large slice of his life behind. He noticed details of the nineteenth-century woodworking for the first time since his freshman year, and he realized that there was something universal about a classroom building after hours — the smell of floor wax and dust, the fading light filtering into the dark hallways, and the echoing of his solitary footsteps on the worn oak stairs. These were the things he'd miss. There was a sense of peaceful community in these old buildings.

Alan stepped out into the glaring West Texas sun and quickly reached for his sunglasses. It was close to 4:00 in the afternoon, but the relentless waves of heat showed no sign of letting up. The people who chose to make this arid, barren, and beautiful land their home were physically hard men and women. They had neither backed down from the harsh elements or the marauding Comanches. Alan sprang from that stock, so he wasn't bothered much by the dust and heat; it just felt like home to him.

Alan entered the cool, air-conditioned interior of the Union building and went directly to the Union Grill. There was a scattering of summer-school students and a few faculty members sitting in small groups sipping coffee and cold drinks, mostly avoiding the broiling heat that blanketed the campus. Their conversations picked up intensity as Alan walked by. Apparently, the word had spread.

Alan went through the serving line and bought a piece of apple pie and a cup of coffee. He found a table that offered some degree of privacy and sat down to wait for Pete Corelli. Shortly, Pete came into the Union and headed toward Alan's table. "You'd never notice that Pete had an artificial leg if you didn't know it," thought Alan. "He's still as agile as he was when he played quarterback at Navy."

Pete motioned that he was getting some coffee, and then he headed over to Alan's table. Pete was one of those guys who never seemed to age. He was a little over six feet tall, and he still weighed the same 195 pounds that he carried at Annapolis. He had sandy hair, a smooth and innocent face, and a boyishness that had fooled many opposing linebackers, as well as several dozen deceased Iraqis.

Pete pulled a chair out and said, "Okay, let's hear the whole story. Don't leave out a thing."

Alan gave him the extended version of the morning's events, while Pete listened intently, a wide grin splitting his handsome face. "Alan, that's the damnedest tale I've ever heard. You really told them to take their job and stick it?"

"Well, I guess I did — in so many words. That was certainly the essence of the conversation."

"It's only been five hours, and you're already a legend on campus. All of the toadies are appalled, and the rest are just plain envious. You're my hero."

"C'mon, Pete. You wouldn't give a damn about tenure, and you know it."

"You're right. Daddy granted me tenure when he left me 73 producing oil wells, but I love it when someone twists the tail of the powers that be."

"As much of a problem as you have with authority, I've always been amazed that you managed to survive the Naval Academy without walking the plank."

"Being an All-American quarterback and having a 4.0 GPA will excuse a lot of sass and sarcasm. Besides, they knew I was going to take my commission in the Marine Corps, and the navy would be rid of me for good. Enough about me, what do you plan to do with the rest of your life?"

"I plan to trade my own securities account, and, if possible, build enough capital to try to do something worthwhile for humankind. That's it in a nutshell."

"Nutshell probably fits this to a tee. I'm glad you're limiting your ambition to these small tasks and leaving world peace and poverty to Bill and Melinda, and me."

"Do you really think I'm a nut case?"

"Yeah, you probably are, but it sounds just like something you'd do, and it ought to be interesting watching you do it. So, you gonna require any investors to pull it off? I've got more money than God, and you can have whatever you need."

"I appreciate the offer, man. Ellis Fields offered to invest, as well, but I can't allow either of you to get involved. There's a serious element of risk beyond the financial liability, so I think I'll have to go down this path on my own."

"Damn, Alan, this sounds a bit mysterious, not to mention ominous — just the kind of shit I love. You know how bored I can get, and, as you've said many times, when I'm bored, I'm dangerous. Lay it out there and let me decide if I can stand the heat."

"Well, I do need someone to act as a sounding board, someone to bounce ideas off of. If I share the full scope of what I'm planning with you and you have any reservations, then will you agree to forget that we ever discussed it? I still can't allow you to invest, so there won't be a direct connection from me to you if there ever is an *A. Brooks vs. the U.S.*"

"That doesn't really scare me much. I figure the leg I left in Fallujah cuts me some slack with Uncle Sam. Like I said, tell me what you're up to, and I'll decide if I want any part of it. You and I go back too far for you to hold out on me now."

THREE

OVER THE NEXT HOUR, Alan laid out the entire plan for Pete Corelli, at least as far as he had thought it through. When Alan finished, Pete just sat silently, staring blankly into space. Finally, Pete said, "A couple of things come to mind. First, you're *assuming* that what you're planning is illegal, but, since it's never been done and there's no statute dealing with it, you're just guessing."

"It's been my experience that when a person takes something that doesn't belong to him, most people are going to call it stealing. That's what I'm guessing," Alan said.

"Maybe yes, maybe no. If I think I own something that's worth $10.54, and I move it from point A to point B, and I still have $10.54, what's been stolen from me? The fact that the real value was $10.54007 but the $.00007 disappeared doesn't alter the fact that I still have exactly what I thought I had. Where's the crime in that?"

"Corelli, that's the most convoluted rationalization I've ever heard. You should be on Wall Street."

"It may be a rationalization, but you can't refute the logic. Let's move on to the other issue that I thought about. There may be a fixed amount of excess decimals in the system — so when you've harvested them all, the game will be over."

"Well, I have to admit that I haven't considered that possibility, but, off the top of my head, it seems very unlikely. As long as one multi-decimal amount is multiplied by another amount, even if the second is exactly even to the cent, the product will likely have multiple decimal points. The only way we'll ever know is through experience."

"The third thing on my mind is much simpler. Do you honestly think this thing will be a success?"

"Yes, based on everything I've worked through so far, I think it will, but I can't be certain until I run a real-time test."

"And exactly when do you propose to do this?"

"As soon as I can get everything set up...maybe a couple of weeks or so."

"Okay, count me in."

"Damn, Pete, and I was worried you wouldn't give the risk a thorough analysis and would just jump in!"

"Don't be a bore. Tell me how I can help get this thing going."

"I'll need to find office space to house the securities trading firm that will be my official source of income. I'll actually do some trading, so I'll need a fully functional trading operation, Bloomberg, Intex, and Trade Web — that sort of electronic stuff. I'll also need a world-class communications system, with built-in redundancy. I can't risk having the system go down. I'd been planning on using the large mainframe computer here at WTSU, but I killed that plan this afternoon."

Pete thought for a moment and then nodded. "It just so happens that I own a couple of downtown buildings that might work for the trading operation. Leave the space and the communications system to me. I'll have you ready to move in by the end of next week. You'll need to give me a schematic of where you want stuff placed, and I can take it from there. You'll have to arrange for the electronic crap. I don't know Bloomberg from boomerangs. I'll buy whatever computers you need and lease them back to you, so figure it out and let me know."

Alan had seen Pete with a new project before, and there was no slowing him down. The good news was that he would deliver exactly what he promised, and the whole business would keep him fully engaged for at least the next 10 days. That would give Alan enough breathing room to line up the systems and put the final touches on the algorithms.

Now that Pete had a project to work on, he was ready to move into action, so he began to gather up his stuff to get on his way. "Great," he said. "I'll get busy on my end, and I'll give you a progress report in a day or two. When do you finish up here at Pecos High?"

"I'm not teaching second-semester summer school, so I plan to be packed and gone over the weekend."

"I'll have you a place ready to go by the end of the month for sure," Pete said, as he threw Alan a wave and walked hurriedly toward the exit of the Union Building. Alan observed that Pete's limp was almost unnoticeable. There was nothing like involvement in a conspiracy to bring back the old Pete Corelli.

Alan walked over, got another cup of coffee, and returned to his seat. He debated going ahead and eating dinner while he was there, but he finally decided that Maria would already be preparing food at the ranch. He sipped his coffee and mused, "Like the dog who loved to chase cars, it appears that I have finally caught one. I have my teeth firmly embedded in the tire, so now what? I guess I better get busy lining up a company, setting up a bank account, and ordering some electronics. Corelli won't be happy if I hold things up."

Alan left the Union, thinking about the outline of an action plan as he walked to his pickup. Even with the sun setting behind the trees, the door handle was still hot to the touch, and the air inside the truck was probably over 120 degrees Fahrenheit. It would eventually cool off, and, by midnight, it would be in the sixties. That's the way it worked in the desert.

Alan rolled the windows down and didn't turn on the air-conditioning system, in spite of the heat. He put in a Willie Nelson disc, turned the truck toward his ranch, and let the wind blow in his face as he drove.

Following State Road 20 west out of Pecos Springs, Alan drove into a Texas sunset that painted the distant mountains in a thousand shades of pinks, purples, and corals. The desert air's flowing through the open windows bore the scents and aromas of the dying day, and it felt warm and soothing on his face and arms.

Alan turned north off 20 onto a white rock road leading to a wrought-iron entrance that read "Circle B Ranch." The road continued north, then disappeared behind a distant ridge. Alan topped the ridge and looked down on a panorama that stretched for miles in every direction. In the distance, his ranch house and headquarters sat along a cottonwood-lined creek. In West Texas, the land is measured in sections, not acres, and everything visible from the crest of the ridge belonged to Alan.

The good news was that Alan owned a hell of a lot of land, something like 16,000 acres. The bad news was that it didn't have a single oil well on it, and you'd be lucky to feed a steer on 10 acres. The ranch was beautiful but economically marginal. Alan not only kept the ranching operation for sentimental reasons, but also to employ the two Mexican families who had worked the cattle for over six generations. These folks were Alan's oldest friends and the closest thing he had to family.

Alan waved to Cesar Alvarez, who was loading bags of feed into the back of his dusty pickup, and Cesar grinned and waved back. Alan parked his truck at the old hitching rail that ran along the front of his house. The original house had been built in the 1850s when the first Brooks settled on an abandoned Spanish land grant, in what was still Indian Territory. The original structure was made of 12-inch-thick limestone walls with narrow windows that resembled gun ports, which is exactly what they were.

This was Comanche territory, and, until the 1890s, the only protections for the settlers were their fortified home sites and two Texas Rangers. The old building had a slate roof built on six-inch ironwood timbers, cut and hauled from the distant mountains. The ironwood rafters and slate roof made it darn near impossible for the Comanches to employ their favorite tactic, set the roof on fire and take down the fleeing defenders. Ironwood was akin to asbestos. The Brooks house had been attacked many times over a 50-year period, but it had never been breached.

After the Indians had been killed or driven onto reservations, the slate roof had been replaced with brown half-pipe roofing tiles that had been made on the property. The dirt floors were replaced with hand-sawn hardwood and, after a hundred years of constant polishing and buffing, shone with a deep patina. Over the years, the house had been added on to and modernized, but the main living area, with its huge walk-in fireplace, was in the original building.

A large, deep veranda encircled the entire building, providing shade and shelter from the few, but violent, thunderstorms that were common in the high desert. The house was nestled in a grove of oaks that had been planted at the turn of the 20th century and had been carefully maintained and replaced over the years. The oaks provided a 20-degree cooling differential in the summer and served as a windbreak when the Alberta Express howled down from Canada. There was an old saying that the only thing between Texas and the North Pole was a barbed-wire fence somewhere in Kansas, and it was busted.

Alan entered the house and was greeted by Maria Alvarez, Cesar's plump and pretty wife, and Alan's housekeeper and cook. Her mother, Inez, had been Alan's nanny, and, when she became too sick to work, Alan had built her a small bungalow along the creek bottom so Maria and Cesar could care for her. Alan made sure he dropped in to see Inez at least a couple of times a week. He was still her "Bebe," and she was the only real mother he had ever had.

Alan hung his hat and jacket on the wooden pegs by the door as Maria asked, "Can I get you something to drink before dinner, Señor?"

"That would be nice. How about a double martini? By the way, what's for dinner?"

"Roast lamb and potatoes, just like you like them."

"Gracias, Maria. I'll have the martini out on the veranda; I want to catch the last of the sunset."

Maria smiled and said, "Si, Señor," and swept back into her kitchen to mix his cocktail.

Alan pulled one of the substantial oak rocking chairs closer to the porch rail and sat with his boots propped up facing the setting sun. He thought about the many times he had longed to be right here during his deployments in Iraq and Afghanistan. The scenery in those war-torn lands was very similar, but it was rare to get shot at in Texas — rare, but not unheard of.

The sunset was beginning to fade into purple dusk when Maria handed Alan his martini. He took a sip and sighed. There was no doubt that in addition to being the best cook in Texas, Maria made a mean martini. He was enjoying his drink and admiring the advancing evening when he heard the distant jangle of the telephone. He chose to ignore it and hoped whoever it was would just go away. No such luck.

Maria stepped through the screen door and said, "Señor Alan, the telephone is for you. It is Señor Corelli." She handed him the portable phone.

"Hey, Pete, what's up?"

"I think I've got you an office. You know that old bank building I own on the corner of Main and Austin? I just left there, and I believe that, with just a little work, it would be perfect. Since I'm the landlord, I think I can arrange whatever renovation and build-out you'll need, and amortize it over the length of the lease. I'm having my real-estate guy draw up a 20-year lease with no security deposit and six months of free rent to give you a head start. Whattaya think?"

"What do I think? It sounds too good to be true. Would you make the same deal for somebody else?"

"Of course I would! My mother could get this deal if she were still alive and would put up some collateral."

"I'm not going to argue with you, man. This is a generous offer, and I'd be a fool to pass it by. Draw up the lease, and I'll sign it right away."

"There is one other idea that I wanted to run by you. I'd be willing to give you a $500,000 equipment credit and roll it into the lease payments if that would help get the computers and communications gear faster."

"Again, I'm not gonna argue with you. I'll accept your offer, and it'll certainly speed things up."

"Great. I'll set up an account at the Pecos State Bank & Trust tomorrow, and you'll have good funds immediately. Can you meet me there about 10:00 in the morning?"

"Pete, can you do it that fast? I can wait till you have time to talk to the bank."

"I can pull it off. I know the President of Pecos State pretty well. The bank only has one shareholder, and that happens to be me."

"Well, I can see where that might speed things up a bit. Is there anything around here that you don't own?"

"Nothing of any importance that I can think of. If something comes to mind, let me know, and I'll buy it."

"It's good to be king."
"It certainly has its moments. Ciao! See you in the morning."

FOUR

LAN AWOKE THE NEXT MORNING just at sunrise. He splashed some water on his face and dried it on the towel by his sink. After he'd slipped into a pair of old jeans and a warm flannel shirt, he pulled on his boots and went into the kitchen to make a pot of coffee.

Alan liked to take an early-morning ride if he had an opportunity, and Maria and Cesar had anticipated this. The coffee was made, and Alan saw his favorite horse, Lucifer, saddled and tied to the hitching rail just outside the kitchen door.

"Buenos dias, Señor," said Maria. "The coffee is ready."

"Buenos dias, Maria. Thanks for the coffee. I'll take a mug with me during my ride."

"Si, Señor. Breakfast will be ready when you get back."

Alan mounted Lucifer, the large black stallion that he'd raised from a colt, and he could feel the horse's power ripple through the western saddle that had belonged to his grandfather. Lucifer was as strong as a Clydesdale, and as fast as a thoroughbred. He was also mean as a snake to anyone but Alan and Cesar. Alan whistled, and Otto, his large brown and black German shepherd, trotted out to join the ride.

There were many trails that he could take, and this morning Alan decided to use one of the short routes that would take about an hour. The sun was just peeking over the eastern horizon, beginning to color the distant Guadalupe Mountains with a pink and gold wash. The air was still cool from the night and wouldn't warm up until the sun had been up a couple of hours. He rode down the hill behind the house until he came to the small creek, which lay hidden in the cottonwoods.

Alan usually allowed Lucifer to work his way along without much human interference, and this was the case today. The big horse ambled along the creek bank, keeping an eye out for a place to cross, and Otto let him lead the way. The breeze in the cottonwoods rattled the leaves and carried with it the faint aroma of the honeysuckle that grew along the abandoned fence line that followed the slow-moving creek.

Lucifer began to ford the little creek and was soon picking his way up the opposite bank. The horse had moved about 10 feet into the creek-side brush when Otto ran through a patch of low scrub. The whole world exploded in a cacophony of rapidly beating wings and blurred brown missiles, scattering in every direction. Lucifer seemed to jump straight up, with all four legs leaving the ground. When he regained his footing, he reared up and nearly unseated Alan. It took a minute or two to settle the stallion down and reassure him that the covey of quail would not be back.

It was clear that the bobwhites had unnerved the big black horse, and he began to dance sideways as he moved up the creek bank. Alan was a good horseman, and he had no fear of losing control, but he didn't want Lucifer to stay so spooked. The best thing would be to take a little gallop and work off some of the adrenaline.

Once clear of the creek, Alan turned down a small dirt road that meandered west toward the distant mountains. Alan knew that this would lead to a small tank in a meadow, about a mile away. He tapped the big horse with the heel of his boot and felt the almost instant surge of brute power as Lucifer moved from a walk to a full-out gallop. Otto could not keep up but trailed behind them at a full run.

The big horse stretched out and hit a gear that Alan had only seen a couple of times before. Alan rode down in the saddle and gave the horse his head. With the wind in his face and brush flying by, Alan felt the sense of speed and power that every man who has ever ridden a great horse has experienced. It was exhilarating, and probably habit-forming.

As the horse and his rider neared the meadow, Alan began to rein in Lucifer from a gallop to a trot, and finally to an easy walk. The breeze was in their faces, and both horse and dog suddenly picked up the scent of something. It was then that Alan noticed the large, black vultures on the other side of the tank. They were obviously eating.

Alan rode around the tank and stopped where he was upwind of the birds and out of the scent stream. Horses don't like the smell of death, and it tends to spook them. Alan dismounted and allowed Lucifer to start to graze on the deep, green grass. Alan moved toward the scene, and soon his approach flushed the vultures, which flew off a couple of hundred feet and sat looking back at him.

In the knee-high grass, Alan could see a brown shape, all but hidden from view. When Alan got within six feet, he saw that it was the body of a small horse. The little horse had been shot once in the head, and there was no tack to be seen. Someone had shot his horse and left on foot, carrying all his gear. Looking more closely, Alan could see a badly swollen back leg and the telltale marks of a snake bite.

Alan thought, "Looks like a mercy killing that sat someone afoot in the middle of my property. This happened a day or so ago, and whoever it was is long gone. The question is, what was he or she doing on the Circle B in the first place? I'll check with Cesar and his men. Maybe they know something. We'll need to get a crew up here to bury the horse before it gets too ripe."

When he returned to the house, Alan dialed Pete Corelli's cell phone, and, after about 10 rings, a groggy voice answered. "Corelli here. Who in the hell is calling in the middle of the night?"

"Good morning, Pete. It's Alan, and it's 7:45 a.m., not the middle of the night."

"Brooks, you and I will never agree about what constitutes night. I hope you have a damn good reason to wake me up."

"I promised to meet you at the bank this morning, but something's come up that may delay me for an hour or two."

"Damn, the bank isn't even open yet. Couldn't this crisis wait till a decent hour?"

"Pete, I have no idea how long this will take. I went for an early-morning ride and found a dead horse in my upper meadow. The horse had been snakebit, and his rider had to shoot him. I've gotta dispose of the body and then see if I can find his owner. Thought I better give you a heads-up that I'll be along as soon as I can."

"Brooks, you really piss me off. Your life is one big adventure, and mine is as dull as dirt. I've never found a dead horse around my place, but you act like it's a weekly occurrence for you."

"I have been granted an interesting life, while you are burdened with great riches. Wanna trade?"

"Hmm, I'll have to get back to you on that. Call me when you're ready to go to the bank."

"Thanks, man. I'll be there as soon as I can."

Alan called all of his ranch employees together and questioned them about what they'd seen and heard, but the inquiry netted him nothing. No one had seen anything unusual or heard the shot, and the fact that no one had heard the report of a weapon troubled Alan. "Mighty strange indeed," he thought.

"Cesar, I need to get into town to meet Pete Corelli. Can you and the boys handle this from here?"

"Si, Señor. We'll take the backhoe and bury the horse. I'll look carefully for any signs of someone still on the ranch."

Alan went in to see if there was any chance of getting a little breakfast. It was almost 10:00, and Maria had probably cleaned the kitchen and was working on lunch. The thick-walled ranch house was still cool, and the wide veranda kept the worst of the West Texas heat at bay. The house was air-conditioned, but Maria rarely turned it on until mid-afternoon.

Alan stuck his head into the kitchen, and Maria said, "Oh, Señor Alan! Are you ready for your breakfast yet?"

Upon reflection, Alan decided that his acceptance of breakfast was unfair to Maria and politely replied, "I need to get a quick bath and go meet Pete Corelli. I think I'll skip breakfast and grab an early lunch in town. Thanks anyway. I'll see you tonight for dinner."

"Si, Señor. I'm planning on having grilled chicken, if that's alright with you."

"Your chicken will always work for me, Maria. Wring enough necks for everybody, and we can get Cesar to fire up the big grill. We haven't had everybody for dinner in a while."

Maria kept a well-stocked henhouse, filled with yard chickens. Her chickens were free to eat bugs, and God only knew what else, but they would be served within hours of their demise, and their flavor was impossible to get in a store-bought bird. She also kept everyone supplied with fresh eggs that tasted like REAL eggs.

Alan picked up the phone in his bedroom and dialed Pete's number. Corelli picked up on the second ring and said, "I was just about to call you. We have an appointment at the bank at 3:00 this afternoon, which will give us time to check out the old bank building and decide if it'll work for you. By the way, did you find out anything about your mystery horse?"

"First, let's meet at the C&P for lunch. I haven't had time for breakfast. We can see the office building and still make the bank by 3:00. Second, no, I still don't know what happened, but it was probably someone just passing through. Who knows?"

"Sounds reasonable to me; I'll see you at the Choke & Puke about noon. Try to stay out of trouble until then."

"See you at noon," Alan said and hung up the phone.

The C&P was local shorthand for Charley & Pearl's. It was located in an unincorporated area, about three miles on the east side of town known as Slap Out, Texas — as in, "slap out in the middle of nowhere." The diner shared the little crossroads with a Shell station and a Texas co-op farm store.

The C&P was far and away the best meat-and-three in about a five-county area, and five counties in West Texas would just about swallow most of New England. On the other hand, there were more people in Rhode Island than in the entire five counties, so it probably all evened out in the end.

Alan drove through town, following Highway 192 east until the little settlement fell into view. The C&P was in a low concrete-block building that was painted the same shade of yellow as the center line on 192. It had a green tin roof and large plate glass windows that stretched across the front. There was one neon sign in the window that merely said "EATS." A large gravel parking lot was almost full, and Alan had to park in the back and walk around the building.

The sun beat down on the bright, yellow structure, and the glare darn near blinded him. He was, however, able to notice Corelli's shiny black Jaguar convertible parked in the shade of the only oak tree in sight. Things just seemed to fall into place for Pete. Alan entered the café and was immediately assailed by the smells of hot, homemade yeast rolls and frying chicken. If he weren't already hungry, then the C&P would bring it on for sure.

Alan removed his sunglasses and spotted Pete sitting at a table for two near the back wall, where Alan pulled out the empty chair and took a seat. Pete said, "Sorry, I just couldn't wait for you any longer. I had Pearl bring me an order of the rolls. You gotta try one."

Alan snagged a hot roll, pulled it apart, put a chunk of the real, creamy butter on it, and sampled the yeasty tastiness. He smiled at Pete and said, "Damn, that's good! Give me a cup of Charlie's New Orleans coffee, and I could eat the whole basket."

"You better order your own basket, if that's your plan. These things are addictive."

Pearl walked up holding her order pad and opened with, "What can I get you boys to drink?"

"I'll have un-sweet iced tea," Alan replied.

"Make it two, and what might the Choke and Puke have on special today?" Pete asked this mockingly, knowing that Pearl hated that nickname for her place, but Corelli just could not help himself.

Pearl glared at him and growled, "The lunch special is Charlie's pot roast and new potatoes; the soups are broccoli/cheese and chili; and the veggies are collard greens and corn on the cob, smart ass."

Pete smiled slightly and teased, "Moi? Why, Pearl, I'm shocked by your attitude!"

"You're gonna be even more shocked when I throw your gimpy little ass outta here."

This was more than an idle threat; Pearl had Pete by four inches and sixty pounds, most of which was not fat. He knew just how far to push her — maybe just a little more. "Pearl, be honest with me. Has anybody ever ordered the broccoli/cheese soup? I always figured y'all put it on the menu because you knew one pot would last forever."

"We put it on the menu to add a little sophistication. I never expected someone with your redneck taste to order it, and, yes, we sell quite a bit each week."

"Pearl, you start down a slippery slope when you compromise like that. Next thing you know, it'll be the 'quiche of the day, served with assorted roots and an arugula salad.'"

Pearl glared at him and said, "Pete, why don't you just order lunch, since neither one of us has any idea what the hell you're talking about."

"You know, Pearl, I believe you're right. I'll have the Choke and Puke special with the veggies."

"How 'bout you, Alan?"

"I'll have the same, Pearl; you oughtta toss his butt into the parking lot, you know."

"I'd love to, but he owns the building. We just rent it from him."

"Shit, I shoulda known."

Pearl headed to turn their orders in and to see about the rest of her customers, and Alan looked over at Pete. "You shouldn't give Pearl such a hard time...after all, she is your tenant."

"Considering the little bit of rent they pay, she can put up with a little bit of ribbing. Besides, she's secretly in love with me."

"She hides it well."

"Well, enough about me."

Alan's cell phone began to vibrate on the table, and he reached down and answered it: "Alan Brooks."

The call was from the business office at WTSU, inquiring about the date that Alan's office would be vacated and available for reassignment. Alan told the lady that he would be out by Monday morning and would come by at that time to complete any paperwork needed to make his departure official. Alan shut his cell phone off, turned to Pete, and said, "That was WTSU trying to talk me into staying on, but I held firm."

"You know, Brooks, I really like playing with you. You can get into more interesting shit in one morning than the average guy can in a year. Your whole life gets stranger and stranger. What do you do...run down the rabbit hole every day?"

"Like I said, I was granted an interesting life, and you were blessed with great riches. I'm still willing to swap."

"I sorta like having my cake and eating it too. I think I'll just pal around with you and find ways to piss away some of those great riches." Pete looked at his watch and said, "We better head back to town and look at the old bank building to see if it'll work for you. Then we can go to the actual bank."

Pete told Pearl to put lunch on his tab and then said to Alan, "I'll meet you at the bank. Pull into the alley and park in the back."

FIVE

A LAN FOLLOWED PETE back into town and parked beside the Jag in one of two reserved parking places in the bank's parking lot. They met as Pete was opening the door, and they entered a dark hallway. Pete turned on the overhead lights and walked past a couple of empty rooms on either side of the hall. He pushed open a heavy oak door and flipped on the primary lighting system for the bank lobby.

There, spread before them, was a time capsule of Art Nouveau opulence. The building had been constructed in 1902, but the bank had failed in 1929, and, apparently, remained today just as it was on its last day of operation.

Pete asked, "Well, whatta you think?"

"Wow, this place is like a museum! Have you ever seen it before?"

"I have to admit that I haven't. Gramps just shut it up when the bank failed and never gave it another thought. I've never taken the time to come over here to check it out, but, I believe, with a little remodeling, it can be just what you need. In addition to the main floor and the lobby, there are two upper floors and a basement where the vault is located."

"Pete, this could be a showplace! I love it. It'll take some work, but I think it'll do just fine."

"Good. Let's go over to Pecos State and sign some papers."

The two men spent the better part of an hour reading and signing loan documents and leases. When they finally finished, Alan owned a lease on the old bank building and had an appointment to meet with a local architect to work out the remodeling plan. He also had a new bank account in the name of Brooks Capital, LLC, with a balance of $500,000. Pete's attorney had filed the LLC papers with the Texas Secretary of State, and Alan was formally in business. There was nothing holding him back now except the failure of the theory.

It was late afternoon when Alan left the Pecos State Bank, and his mind was racing through all the things he needed to get done in order to beta-test his system. Before heading home, he decided to stop at Shorty's, the local coffee shop, to grab a cup. He was finishing his coffee and about to leave for the ranch when a pretty, young woman came into the shop and immediately spotted him. A big smile lit up her face, and she walked over and pulled up a chair at his table. "Well, I didn't expect to see you in Shorty's. I thought you'd be hanging out at the unemployment office."

Alan shook his head and grinned. He and Ellen Sikes had been friends all of their lives. Ellen was on the tall side, with short, blond hair and a perfect complexion. She ran track and played basketball in high school, and, after graduation, she left Pecos Springs for the University of Missouri to major in journalism. Her dad was the *Pecos Springs Clarion's* owner and publisher, and she was back in town to serve as editor of the paper. Ellen didn't miss much. In response to her greeting, Alan replied, "I've decided to change careers and become a sportswriter; in fact, I was just headed over to see you about a position."

"Just because you could play it, doesn't mean you can write about it. Besides, we're not in the habit of hiring unemployed rookies. Maybe you could work for a smaller paper and get some experience…then check back in a few years."

"Ellen, I doubt that there's a smaller paper in the entire State of Texas. I will also point out to you that I was sports editor of the *WTSU Bugle* when you were a rookie reporter covering sorority parties."

"I do remember, but I'll also point out that now I am the editor of a daily paper, and you are unemployed. Looks like a classic case of unfulfilled potential."

"If you don't tone down the venom, I might get Corelli to buy that rag from your father, and you'll find yourself back on the Greek beat."

"Don't you fret about Pete Corelli; he's been after me since the first grade. I've got him wrapped around my little finger."

"Well, there is that. He's not the only one who'd like to catch you."

"Dream on, stud muffin. You have a better chance of getting hired on at *The New York Times*."

Alan shrugged his shoulders and signaled his surrender to Ellen. She smiled in acceptance of his capitulation and said, "Speaking of my newspaper career, I don't suppose you'd like to fill me in on whatever scheme you and Corelli have cooked up?"

"There's not much to tell. I'm starting a new business, and I'm planning to rent a space from Pete. That's about it."

"Bullshit," Ellen sputtered. "I know both of you better than that, and I know you're up to something big. I'll give you two weeks, and then I want an exclusive interview."

"Like I said, there's not much to tell, but I'll give you a call once I'm all set up, and you can interview me to your heart's content."

"Don't you and Corelli screw around with me. I'll expect to hear from you by Thursday week. I've got deadlines to meet."

With that, Ellen did a one-eighty and headed back to the paper. Alan decided to start for home. The sun was setting behind the Guadalupes when he grabbed his cell phone and called Cesar, who answered on the second ring: "Hola, Señor Alan."

"Hey, Cesar. I'm on my way home, and I'd like to have a meeting when I get there. You think you can have everyone gather at the main house in, say, about 45 minutes?"

"Si, Señor. They're all planning to be here for the grilled pollo that Maria and I are working on."

"That's great. The chicken had slipped my mind. That'll be perfect. I'll have time to wash up before we have a short meeting, and then we'll have dinner. See you about 7:30."

"Si, Señor. Adios."

When he reached the ranch, Alan washed up and changed into jeans and a WTSU football jersey. He walked through the kitchen, where he found Maria preparing the fixings for tonight's cookout. They exchanged a few pleasantries as Alan went out the back door to the big portable grill that was aglow with cherry-red charcoal, just about ready for Maria's and Cesar's famous grilled chicken. Alan caught Cesar's eye and said, "Your fire looks about ready to go. Should we eat first and then have the meeting?"

"No, Señor. The fire needs to die down a little before I put on the pollo. It will be fine to start the meeting as you wished."

"Then, why don't you get everyone together in the living room? What I have to say won't take too long, and then we can eat on the picnic tables out by the big oak tree."

"Si, Señor. I will gather everyone and meet you in the house."

Alan walked into the large living room, where all of the people who lived on the Circle B were gathered. They stood when he entered the room, and he smiled and said, "Everyone find a place to sit. This won't take long, but I want to bring all of you up to speed on what's happened in the last couple of days."

Alan gave a detailed presentation of the facts concerning his resignation and the decision to start a new business, and then he brought up the dead horse. "I'll keep everyone informed as more information becomes available, but, in the meantime, I want each of you to be extra careful as you go about your daily chores; if you see anything the least bit out of the ordinary, be sure to let Cesar or me know right away. Does anyone have a question?"

One of Cesar's and Maria's teenaged sons raised his hand, and Alan nodded to him. "Señor Brooks, why are you so worried about a dead horse?"

"That's a good question, José. The horse was ridden and also probably shot by someone who was on this property without my permission, and I need to find out why they were here. I always like to be safe rather than sorry, so just keep your eyes open."

Alan looked at the group and said, "If there are no more questions, then let's go dig into some grilled chicken!"

***

The next morning, Alan was sitting on the porch having his first cup of coffee when he decided to go back up to the little meadow where he'd found the horse and take another look around. He saw Cesar walking toward the barn and called out to him: "Hey, Cesar! Wanna take a ride with me to look around the place?"

"Si, Señor. I'll saddle Lucifer and meet you after breakfast."

The two men rode at an easy pace and were soon near the little meadow. They dismounted and stood in the exact spot where the horse was shot, and Alan looked at the surrounding terrain with the eye of an experienced military officer. It was clear that the rider had not come from the east. The land sloped downhill all the way back to the creek and the cottonwoods, and, to the west, there was a series of rolling hills, each a little higher than the last, all the way to the foothills of the mountains looming in the distance. Alan said, "Cesar, I think the rider had to come from either the north or the south. The west doesn't offer much cover for about a mile, and then there are hundreds of possibilities. There are a couple of places to the north that would offer good cover just over the military crest of those little hills with the scrub trees. Let's go up there and take a look around."

There was a slight breeze coming out of the north, and suddenly both horses began to act a little spooky, as if they smelled an unfamiliar scent in the air. Just about then, Alan caught the briefest glint in a small copse of trees about a half-mile away. Something had reflected the rising sun — something metal or glass. Alan asked, "Cesar, did you see that flash just to the right of that large pine on the hill over there?" Alan pointed in the direction of the reflection.

"No, Señor, I missed it. Show me where."

Alan pulled a pair of military binoculars from his saddle bag and was refocusing the glasses when there was another flash a little to the right of the first one. Cesar saw this and said, "Señor, there is definitely something, and probably someone, up on that ridge, and I suspect we are being scoped."

"Shit, I think you're right, and whoever it is has no business being up there. Let's see if we can flush him out."

The two men mounted and began to ride toward the concealed position on the hill, and soon they had entered the small grove. Alan turned to Cesar and said, "There's no sign of anyone up here, not even a broken twig, but I know we saw someone. Let's make a wide turn on the other side of the ridge and see what we can find."

Alan and Cesar rode for another 45 minutes, but there was no sign of another human, so they decided to head back to the ranch.

Alan needed to meet Pete's architect at the new office at 1:30 p.m., and he had a couple of phone calls to make before the meeting, so he took a quick shower and put on jeans and a golf shirt. He stuck his head in the kitchen and told Maria he'd eat lunch in town, and then walked into the ranch office.

"The first thing I'm gonna do is call Ellen and confirm our meeting for Thursday week. I'll be better off working with her than against her. At least it'll keep her from bugging me while I try to get my new office set up."

Alan dialed Ellen at the paper.

"Good morning, *Pecos Springs Clarion*. How may I direct your call?"

"Good morning, Mabel. This is Alan Brooks. Is Ellen in?"

"Oh, hi, Alan. She sure is. Let me connect you."

Almost immediately, Ellen said, "I was just about to call you to confirm our appointment a week from Thursday."

"I want to make you a deal you can't turn down."

"Oh, hell, why don't I like the sound of that? What kindda deal?"

"I'll show you mine, if you'll show me yours."

"Alan Brooks, have you lost your frigging mind? Why ever would I want to see your little pencil pecker?"

"Get your mind out of the gutter, Ellen. I'm offering to tell you everything about my new business on two conditions, neither of which involves my very impressive wanger."

"I'm relieved to know that your plumbing isn't going to be an issue. What are the conditions?"

"First, you agree not to print what I tell you until I give you the green light, and, second, you'll allow me to read and comment on everything you plan to print."

"I *knew* you and Corelli were up to something big! Alright, I won't print until you say so, but I have no intention of allowing you, or anyone else, to censor my column, but I will let you comment and make corrections before it goes to press."

"I can live with that."

SIX

THE RECEPTIONIST AT THOMPSON Architecture, LLC, smiled at Alan and said, "Mr. Brooks, Mr. Thompson will see you now if you'll follow me. May I get you a cup of coffee or a coke?"

"A cup of black coffee would be nice, thanks."

Alan was ushered into Seth Thompson's office, a brightly lit, airy space with an intimate seating area at one end, and floor to ceiling windows that ran along the outer wall. Thompson's desk and drawing board took up the other end of the office. Seth Thompson met Alan and invited him to the seating area. "Alan, good to see you again. We've met on several occasions since you returned to town, but you probably don't remember me."

"As a matter of fact, I do remember you. I met you at Pete's summer party; we talked about old, West Texas ranch houses."

"As I recall, you own one of the original fortified houses. There aren't that many left. I'd love to come out and take a look at it sometime."

"You're welcome anytime. Just give me a call and we'll get together."

The receptionist served Alan the coffee, and Thompson had a bottle of water. He broke the seal, took a long drink, and said, "Mr. Corelli has asked me to meet with you to be sure that the planned renovations to the old bank building meet with your approval. I received the technical instructions for the telecommunications and computer systems, and they pose no problem. We're providing conduits for all of them, plus a three-tiered internet connection. You'll have a satellite dish, high-speed fiber optics, and a telephone DSL connection. I have here some renderings of the proposed interior of the building for you to look at, as well."

Thompson handed a set of plans to Alan and said, "Take these with you and look them over. If you have changes, suggestions, or requirements, just let me know, and we can alter things to suit you."

"How soon can this work be done?"

"If you give me the okay, then we can have the contractor start first thing next week; the work should take about 10 days. I've asked our interior designer to prepare a decorating plan that will include furniture and fixtures. If you approve her ideas, then she can be prepared to start in right behind the construction, and you should be ready to move in within 15 working days."

"That sounds good. Let me take a look at these, and I'll get right back to you."

"Great. As soon as we have your final approval, the designer will have her plan ready in about 24 hours."

Alan gathered the plans together and rose to go. He said, "Thanks for expediting all of this; I'll tell Pete that we're on our way."

"Please do. Mr. Corelli can be very persuasive and unrelenting."

Alan looked over his shoulder as he left Thompson's office and said, "Yeah, Pete wants what he wants, and he wants it now. Sometimes it's better to just give it to him than to listen to him rant and rave. Be sure to call me when you want to visit the house."

The two men shook hands, and Alan walked to his pickup. It was almost 4:00 p.m. when Alan sat down at his desk at home and checked his messages. He had a call from Corelli, which he returned but got Pete's voicemail. Alan left a message filling Pete in on his visit with Thompson and the plans to get the office open and told Pete to call if he wanted to. Otherwise, they would talk tomorrow. The sun was just beginning to drop behind the mountains to the west, and Alan poured a glass of wine and went to the veranda to enjoy the sunset.

The next week passed in a blur of construction activity at the old bank building. Alan worked with Thompson and his staff to finalize the renovation plans, and the contractor started on schedule. Alan visited the work site first thing every morning and met with Thompson's interior designer to decide on the final choices of the furniture, fixtures, paint, and materials. As soon as the contractor completed his work, the designer's team descended on the space and began to transform it into a finished product. By the end of the week, the computers and communications gear were installed and ready to go.

Late Friday afternoon, all of the workers were gone, and Alan and Pete were sitting in Alan's new office reviewing the week's work. Alan said, "I never thought they'd get it done on time. Corelli, you're a miracle worker."

"Shucks, it was nothing; anyone could have done it with generous bribes and incentives. Just another example of my compelling personality and Daddy's money."

"No kidding, Pete…you managed to do in 10 days that which, under any normal time frame, should have taken a month or more. Thanks to you, we can test my theory late next week. I'll need a day or two for the shakedown cruise in order to test the system, but I believe everything will go smoothly, and we can see if we've pissed away a ton of your money."

"Alan, I may be flaky, but, when it comes to my money, I'm pretty shrewd. I have A.G. Edwards ready to move its office into this space if you can't make your idea work."

"That's good to know; at least you can eventually recoup your investment if I come up a disappointment."

"Recoup my investment and make a tidy profit to boot. Don't worry about failing. Concentrate on making this damn thing work."

Pete visited for a while longer and then announced that he had a meeting with his life insurance agent and needed to be on his way. Alan thanked him again and walked him to the door. After Pete left, Alan sat at his new desk and booted up one of his desktop computer terminals. First, he called up the master plan to see what logistical and administrative issues remained to be done. The first item that would need his attention was hiring an office manager to oversee the daily operations. This person would have to be privy to the decimal-scrapping scheme in order to do the job, which meant hiring very carefully. Alan thought, "This hire has to be someone I can completely trust, and someone who can keep things on an even keel. There'll have to be other employees as we begin to work on the project, so whomever I hire will have to serve as Chief Operating

Officer. I'll be covered up trying to manage the decimal project, running the trading operation, and keeping the press at bay."

Alan continued musing: "I'd really like to talk to Amy Wilson, but, since she just retired as postmistress, she'll probably want to take some time off. Oh, what the hell — I'll give it a shot. All she can do is say no. I'll give her a call first thing Monday morning. I also need to figure out exactly how to handle the generated proceeds, if the system works. Maybe Pete'll have some ideas. I'd like to move the funds directly to a major financial institution and bypass the local bank entirely. I'd prefer it if no one in town knows my financial situation. I also ought to be ready to run the initial beta test at least by Friday and maybe sooner. I want Pete to be here when I crank it up; he deserves to be in at the beginning, or the end, depending on the outcome."

Alan was startled back to the present by the jangling of his new telephone. "I wonder who this is. I don't think I've had time to give this number to anyone."

Alan picked up the phone and said, "Alan Brooks's office...this is Alan."

"Hey, Alan, Ellen here. Have you got a minute?"

"Ellen, how in the hell did you manage to get this phone number?"

"I sweet-talked Corelli into giving it to me; did you think it was going to be a secret number?"

"No, of course not. I just didn't realize Pete had it. No big deal. What can I do for you?"

"I decided to run a feature story on your new venture in Sunday's business section, and I thought maybe we could move our interview up a week, just to be sure I get the facts straight."

"Do you mean this Sunday or a week from Sunday?"

"A week from Sunday. Even I would be pressed to get a feature story done that fast."

"Ellen, give me a minute to think."

"Take your time; I know how hard it is for you."

Alan thought, "I better try to put her off until after the beta test. I'd look like a total yo-yo if the system doesn't work and she's splashed it all over the Sunday paper."

Alan said, "Ellen, I'd appreciate it if you could delay writing about my new venture until it's had a chance to get up and running, say a month or two?"

"No way. In a month or two, this will be ancient history, and no one will give a hoot. It's gonna run next Sunday. The only choice you have is how much influence you want to have on the finished feature. I can do it without you, but I thought you might like to have the opportunity to make sure I get the facts straight."

"How soon do we need to do this interview?"

"My deadline to submit the finished copy is the Wednesday before publishing. I'd like to have at least a couple of days to put it together. That would be next Thursday, at the latest."

"Okay, come on over to my new office about 2:00 Thursday afternoon and we'll do it — by the way, thanks for asking for my input. I know you didn't have to do that."

"I really try to get it right when I write about something, in spite of the risk of being played. Of course, I know you would never try to play me because you know I'll rip your heart out and sell it in the classified ads."

"Yeah, something like that did occur to me. Actually, I do believe you shoot for accuracy, and I'm glad to tell you my story."

"Good, I'll see you on Thursday, if we don't talk before." Ellen hung up before Alan could say goodbye.

Alan thought, "I guess I better cobble together some plausible trading scheme that will satisfy Ellen and not let her pin me down to anything specific. I'll come up with something by next Thursday, but I better be sure it's based to some degree on facts; she's too damn smart to buy into bullshit. Besides, she probably *would* rip my heart out and sell it. At least I don't want to put her to the test. I better plan on working over the weekend if I want to get all of this done by next Thursday."

Saturday morning, Alan took his coffee out to the veranda and watched the sunrise. He sat with his feet propped up on the porch railing, surveying the early morning desert. His eyes strayed across the little valley in the direction of the hills to the north, and he thought he saw movement near the copse of pines where he and Cesar had seen the reflections.

The light was still pretty dim, and Alan couldn't be sure, but it looked like someone was standing under the pines, looking down into the little meadow where the horse had died. Alan eased himself up and went into the ranch house to get his binoculars. The glasses were U.S. Navy issue and were super high-quality.

Alan returned to the porch and resumed his position as if he'd gone for more coffee. He sat, quietly observing the tree line until he thought he could make out a person watching the meadow. Alan eased the binoculars to his eyes and gently focused them. He could clearly see a human form under the pine branches, and he nearly dropped the binoculars. It was as if he were seeing an Apache warrior from another century.

The man was dressed in baggy pants and a loose-fitting shirt. He had a bright-red sash as a belt and was wearing rawhide boots. His long, black hair was held back by a bandanna. He could have been Geronimo or Cochise. He stood motionless, staring down into the little meadow, holding a long lance with feathers tied just below the tip.

Alan was spellbound; all he could do was watch the figure, hoping not to spook him. As the sun reached full light, the figure looked directly at Alan, raised his lance in salute, and then turned and melted away, as if by magic. One minute he was there, and the next he had simply vanished.

"Well, I'll just be damned," Alan thought. "That was like seeing a ghost from 1855. I doubt there's any use trying to run him down, since he seems to come and go like a spirit. There's just too much going on, and I don't have the time or the head space to deal with all of it. I need to concentrate all my energy on getting my system up and running, so I need to find somebody to help me with whatever in the hell's going on out here. I think I'll give Shiva a call."

Shiva was the code name for a young woman he'd briefly served with in Afghanistan. His SEAL team had been trapped on a remote mountaintop, along with Captain Mary Jo Thibodaux, the team's liaison officer from military intelligence. She'd been injured in the crash of the team's helicopter, and, in spite of her wounds, she, later that night, led a patrol that forced their Taliban tormentors to withdraw with heavy casualties. Many of the warriors sent to Paradise that night had their throats slit by Captain Thibodaux. Alan told Mary Jo's commander that she operated in the dark like Shiva the Destroyer, and that became her handle. She and Alan had kept in touch after they both left the service — he returned to his home in West Texas, while Mary Jo moved to Mobile, Alabama, to open a Civil Engineering practice.

Mary Jo was the clear person to aid Alan on several fronts. In addition to needing someone to help him deal with this bizarre horse/warrior situation, he needed someone to consult with him on the obvious major and multiple security issues he was about to face with the implementation of this trading system. He also needed someone to help him figure his way through the possible illegal deal he was about to undertake.

SEVEN

HASTILY, ALAN FOUND MARY JO'S NUMBER in his cell phone contact list, and, when he called, she answered immediately. "My goodness! They finally ran a telephone line out there?"

"Yeah, just when we were getting comfortable with smoke signals. Have you got a minute? I think I'll be needing Shiva's help with a project I'm working on."

"Great, I was hoping for something to get the old blood pumping," Mary Jo thought.

Mary Jo *said*, "I'm all ears; let's hear it."

Alan gave her the short and dirty version of the past two weeks, and, when he finished, Mary Jo replied, "So, basically, you're unemployed, but you're about to save the world. However, you're going to do it illegally; your ranch is under siege; and, as usual, you need some adult supervision. That about cover it?"

"I might not have used that exact phrasing, but it's close enough. You mentioned that, in addition to your Civil Engineering business, you occasionally take on some special consulting work, which probably translates as you get bored as hell from time to time and need some action. Think you might want to talk about helping me and possibly getting your adrenaline hit at the same time?"

"Of course, I'll talk to you. I guess I'll have to come out to that godforsaken hole so that you can fill me in on the whole situation."

"That would be perfect; we can discuss your consulting fees once you get here. Either I can afford whatever you charge, or your trip will be on the cuff, but I won't know till later in the week."

"Money won't be a factor. I don't know if you ever knew it, but my great-grandfather left me well fixed for life. Besides, we've been talking about my coming out to visit for a long time, and this looks like the perfect opportunity."

"I'll be looking for you as soon as you can get here. I hate to rush you, but how quickly can you come?"

"Is there an airport anywhere nearby?"

"The closest commercial airport is El Paso. It's about 90 miles west, and I can pick you up."

"How about a private field that can handle a small jet?"

"Yeah, West Pecos State University, my employer until recently, flies small jets in and out of the municipal airport. It's listed as Blister, Texas."

"No shit? Blister?"

"Yeah, and there's nothing you can say that I haven't already heard on that subject."

"Okay. Plan on picking me up tomorrow afternoon. I'll call when I'm an hour out."

"Are you going to charter?"

"No. I'll be flying my little Cessna Mustang."

"You own one of the little Citations, huh? I shudder to think what this is gonna cost!"

"I told you not to worry about the money. Just come pick me up and provide me with room and board."

"Room and board we got plenty of."

The friends chatted for a few more minutes, mostly about their mutual friends, and then Mary Jo said she needed to start packing and making her flight plans. Alan assured her that he'd meet her plane, and they broke the connection. He sat for a moment and thought, "It's amazing. I feel better already. Mary Jo may be the shrewdest, and certainly most fearless, strategist I've ever known, and I have a feeling it might be good to have her alter ego, Shiva, on our team too. I just hope I'll be able to pay her fee."

Alan finished his coffee, shaved, showered, and dressed in jeans and a football jersey. He drove into town, parked behind his new office, and let himself in the back. He headed to the lobby entrance, flipping lights on as he walked. When he entered, he stood transfixed. The space had been carefully restored to its Art Nouveau elegance. The lobby had been transformed into a spacious reception area, with several glass-fronted offices on one side, and Alan's large and beautifully decorated office on the other. Seeing everything with all the lights on, Alan realized what a professional job the Thompson firm had managed in a very short time.

Alan crossed the lobby space and opened the door to his private office. Pete's grandfather's large walnut desk faced the entrance. Behind it stood a matching credenza that held the computer terminals and communications equipment that would make this the heartbeat of his new operation. Alan sat in the large leather chair, leaned back, and smiled to himself. He thought, "If this scheme doesn't work, it won't be because Corelli chintzed on his part of the deal. I've got everything I asked for, plus some extra stuff that I don't have a clue about. Since Mary Jo is coming out tomorrow, I think I'll go on and give Amy Wilson a call to see if she has any interest in coming on board. I need to have someone lined up before I start testing the system."

Alan grabbed the phone book and looked up Amy Wilson's home number. He dialed it, and on the second ring a voice said, "Good morning. This is Amy Wilson."

"Good morning, Amy. This is Alan Brooks. How're you this fine summer day?"

"Alan! Hello! I'm just fine. To what do I owe this pleasure?"

"Well, I'm starting a new business venture, and I want to talk to you about possibly joining me as my operations manager. I know you've just retired and probably haven't even had a chance to settle into your new routine, but I think we would work well together, and I hoped you might have an interest in at least talking with me."

"I'm flattered that you've thought of me, Alan, but I can't imagine what I could offer your operation unless you plan to do a lot of mailing and shipping. If that's the case, then I'm your girl. What sort of business are you starting?"

"I suppose it could best be described as a securities trading company. To some degree, it'll resemble a privately held hedge fund, but that's really irrelevant to my interest in having you come on board with me. I admired your ability to maintain order in the chaos of the Postal Service. If you can manage that zoo, then anything I do will be a piece of cake for you."

"Referring to the Postal System as a zoo might be a little harsh, but it certainly was an ongoing challenge...that's for sure. What sort of time frame are we talking about?"

"Well, that could be a bit of a problem. I'll need someone as soon as possible, and, preferably, I'd like to have you start early next week. Is there any chance you could meet with me on Monday morning, let me give you a data dump, and discuss salary and benefits?"

"Alan, as I said, I'm really flattered that you thought of me, and I heard that you had resigned your teaching post to do something on your own. You're right when you say that I haven't settled into a retirement routine, and I'm not at all sure I want to, so, yes, I'll be glad to talk with you on Monday. Where would you like to meet?"

"Could you come downtown to my new office? It's in the old bank building on the corner of Main and Austin. Just park in one of the reserved spaces in the back and ring the doorbell; I'll come and let you in. Thank you, Amy. I'm looking forward to our talk. See you on Monday."

Amy replied, "See you then," and hung up the phone.

"That went better than I expected. I might just have a chance with Amy, and Mary Jo can sit in on the interview."

***

After she finished her conversation with Alan Brooks, Mary Jo called Carson Aviation and asked Doug Hastings to have her twin-engine Cessna Mustang ready to leave on Sunday morning. She added that she'd file a complete flight plan online later. She noticed that Allie Burke, the office manager for Thibodaux Engineering, was in her office, and Mary Jo tapped on the doorframe and stuck her head in. "Good morning, Allie. Didn't know you'd be in on Saturday."

"Not going to be here too long. Just needed to catch up on some filing. I hate to do it, and it piles up until I can't find a damn thing."

"Well, I'm glad I caught you. Wanted to give you a heads-up that I'll be flying out to Indian Territory tomorrow, and I'll probably be gone a couple of days."

"Finally going to see Alan Brooks, huh? Doesn't he live in some little town with a funny name?"

"Yeah, believe it or not, he lives near Blister, Texas. Sounds inviting, doesn't it?"

"Yeah! Be sure to send us a postcard."

"If they have a post office. Is there anything on our schedule that needs attention next week?"

"Not really. We're putting the finishing touches on the sea wall in Gulf Shores, and the catfish operation in Greensboro is moving right along, so, no, there's nothing urgent. Have fun and try to keep your scalp attached to your head."

"I'll be flying out early tomorrow morning. Would you let Laurie know that I'll be gone? Once I get out there, I'll let y'all know when I'll be back."

"No problem. I'll call if I need you."

"Okay. I'll let you get back to your filing."

Mary Jo went into her office, booted up her computer, pulled up a site that served private aviation, and logged in. She calculated the air miles from Mobile to Blister, Texas, to be just under 1,100, and the range of her little Citation was 1,400 air miles. She could do it nonstop if she caught the winds right, and, if not, she could stop for fuel in Midland/Odessa without straining the little jet's range. She determined her flight time to be around four hours, even with a possible refueling stop.

Mary Jo decided to leave at least by 8:00 on Sunday morning, and, with the hour she'd gain going from Central to Mountain Time, she could be in Blister by 1:00 or so. She filed her flight plan and sent an email to Alan letting him know that she'd arrive around 1:00 p.m. and gave him her plane's tail number.

While Mary Jo was planning and packing for her trip, Alan spent the rest of Saturday closing his office at WTSU and making sure he'd taken care of all the separation paperwork. That evening, he fired up the grill and cooked a two-inch-thick porterhouse for himself. After eating the whole two pounds of beef, he mixed a bourbon on the rocks and sat on the front veranda, watching the millions of stars that twinkled in the desert night until sleep overtook him.

Just after noon on Sunday morning, Alan drove his pickup to the Blister, Texas, airport and parked at the Fixed Base Operation, which served private aviation. He gave the tail number to the gal at the desk, and she told him that Mary Jo was a little over an hour out. Alan took a seat and picked up a copy of the latest issue of *Texas Parks & Wildlife*. Alan's phone rang, and Mary Jo told him that she'd be landing in about 40 minutes.

Alan was leaning against the fence as the little jet followed the plane handlers and parked in front of the terminal. Mary Jo deplaned, took a garment bag and a small roll-on suitcase from the baggage bin, and walked across the tarmac towards Alan. He watched as she moved smoothly toward the terminal, and he marveled at her animal-like grace. He held the gate open, took her suitcase, and said, "Welcome to paradise."

Mary Jo looked up at the glaring West Texas sun, shielded her eyes, and replied, "Funny how it feels just like my vision of Hell. Now I see why you loved Afghanistan."

"You should be comfortable. I checked the weather in Mobile this morning, and it was 96 degrees with 90% humidity. At least we have a dry heat, even if it is 106. It's good to see you, Mary Jo."

"I'm glad to see you, as well. You look great."

"So do you. I see you keep in shape, despite having a desk job."

"At least I have a job, unlike certain people I know."

"We're going to be talking a lot about that sad situation over the next day or two. I'll put your stuff in the truck while you tend to your plane. Meet you out front."

The friends were pulling out of the airport parking lot when Alan asked, "Have you had lunch?"

"No. I ate a protein bar an hour or so ago, but I'm a little peckish now that you ask."

"There's not much open on Sundays out here, but I know where we can get a dynamite cheeseburger and a cold beer, if you're interested."

"When in Rome…"

Alan stopped at the Shell station opposite the C&P at Slap Out. Mary Jo took a look at the sign broadcasting Slap Out Shell and asked, "So you suppose they're slap out of gas?"

"No. You're sitting in Slap Out, Texas."

"I guess Slap Out is a suburb of Blister, right?"

"C'mon, smart ass. You're gonna love their burgers."

After slamming down a bacon cheeseburger, fries, and a couple of cold beers, Mary Jo leaned back in the booth and said, "Okay, I'll have to admit that was an outstanding cheeseburger. Must be the desert air."

"Better be careful, you might just learn to like my part of the country. There's room to roam at will out here."

"Yeah and, from what you said on the phone, people are roaming all over your place, including Indian ghost soldiers and horse killers."

"There's a whole lot going on for me right now, so let's order another beer and let me fill you in on why I wanted you to come help me."

"Sounds like a good way to start."

Alan spent close to an hour walking Shiva through everything that had happened since his resignation from WTSU. Mary Jo asked a few questions about the decimal-scalping system and then said, "Okay, from what you've told me, I'd say you have multiple issues that might necessitate my help. First, you've got to set up and test your theory. If it doesn't work, then we'll all have a nice visit and go back to our normal lives — no harm, no foul. If it *does* work, then you'll have to be sure you can collect a large amount of money and get it in the world financial markets without attracting a lot of attention, *and* you need a way to protect your intellectual property. It so happens that I may just have the answer to part of the problem close at hand, but we'll get into that later. You also have some strange business going on at your ranch. Who do you think shot that horse, and do you think it's connected to what you're doing with your system?"

"No, I doubt that there's any connection, but I have to admit that the timing is a *big* coincidence, and you know how I feel about coincidences; I don't believe in them."

"How about the mysterious Native American? Who the hell is he?"

"I don't think he represents a threat of any sort. My best guess is that whoever he is, he came from the small Apache reservation that borders my land to the north. There've never been more than a couple of dozen families from the Jicarilla, a small clan that's part of the larger Chiricahua tribe. Texas allowed them to stay on their ancestral lands because it's one of their holiest of holies."

"Have you ever seen any of them on your land before?"

"No, but you have to realize that I've got over 16,000 acres, and we live on the southeastern section. There's a lot of open desert north of us. We've always had good relations with the Jicarilla, and if there's a problem, then I certainly don't know what it is."

"Okay, we'll deal with that a little later. You mentioned that you have an interview set up for tomorrow morning with a possible candidate for operations manager. Seems to me that this will be a key position, and whoever holds it will have to be fully briefed on the legal implications. Personally, I agree with Pete Corelli. I don't see a legal or moral problem, but it's only fair to be sure she goes in with her eyes wide open."

"I'd like you to sit in on the interview. I'll introduce you as my security consultant."

"I'd like to do that. If I'm going to be able to help, then I'll need a good read on all of the players. Let's deal with getting the company set up and testing your theory, and we can deal with the stuff at the ranch a little further down the road. By the way, I hope I'll get to meet Corelli. He sounds like an interesting fellow."

"Oh, you'll meet him tomorrow, and you can bet he'll find you just as interesting."

The two friends chatted for a while longer and then drove back to the Circle B. The afternoon sun was approaching the Guadalupe Mountains to the west, and everything was bathed in an ethereal light. They sat on the porch and watched as the sun slid below the mountains, and, finally, Mary Jo said, "Okay. I have to admit it. This is really a beautiful place. I've never seen light that has as many hues as tonight's sunset had. I can see why you love this country so. It has its splendor."

"Yes, it does. Let's turn in for the night. If you'll get up early, then we can take a ride, and you'll see an altogether different kind of beauty. You do ride, don't you?"

"I've been riding since I've been walking. I love it."

"Good! Let me show you your room, and we'll meet again in the morning."

EIGHT

MARY JO AWOKE TO THE SOUND of people moving about and the aroma of freshly brewed coffee. She took care of her morning ablutions and then wandered into the kitchen. A pretty, plump, Latino lady was rolling biscuits out on a flour-covered pastry board, and bacon was frying on the stove. Mary Jo smiled and said, "Good morning. You must be Maria. I'm Mary Jo."

"Si, Señorita. Señor Alan told me to expect you for breakfast. Since you sleep so late, he wanted to eat when you finally got up."

Mary Jo looked at the clock on the wall and saw that it was 6:30, and she thought, "I wonder what in the hell time everyone gets up around here?"

Maria poured a large mug of steaming coffee and handed it to Mary Jo, just as Alan came bursting through the back door. He smiled and said, "Good morning, sleepy girl. I gather you are well rested."

Shaking her head, Mary Jo replied, "I did sleep very well, but, for heaven's sake, it isn't exactly noon!"

"No, but we've got places to go and people to see. Since we missed the sunrise this morning, I thought we'd postpone our ride until tomorrow. We'll eat breakfast and head on into town."

"Whatever you think," Mary Jo said, as she took a seat at the kitchen table.

Maria had made biscuits, bacon, sausage, and ham, along with hash browns, grits, and refried beans. She came to the table and asked Mary Jo how many eggs she wanted and how she wanted them fixed, and Mary Jo replied, "I'll just have one egg, softly scrambled, please."

Maria shook her head and said, "You ought to eat a good breakfast, Señorita."

Mary Jo looked around the table and said, "Maria, I believe I can find enough to keep me going, and it all looks scrumptious."

Maria turned back to her stove, muttering something under her breath as she went.

After breakfast, Alan and Mary Jo got in the pickup and started to town. It was just after 8:00, but the sun was bearing down, and the mercury was steadily rising. Alan parked in one of the spaces next to the back door and fumbled to find his key. He opened the door and held it for Mary Jo. When they entered the main lobby and Alan had turned on all the lights, Mary Jo gasped, "My gracious, this is spectacular! How long have you been working on the restoration?"

"You'll be shocked to know that two weeks ago this space hadn't been occupied since 1929. Corelli can work miracles."

"Yes, he can. I can't wait to meet the talented Mr. Corelli."

"Wait till you see my office, but, first, let's make a pot of coffee."

Alan made the coffee as Mary Jo wandered around the first floor of the building. When he handed her a steaming mug, she said, "If I'm going to be in charge of setting up security, then I'm going to need an office and commo hookups."

"Not a problem. There are several open offices on the second floor, and I can get phone and internet service in there by this afternoon. Want to take a look?"

The friends toured the upper floors of the building and then returned to Alan's office. He sat down behind his desk and motioned for Mary Jo to take one of the chairs that faced his desk, and then he pulled open a drawer, retrieved a set of blueprints, and handed them across the desk to her. "These are the drawings for all of the communications networks, as well as the building plans," he said.

"Great, I'll take these and start a risk analysis as soon as I have an office. What time are you expecting Mrs. Wilson?"

"Anytime now, and I believe it'll be Ms. Wilson. As far as I know, she's never been married."

The back doorbell sounded, and Alan stood and headed toward the ringing. "That's probably Amy now; keep your seat and I'll go let her in."

Alan opened the door and greeted Amy Wilson. "Good morning, Amy. I'm glad to see you. I appreciate your meeting with me on such short notice. Let's go to my office and visit awhile."

"Just lead the way. I'll be close behind," Amy replied.

Alan said, "Let's stop by the kitchen and get you a cup of coffee. You do drink coffee, don't you?"

"Coffee will be fine. Why don't you let me make it?"

"One thing that you learn early in a career as a marine is how to make coffee under almost any circumstances. I have a pot ready to go." Alan poured Amy a cup. "There's someone I want you to meet," Alan said as he led her into his office. When they came in, Mary Jo stood up while Alan made the introductions. "Amy Wilson, this is Mary Jo Thibodaux. Mary Jo and I once served together, and now, among other things, she's a security consultant. She'll be responsible for setting up the security on our systems."

Mary Jo extended her hand and said, "I'm glad to meet you Ms. Wilson; I hope you don't mind my sitting in this morning."

Amy took her hand with a firm grip, smiled, and said, "Please, call me Amy, and I'm fine with your being here."

The three took seats around a low coffee table, which was flanked by four Queen Anne wingback chairs. Alan looked across the table and noticed what an attractive lady Amy was. Her short, silvery gray hair framed a pretty face, which showed few visible signs of her sixty-plus years. Her outfit, tweed slacks and a coral blouse, accented by a cardigan sweater that was draped over her shoulders, complemented her trim figure. There was some conversation about her career with the Postal System, and they made small talk about the local scene until Amy took a sip of her coffee and said, "Alan, fill me in on your life since you finished WTSU."

"Sure, I'll be glad to; it's a pretty dull tale. I graduated from WTSU with a B.S. in Electrical Engineering and accepted my Naval ROTC commission as a 2nd lieutenant in the Marine Corps. After basic officer school, I served with a marine infantry unit as a platoon leader and, finally, as a company commander in Iraq. After my deployment to Iraq, I attended the Special Warfare School and qualified as a Navy SEAL. I gave up my commission in the Corps and became a naval officer. Later, I led a Special Operations team in Afghanistan, and that's where I met Mary Jo."

Alan continued, "I was wounded near Kandahar and evacuated back to Walter Reed for my recovery. I transferred to the inactive reserve, started graduate school at Stanford, and subsequently earned a master's degree in Electronics, and later a Ph.D. in Applied Engineering from MIT. I've been teaching Electrical Engineering under Dr. Fields at WTSU since 2000. As you've probably heard, I resigned that position several weeks ago in order to start this business. That's the short version of my life since WTSU."

"Well, I find it interesting that you failed to mention two Silver Stars and a Navy Cross as you recapped your experience as a marine officer. I've read the accompanying citations for these decorations. I should think you'd be flaunting them."

"In both Iraq and Afghanistan, I saw guys put themselves at risk for their buddies but receive no decorations. Any recognition that I got should be shared by every man with whom I served. I just happened to be selected to hold them in trust. You must have done a little research before our meeting."

"I have to confess to googling you before I came over. I don't want you to think I'm interviewing you, but I just wanted to have an understanding of you and what you've been up to."

"I completely understand, and I'll be glad to share any additional information, so please feel free to ask. I find it surprising that you had any knowledge or interest in my Marine Corps career."

"I have a confession to make; it'll come out eventually anyway. I'm a serving officer in the U.S. Naval active reserve. I'll be retiring in two years, but, for now, I'm still active."

"Oh, a swab jockey! I'd never have guessed that a nice lady like you could have gone so wrong."

"That will be Captain Swab Jockey to you, Commander. Once a jarhead, always a jarhead."

Alan stood and snapped to attention. "Yes, ma'am, Captain Wilson. I meant no disrespect with the swab jockey remark."

"None taken. At ease, Commander. We needn't stand on military courtesy when out of uniform. You may refer to me as ma'am or

Captain if it makes you comfortable, but Amy works fine for me," she said with a smile.

"Then Amy it is, but the specter of those eagles will always tint my attitude toward you."

"Actually, I may be trading the eagles for a star or two. I'm on the Admirals List, awaiting Senate confirmation."

"I'm not easily intimated, but you're starting to scare me. Is there anything else I should know about you?"

"Not really, unless you want to count my Ph.D. in International Affairs and my work with the CIA."

"I'm afraid to ask what you did for the CIA; I suppose if you tell me, you'll have to kill me."

"There is that, but, for the most part, I was a policy wonk, and I served as an advisor to the agency on issues relating to international trade. No parachuting behind enemy lines or insertions by submarine for me, both of which I suspect you've probably done."

Amy turned to Mary Jo and said, "Since Alan says that the two of you served together in Afghanistan, I assume you have a strong military background too."

"Yes, ma'am. I'm originally from New Iberia, Louisiana, and I went to LSU on a track scholarship. I graduated with a B.S. in Civil Engineering, and I accepted my ROTC commission in the army. After training as an infantry officer and jump school, I wanted to find a place closer to the action, and I was accepted for military intelligence."

"I suppose it was in this role that you ran across Commander Brooks?"

Alan spoke up and said, "My SEAL team was trapped on a mountaintop, and Mary Jo was our liaison with army intelligence. In spite of serious injuries, she led a nighttime patrol that resulted in our ultimate relief. Mary Jo received the Silver Star for her work that night."

Amy said, "Interesting. Why did you decide to leave the service?"

Mary Jo said, "I spent several months in an army hospital after my injuries and then returned to my unit in the States. I became a senior counterintelligence agent, working in operations all over the world. In 2007, I was promoted to Lieutenant Colonel, but I didn't like the administrative work. Too much bullshit. I decided to get out, and I moved to Mobile, Alabama, to set up a Civil Engineering company. As they say, the rest is history, a history that I'm sure you can check out through your CIA buddies."

"Miss Thibodaux, does my connection with naval intelligence and the CIA cause you some discomfort?"

"I'm not sure. Let's see how it plays out when Alan explains what he has in mind."

Alan said, "Amy, let me fill you in on what we'll be doing here at Brooks Capital, LLC. I have two projects that I'll be attempting to perfect, and the second is totally dependent on the success of the first. The core business, and hopefully my source of investment capital, will be implementing a securities trading system that I've developed but haven't completely proven. This will be my day-to-day business."

Amy asked, "Is this anything like a hedge fund?"

"Yes and no. I'll be using some of the trading systems that are common to almost all investment funds, but I'll only have my own money at play. There'll be no limited partners. This is the major difference between what we'll be doing and most hedge funds. Because there won't be shareholders or investors involved, we'll be flying completely under the radar of the usual regulatory agencies, such as the Securities Exchange Commission. This will make our job a whole lot simpler."

"Well, all of that seems to be pretty straightforward. I can probably pick up the necessary knowledge I'd need to help you keep it all in order. What's the second project about?"

"I want to use any excess capital that I might be able to accumulate to do basic research on important issues that will affect people worldwide, such as clean, abundant water, cheap energy, and good medical care. Sounds cliché, but there it is."

"So, the work yet to be done to save the world is dependent on financing provided by Brooks Capital?"

"Yeah, that's pretty much the idea. Think you might be interested?"

"Interested in being involved with possibly changing the world? Yes, I think so. What do you need to know about me?"

"That you're interested is the most important thing. I've known you forever, and I have great respect for the job you did with the post office. I suppose the next step would be to make you an offer, but, first, we need to come to an understanding that may affect your decision. Simply put, if my trading system pans out, then we're good to go for the long term; however, if it doesn't, then this will be the shortest job you've ever had. I'm going to make you an offer, assuming that everything works. If it doesn't, then we'll just shut the whole thing down and go on with our lives. Will that suit you?"

"Of course. I don't have a problem with working it like that. I have a feeling that you'll make this happen, and we'll all have a great adventure. I'm pleased that you're willing to allow me to participate. Anything else I need to know?"

"As a matter of fact, there is, and this is going to get a little heavy, but it has to be put on the table. I haven't been entirely truthful with you about our operation, so I need to rectify that. I'm going to tell you something, and then I want you to do one of three things: either leave now and agree never to discuss what I'm about to tell you with another person; take any action that your conscience requires; or commit to helping me maintain the system and never discuss it with any outsiders, including your intelligence connections. Can you agree to one of these three options?"

Amy thought carefully for several minutes and finally responded. "I'll be free to follow my conscience and do whatever I feel is the right thing — did I hear you correctly? And you do understand that I can do nothing that is not in the best interest of the United States?"

"That's a given. We've all taken the same oath," Mary Jo added.

Alan's stomach did a flip, but he decided to see it through. "Yes, and that includes reporting my activities to any authority you feel needs to know."

"I can't promise what my reaction will be, but, if you trust me enough to take the chance, then I'll be as fair as possible."

"That's good enough for me. Here goes."

Alan spent the next 15 minutes giving Amy a rundown of Wu's system and how it would work. He included the possibility that it might be illegal and the near certainty that it was immoral. When he had finished, he folded his hands and said, "Amy, if you need some time to think this over, then take as much as you need, but I'd appreciate an answer before the day is done."

"Alan, I don't need to think about this at all. It's clearly immoral, probably illegal, and it sounds like it'll be a blast. Count me in on the third option," she said with a huge grin. Alan must have looked stunned. "Hello, Alan. You seem surprised at my reaction."

"Not surprised as much as relieved and supremely pleased. This a major commitment on your part."

"I'm glad you're pleased but stop and think about it. I'm a relatively attractive matron 'of a certain age.' My life has been spent in government service, and my personal relationships have been limited to affairs that, for one reason or another, never panned out. At this late stage in my life, here comes a chance for adventure and excitement. I'd be nuts to let it go by, and, besides, what's the worst that can happen? A little legal inconvenience maybe, but I'll never serve a day. I'll roll on you before the FBI can start asking the first question."

Alan laughed and said, "Corelli will probably knock you down trying to get to the first of the 'I'm gonna roll on Alan lines.'"

"Too bad, chief. It's lonely at the top, and that's why you'll make the big bucks."

"Speaking of bucks, there'll be enough to make us all rich under the comp plan I have in mind. I propose to pay you a salary of $175,000 per year, full medical insurance coverage, disability insurance, and long-term health care. You'll get four weeks of vacation, all of the normal local, state, and national holidays, plus the Marine Corps' birthday. Also, I'll give you an annual bonus equal to one half of one percent of the company's net profits. Based on my expectations, this could mean an additional $50,000 to $100,000 per year, and maybe more. If we get up and running, then we'll look at 401(k)s and retirement plans, and I'll also provide $1,000,000 of whole life insurance, with you as the owner."

"Alan, this is most generous. Are you sure you'll be able to afford something like this?"

"Look at it this way; the trading system is a binary event. Either it'll work, or it won't. If it works, then there'll be no problem with what I'm proposing. If it doesn't, then the whole issue is moot. I hope you're willing to take a chance for a week or so, and let's hope I can make this deal a success."

Amy asked, "When do you want me to start?"

Alan replied with a grin, "It appears you just did."

NINE

ALAN SUGGESTED THAT AMY go home, change into something more comfortable, and meet back at the office after lunch. When she'd gone, Alan looked at Mary Jo and said, "So, what'd you think?"

Mary Jo paused for a moment. "At this point, I'm not sure. She'd done her homework on you, and that's a plus. The fact that she's a spook concerns me a little. I'd like to wait until I've gotten to know her better before I make a judgment. No doubt she'll know more about me when she comes back this afternoon, so let's see how it goes."

"Well, since you're head of security around here, I'll defer to you. Speaking of security, there's something else we need to talk about."

"Yeah, what's that?"

"*If* the system works, as I hope it will, then it could create thousands of dollars every day. I'll need to deposit that in a bank where it can be held until I need it. Eventually, I want access to the international banking system without creating any undo concern on anyone's part. Any thoughts on that?"

"Personally, I don't, but I know and trust someone whose family's been dealing with this sort of thing for centuries. Do you remember Col. Will Ransom, my unit commander?"

"Yeah, I met Will when we were cleaning up after you slit the throats of about a dozen turbaned warriors. As I recall, he's out now, farming in Mississippi."

"He is. He owns about as much land in the Mississippi Delta as you have out here. The only difference is that his sits on top of one of North America's largest aquifers. Anyway, when Shell Oil settled my grandfather's lawsuit, and I got that windfall of money, I asked Will if he could recommend someone to manage it for me. He introduced me to the Dalhousie Merchant Bank, and they've managed my funds ever since."

"You mentioned that you use them. I assume you're pleased with their operation."

"More than pleased."

"Think they'd be interested in working with me?"

"I'll call them and find out. Emile Dalhousie is the North American head of the firm, which is headquartered in Bordeaux, France."

"Where's the U.S. branch?"

"In Mobile and has been since the early 1700s. I'll give Emile a call this morning and see what he says. If for some reason he can't do it, then I'm sure he can recommend an alternative."

"Mary Jo, I realize all of this has been rushed, but I'd like to have an answer before we run the beta test on the system."

"When are you planning on testing it?"

"I hope we can make the first run on Friday afternoon."

"Okay, let me use a phone, and I'll give Emile a call and check it out."

Alan led her to what would be Amy's office and closed the door. Mary Jo dialed Emile Dalhousie's private number and waited as it rang. A pleasant female voice said, "Good morning. Emile Dalhousie's office. How may I help you?"

"Good morning, Melissa. Is Emile available?"

"Oh, hi, Mary Jo. I didn't recognize the number on caller ID. Emile is somewhere in the building. Let me page him."

"Great. You didn't recognize this number because I'm deep in the heart of Texas."

"Better you than me. I'll see if I can run Emile down. I'm putting you on hold for a sec."

It was less than a minute when Emile picked up and said, "Good morning, Mary Jo. Melissa tells me you're in Texas."

"Yeah, I'm out here helping a friend set up a new business, and I may need some help."

"You know I'll do anything I can."

"My friend Alan Brooks is about to test a radically new securities trading system, and, if it works, it could generate several million dollars a year in free capital. He plans to use the money to work on developing clean energy and clean water sources, and he wants to have his funds available worldwide on short notice. He needs an international banking partner, and, of course, I immediately thought of Dalhousie."

"I appreciate your confidence, and, as you know, we're certainly international in scope. At your behest, we would be glad to advise Mr. Brooks, but I have to add that I'm skeptical of any market trading system. I've never seen one that works on a consistent basis."

"Emile, I have no basis to evaluate Alan's system, other than to say that he holds a Ph.D. from M.I.T., and he commanded a SEAL team in Afghanistan. He and I served together when I received the wounds that sent me to San Antonio. He also knows Will Ransom, and I believe Will would vouch for him."

"All recommendations that lean in his favor. What would you like for me to do?"

"Alan plans to test his system later this week, and I'd appreciate it if you'd come out here and help him. I can fly back to Mobile and pick you up this afternoon, and we can be back here in the morning."

"That won't be necessary; I can take the Lear and arrive by noon tomorrow. By the way, where is 'out here?'"

"There's a municipal airport that can take a Gulfstream. It's listed as Blister, Texas."

"Blister. Really?"

"Try to keep a straight face when you tell the flight crew that you're going to Blister."

"I'll text you with my flight information later in the day; can I reach you at this number?"

"Probably, but it would be better to use my cell."

Mary Jo signed off with Emile and walked back to Alan's office.

"Emile Dalhousie will be here in the morning. We'll need to pick him up at the airport."

"Here or in El Paso?"

"Here. He'll be coming in on the firm's Lear."

"Am I the only person flying commercial anymore?"

"Probably, but if all works on Friday, that'll soon come to an end."

"Let's don't count our jets before they hatch. It's bad luck."

"I'm hoping that luck doesn't come into play."

"Whatever. I just talked to Corelli, and he's going to meet us for lunch."

"Good, I can't wait to meet the Wizard behind the curtain."

The friends walked the two blocks to Shorty's and found Pete waiting for them at a table under the awning. Pete stood and broke into a wide grin. Alan said, "Damn, Corelli, you're drooling. Try to hold the letching to a dull roar. Meet Mary Jo Thibodaux, our security consultant, who, by the way, carries an ivory-handled straight razor."

Pete rubbed his chin. "You might know it; I just got a shave over at the hotel. It's nice to meet you, Mary Jo, even if you hang around with this old biddy."

"Nice to meet you too. Your reputation precedes you."

"I doubt that Brooks has done me justice. I'll have to see that you get to know the real me."

"Then I'll expect you to leap tall buildings and outrun speeding bullets."

"That sounds doable. Let's go in and get some lunch."

After everyone had ordered, Pete turned to Mary Jo and said, "Brooks tells me you have some unusual skills."

"I'm sure he has. He's the one who hung that horrible name on me."

"I suppose you're talking about Shiva the Destroyer?"

"That's the one."

"If Alan's trading system works, we're definitely gonna need some serious security, and you're probably just the person to set it up."

"I'll do what I can, but eventually you'll have to bring in the professionals. I can hit the high spots, but, when it comes to communications gear and computers, you'll need some techno-nerds."

Alan finished his cheeseburger and said, "By the way, Mary Jo's set up a meeting with her financial advisory firm for tomorrow morning. Think you can join us about 11:00? I'd like you to sit in."

Pete said, "As far as I know. I'll plan on being there. How's the office working out?"

"Great so far. I hired Amy Wilson as Chief Administrative Officer this morning, and she's starting when we get back."

"That's great. Amy's an administrative maven."

"Did you know that she's a captain in the Naval Reserve and is on the Admirals List?"

"No shit? I guess everybody in West Texas outranks me. How about you, Mary Jo? I guess you're a full colonel?"

"Not me — just a simple lieutenant colonel, but don't feel the need to stand on titles."

"Yes'm. I'll bear that in mind. Speaking of things military, Brooks, have you figured out who the mystery warrior haunting your ranch might be?"

"Not yet, but, as soon as we get the system up and running, Mary Jo's going to find out."

"Gonna sic Shiva on him, huh?"

"That's the plan. I'm not too worried about him. If he meant us harm, then he'd have already made his move. I suspect we'll hear from him when he's ready to talk."

"Well, I've enjoyed meeting you, Miss Thibodaux, but, in spite of what Brooks would tell you, I do have to do some work now and then. I'll see you two in the morning. Gotta run."

Pete took Mary Jo's hand, brushed it with a kiss, waved at Shorty, signaled that the lunch bill should go on his tab, and breezed out of the café. Alan and Mary Jo smiled at each other.

The two walked back to the office and noticed Amy's car parked out back. When they entered the lobby, they could see Amy rearranging her own office and adding some personal touches. When she saw them, she stuck her head out and said, "Mary Jo, do you have a minute?"

Alan grinned and said, "Looks like it's your turn in the hot seat. See you when she's done."

Mary Jo walked into Amy's office and took the seat offered to her, as Amy sat down behind her desk. "I think we were both caught a little off guard this morning. There was a great deal that you and Alan didn't know about me, and I knew virtually nothing about you. I remedied that during lunch, and I think we should start over."

"You're right...we had no idea of your intelligence connections, and, to be honest, they worry me a bit."

"I can certainly see how they would, considering the sensitive nature of Alan's venture. First, let me tell you what I've learned about you, and then you can ask me anything you want. I'll tell you the truth, and, if you hit on matters I can't discuss, then I'll remain silent. Will that work?"

"Yes, that sounds like a plan."

"I've got a fairly comprehensive resume of your activities since high school. You lost your parents when they were in a car wreck, and you grew up with your aunt and uncle in New Iberia. I know that you attended LSU on a track scholarship and that you excelled in Civil Engineering and ROTC. You accepted a commission in the army, volunteered for jump school, and later served with the 187th Parachute Infantry."

Amy continued, "You were chosen for training as an intelligence officer and became a counterintelligence agent. You were seriously wounded while supporting a Navy SEAL team. In spite of your injuries, you managed to lead a combat patrol that relieved the SEALs, and you alone killed at least eight of their warriors in hand-to-hand combat. You were decorated with the Silver Star for your bravery and returned to duty until you were promoted to lieutenant colonel, but you opted to leave the service. During this time, your grandfather's suit against the oil companies was settled, and you received a sizable amount of money that has allowed you to live well and open an engineering consulting firm in Mobile, Alabama. Recently, you've accepted other consulting assignments, which fall more in line with your former life in the army. Does that pretty much cover it?"

"As they say, it's close enough for government work. Yes, you've pretty well nailed me."

"There's just one more thing I should mention, and this led me to remember where I've seen you before. There's a man I know professionally, who practices law in Mobile. He and I have worked together over the years, and I trust him implicitly. It seems that you've made quite an impression on him, and he tells me that I should be comfortable working with you. Do you have any idea of whom I speak?"

"Sounds like you've been in touch with General Litton."

"I have indeed, and I've rarely heard him carry on about someone as he has about you. You should be flattered."

"I am. General Litton and I had an opportunity to work together on one of my consulting assignments earlier this year. The General is something else."

"You can bet your ass on that. He told me I should stay out of your way if you pulled your razor."

"Well, let's hope it never comes to that. The General is pretty good in a tight spot himself, and now I recognize you. You were at the White House when General Litton's second DFC was upgraded to the Medal of Honor."

"Yes…when I asked Jack who you were, he said that you were a young woman who had helped him with a little problem recently, and he added that you were our kind of people. That's high praise from Jack Litton."

"I guess this means that I've passed the smell test?"

"I'll be looking forward to working with you. Now, it's your turn."

"The fact that you have the confidence of General Litton is all I need know to trust that you're a person who'll keep her word. The only reservation that I have is what would happen if you found yourself with a question of loyalties."

"I can tell you that if the security of the country is ever in jeopardy, I'll take immediate action to shut this whole thing down and never look back. There is another side to the coin of my intelligence experience though. I have a great source of information at my fingertips, and, once again, if the United States is not threatened, then we can take advantage of it."

"I can see how that might be helpful. Alan's plan to seek methods to produce clean energy and water shouldn't pose any threat to the U.S."

"I agree, so if you're comfortable that I can juggle my responsibilities as Chief Administrative Officer and my duties as an intelligence officer, then we're good to go."

"I say let's do it and play the details out as they come up. I'm a big proponent of rather than asking permission, seek forgiveness."

"I think we'll enjoy working together, Mary Jo."

After their conversation, Mary Jo walked down the hall and knocked on Alan's office door.

"C'mon in. How'd your visit go with Amy?"

"She's the real deal, and she and I have a mutual friend who's vouched for both of us. His opinion removes any doubt that I had."

"Well, I have to confess that I've been worried that you couldn't get comfortable with her spookiness."

"Quite the contrary. I think that'll prove to be a real asset in the long run."

TEN

ALAN AND MARY JO DROVE through the gates of the ranch, with several hours of full daylight left, planning to take the ride they'd missed in the morning. Alan stopped by the stables and asked Pablo, the stable hand, to saddle two horses and bring them up to the house.

"Do you want Lucifer, Señor?"

"No, he's too hard to handle. Bring Janie and Streak."

"Si, Señor. I will bring them myself."

"Gracias, Pablo."

Mary Jo overheard the exchange and asked, "Who's Lucifer?"

Alan said, "He's a stallion we've raised from a foal. He's fast as the wind and has the disposition of a Tasmanian devil. I love to ride him, but not when a second rider's along. He's too damn headstrong, and he doesn't play well with others. Janie and Streak are good strong horses, and they're a lot more fun to ride."

"I'd love to ride Lucifer sometime," Mary Jo replied.

"We'll have to see how that works out. In the meantime, let's go in and change, and I'll meet you back here."

Mary Jo put on a pair of jeans and a football jersey and slipped into her tennis shoes. When she walked into the den, Alan took a look at her feet and said, "Mary Jo, this is West Texas. You won't make it a hundred feet in tennis shoes. We've got so much out here that can hurt you — even steel shank boots can be pierced. Let me see if I can find a pair of boots that'll fit you."

Alan rummaged around in a hall closet until he found a well-worn pair of women's cowboy boots. He handed them to Mary Jo, along with a fleece-lined Levi jacket, and said, "Here, try these on. They should come close to fitting...and bring the jacket. When the sun goes down, it can get pretty chilly out here."

While Mary Jo was working her feet into the borrowed boots, Alan walked to the kitchen.

"Maria, Mary Jo and I are going for a late-afternoon ride, and it'll be after sundown when we get back. Could you rustle up a couple of bowls of your chili for our dinner?"

"Si, Señor. Would you want a couple of tamales to go along with it?"

"That would be great."

When Mary Jo and Alan went outside, they found Pablo waiting with the horses. When they'd mounted, Alan whistled for Otto to come along. The riders took their time and followed the creek until they reached the little meadow where the dead horse was found. The sun was hovering just above the mountain peaks to the west, and the wildflowers that were scattered along the small pond scented the evening air with their sweet aroma. The two friends sat still in their saddles and savored the moment before Alan pointed to the ridge to their north and said, "It's up there that I saw the Indian, and it was just about this time of day."

Mary Jo peered at the distant ridgeline and asked, "Can we get up there from here?"

"Yeah. There's a little draw about a quarter of a mile to the west, and there's a game trail leading to the top. It's a little steep, but Janie and Streak can handle it, if you can."

"You just can't believe I can ride, can you?"

"I'm sure you can in Louisiana, but this is Texas, and that's the same difference as playing Triple A versus the Majors. But you shouldn't have a problem if you'll sit back and let Janie do the work."

The two approached the rocky game trail, and Alan began to move to the front. Mary Jo gave Janie a light kick to her ribs and raced ahead. As she passed Alan, she shouted, "See you at the top," and expertly guided Janie up the steep trail.

When Alan and Streak reached the ridge top, Mary Jo grinned and said, "How'd I do, Tex?"

"Not bad, for a flatlander."

"Does that mean I can ride Lucifer?"

"We'll just have to see how you come along, but you're not ready for prime time just yet."

The riders followed the ridge top, letting the horses pick their way along, until they came to the small copse of pine trees and then entered their shadows. The rock path became cushioned with pine needles, and the aroma of resin filled the summer evening. The two moved quietly along in single file until Alan held up his hand, signaling a stop. Mary Jo eased beside him to see what was up, and she saw it too. There was a lance stuck into the ridge top. The lance had eagle feathers attached. Alan got off his horse, pulled the lance out of the rocky soil, and held it up. "Looks like someone wants to have a little talk."

"What makes you say that?"

"Leaving a war lance stuck in the ground is the Apache way to signal that there's no danger and that he wants to have a parley."

"Okay, but where and when?"

"Don't know, but I'll leave a reply, and he'll let us know."

Alan untied the bandanna from around his neck, tied it to the lance, and then stuck it back in the ridge top. He remounted Streak and signaled for Mary Jo to follow him. The sun was completely behind the mountains, and a chill had settled in, so Shiva pulled on the Levi jacket and fell in behind Alan, asking, "Where are we going now?"

"Home. It's chili time."

The friends ate their chili and tamales on the front veranda and watched as the night sky filled with a zillion stars. When they finished their meal, Alan took the empty bowls in and returned with two snifters of brandy and two Indian blankets. He handed one of each to Mary Jo and said, "Just sitting and watching the night is one of my great joys, but it can get a little nippy. The brandy and blankets will help."

Mary Jo took a sip of the golden liquid, sighed, and watched as a shooting star went from horizon to horizon. Finally, she broke the silence. "You're right about the unique beauty of the high desert, and now I can see why you loved Afghanistan."

"Yeah, I felt at home there, and I loved the native people. They reminded me of our Apaches. They're hospitable and friendly, if left alone. I wish everyone would leave them in peace, but I doubt that's ever going to happen."

"Well, they're certainly like your Apaches in one sense; they don't like outsiders messing with them."

"Yeah, you'd think the world could've figured that out by now."

"The folks out here seem to have found a way to coexist with your Apache neighbors."

"The Apache may have an official reservation, but they roam at will across their traditional homeland. They don't recognize the Rio Grande as a national border, and they move back and forth from Mexico to the United States, as the mood suits them."

"At least they aren't pillaging and burning as they go."

"True. For now, at least, they're honoring the truce, but I'll just bet they're waiting for another crack at throwing our asses back to Dallas."

They sat and chatted through a second snifter of brandy before eventually calling it a night. Mary Jo had fallen asleep in her chair, and Alan gently nudged her to head to bed.

On Wednesday morning, they ate breakfast and then drove into the office. Amy's car was there when they arrived, and, as Alan got out of his vehicle, he said, "Shit! Captain Wilson is already at the helm. She must be one of those morning people."

"This from the man who reprimanded me for sleeping until 6:30 a.m.," Mary Jo retorted. "Just be glad she's reliable and on time."

"Yeah, guess you're right," Alan said as he opened the back door.

All of the lights were on, and the aroma of freshly brewed coffee filled the air. Amy was sitting in her office tapping away on her computer, and Alan knocked on her door. "Good morning, Amy. If you've got a minute, I'd like to have a quick meeting, as soon as Mary Jo and I get a cup of your coffee."

"No problem. Where do you want to meet?"

"Let's do it in my office. We'll be there in a sec."

When they'd all sat down in his office, Alan said, "Amy, this morning, a gentleman from Mobile, Alabama, who may help us keep up with our 'hoped for' profits, is flying in to meet with us. His name is Emile Dalhousie, and his family has been in the merchant banking game since Rome ruled the world. Mary Jo, do you know what time we need to pick up Mr. Dalhousie?"

Mary Jo pulled out her cell phone and checked her text messages. "They left Mobile at 0900 CDT, and their ETA is 0945 MDT. We probably need to head out there pretty soon."

"How in the hell are they getting here in an hour and 45 minutes?"

Amy spoke up and said, "Piece of cake if you've got a Lear that cruises close to 600 MPH."

"Well, I guess we better head on out there. Amy, we'll finish this later, unless the meeting with Emile Dalhousie brings you completely up to speed. Will you give Pete a call and remind him of the meeting?"

"Will do, and I'll make a fresh pot of coffee."

Alan and Mary Jo watched the Lear make a perfect landing and taxi into the terminal. A golf cart arrived just as the front door opened, and stairs descended to the tarmac. Emile Dalhousie and an attractive woman got in the golf cart and sped toward the terminal, where Alan and Mary Jo met them.

Emile looked quite dapper in a tan poplin suit, and Mary Jo recognized his assistant, Melissa Green. She watched as Emile helped Melissa exit the golf cart and said, "Good morning, y'all. Welcome to Blister, Texas."

"Good morning, Mary Jo," they replied in unison.

"I'd like y'all to meet my friend and client, Dr. Alan Brooks. Alan, this is Emile Dalhousie and his personal assistant, Melissa Green."

Alan shook hands with them and suggested that they pick up their bags and go right in to the office. Emile smiled and pointed to his briefcase. "This is all of our bags. We'll be back in Mobile tonight."

Mary Jo and Melissa managed to squeeze into the small dual cab of the pickup, while Alan and Emile took the front. When they got to the office, Alan showed them into the conference room, where Amy and Pete Corelli were talking and drinking coffee. Both of them stood as Alan made the introductions, and, after Amy offered coffee and everyone was settled in, Mary Jo began, "I think the first order of business would be to ask Emile to tell us about his firm. Emile, would you please?"

Emile straightened his cuffs and said, "For you to have a complete understanding of our firm, I need to give you some of the family history, so bear with me. The first written records that mention the Dalhousie family can be found in the tax rolls of the Count of Bordeaux, dating from the year 816. The family held a commercial charter to trade with the lead mines, located on the British mainland. The few records that have survived would suggest that heavily armed merchant ships transported the wine of Bordeaux and returned with galena, a rich lead, and silver ore. The family remained in the import-export business, managing to steer clear of the ebb and flow of local politics and serving the needs of whoever ruled Bordeaux for the next 600 years. The church records indicated that generation after generation of Dalhousies were staunch members of the Roman Church, and parish archives chronicle their births and deaths."

Emile continued, "In the early part of the 16th century, portions of the family became involved with the Calvinist Reformation and converted to the Protestant Reformed Church of France. By the mid-1500s, these Calvinists became known as Huguenots and were in constant conflict with the Roman Church and the French Kings. An uneasy peace existed until 1572, when a wave of persecution swept France and thousands of Huguenots were massacred. Order was restored by the Edict of Nantes, recognizing Roman Catholicism as the State Religion, but guaranteeing religious freedom to all Protestants. This truce remained in place until 1685, when Louis XIV revoked the Edict of Nantes and began a state-sponsored persecution of the Huguenots. This resulted in a mass Protestant exodus from France. Having anticipated the King's action, minor branches of the family remained Catholic and were able to salvage some of the family's property during the persecution. They lost their commercial charter but were able to conceal a significant amount of gold, silver, and precious stones."

Emile added, "The Huguenot Dalhousies fled to French North America to avoid the King's wrath and established a branch of the firm in Montreal. Later, in 1701, when Jean-Baptiste Le Moyne,

Sieur de Bienville was made Governor of French Louisiana and dispatched to establish French sovereignty over the vast area, he was accompanied by one of the young sons of the Montreal Dalhousies. Bienville chose the site of present-day Mobile as the capital of the colony, and young Dalhousie purchased a large parcel of land in the newly laid-out city. We have offices on five continents and in every major financial center. The average tenure of our clients is 111 years, and our attrition rate is close to zero. We have never lost a client due to dissatisfaction, only death. We rarely accept new clients, but, when we do, we always have a firm endorsement from an existing client. Dr. Brooks, in your case, we have the recommendation of two clients — not only Mary Jo but Will Ransom, as well."

Emile paused, and Pete asked, "Mr. Dalhousie, can you give us some idea how your merchant banking operation conducts business?"

Emile smiled and responded, "Our legal structure, unlike the charter of a commercial bank, allows us to operate as a corporation. We don't have depositors but, instead, shareholders, and the shareholders have instant liquidity, should they choose to sell their shares. In spite of our worldwide investment portfolio, we maintain sufficient cash to redeem all of our outstanding shares. We invest mainly in government securities, but we also enter into joint ventures with a proven stable of partners. All of our shareholders participate in all of our profits and losses."

Pete spoke up and said, "Very interesting, Emile. Thank you."

Mary Jo also thanked Emile and turned to Alan, saying, "Alan, would you walk Emile through your business plan?"

"Absolutely. Mr. Dalhousie, we've all reached this point without formal nondisclosure agreements or contracts of any kind. We're operating on mutual trust, and Mary Jo has vouched for your discretion. What I'm about to explain to you, while unproven, may be highly lucrative, but possibly illegal. If, after our meeting, you feel uncomfortable with participating, then I'll ask that you and Ms. Green return to Mobile and forget everything you've heard. Can you agree?"

"We do," replied Emile.

Alan outlined his proposed system, including how he planned to use any profits generated. When he had finished, he looked at Emile and said, "There it is. Any questions?"

Emile looked at Alan and asked, "Dr. Brooks, tell me why you think your system might be illegal?"

ELEVEN

AFTER THINKING FOR A MOMENT, Alan replied, "At this point, I'm basing it on the simple idea that if you take something that doesn't belong to you, that's stealing, and stealing is illegal in most cultures."

Emile asked, "May I play the devil's advocate?"

"Please do."

"First, for something to have been stolen, it would have had to belong to another person. Would you agree?"

"Yeah, that seems reasonable."

"Okay. Does everything belong to someone?"

"I suppose it does. Either to an individual or a group of individuals," Alan responded.

"How about the earth's atmosphere? Who owns it?"

"I suppose we all do," Alan said.

"Would it be stealing if I built a plant and extracted carbon dioxide from the atmosphere?"

"No, I'd say you have as much right to the atmosphere as anyone else."

"Does anyone have title to the bits of decimal points flying around in cyberspace?"

"No, but at one time, they belonged to someone."

"Does the former owner have a sense of loss where these decimal fragments are concerned?"

"No, they aren't aware that they're missing."

"So how does collecting and using them constitute theft any more than my collecting the exhaled particles of CO_2? Didn't they once belong to someone?"

Alan sat quietly thinking about Emile's theory, but Pete spoke up: "That's what I've been trying to tell him, but you just put my concept into words. You can't steal something that doesn't have an owner. Do you agree, Amy?"

"Well, I'm no lawyer, but it does seem logical to me that collecting what is flying about would be on a first come, first served basis, and, for sure, I'd apply the principle of taking action now and asking for forgiveness later."

Alan said, "Okay then. Is it safe for me to assume that none of you has any hesitation about being a part of this project — at least from a moral perspective?" He looked around the table, and everyone nodded in agreement.

Then Emile said, "Dr. Brooks, there are some legal guidelines you will have to deal with that affect any business handling large sums of cash. Exactly how much do you estimate your system will collect in a given period?"

"My calculations, based on some conservative premises, suggest the possibility of accruing close to $4,000 per 24-hour period."

"Would the system work on a 24/7 basis?"

"No, I plan only to run it on business days, so there's less chance of attracting attention when the system is in full swing."

"So, $4,000 per day for, say, 252 days per year?"

"Yeah, that's what I expect to happen...something like a million per year."

"Your biggest problem is going to come after you initially collect the funds. They can enter the banking system as 'trading profits,' but they will be subject to federal regulations as the funds are moved into the world banking system."

Alan asked, "Will this be a problem?"

"It won't be if you pay taxes on your gains and understand the banking regulations regarding transferring large sums of money."

"Of course. I'll pay any taxes due, but what's the deal about transferring large sums?"

"When you move your profits from the collecting bank to any other institution, including our firm, your bank will have to report every transfer of $10,000 or more."

Alan inquired, "Does this pose a real problem?"

"Not as long as you can account for the source of the funds, if questioned. This regulation is intended to be a red flag for money laundering. There will be an electronic trail left behind every deposit and withdrawal, and they must all tie together. Have you figured out how to disguise your decimal skimming as legitimate trading profits?"

"I hope so — at least, I believe I have."

"On what are you basing your logic?"

"A system of buying and selling options on financial futures."

"Will you actually trade these options?"

"That's my plan unless you have a better idea."

"Perhaps. If you'd like, I can have my financial-strategies people take a look at your system and give us an opinion."

"Yes. If we decide to work together, then I'd appreciate that — assuming we agree that all taxes would be paid and your people vet my options trading, would your firm have an interest in working with me?"

"Frankly, I doubt it. A million a year falls far below our minimum account value, and we adhere to the policy without exception. I am willing to advise you during your startup period, however, and to suggest other relationships for your long-term operation. We'll be happy to do this as a courtesy to Mary Jo and Will."

"I don't think I can argue with your offer. What do you need from me?"

"I'd like to bring my head of trading and a couple of his people out to make sure your system of decimal skimming and options trading can be made to work together. They're among the world's best financial minds. When do you plan to test your system?"

"I'm hoping to run a beta test on Friday afternoon. When can your people do this?"

"Melissa will fly back to Mobile this evening and return with the team early tomorrow morning. I'll stay over this evening, and, if you'll allow me to ask a couple of more questions, I'll be prepared to read them into the system as soon as they arrive."

"Emile, I can't tell you how much I appreciate your involvement, and I hope that, in a couple of years, we'll have accumulated the assets that'll allow us to work with your firm."

"I, too, hope for that outcome, but, in the meantime, we'll do what we can to help."

Pete had listened quietly and finally interjected: "Emile, I want to add my appreciation to Alan's. I'll leave y'all to it, but I'd like to have everyone join me at Lester's for steaks tonight."

Alan looked at Emile and said, "Emile, you can bunk at my ranch this evening, and I think dinner at Lester's sounds good. What do you say?"

"I'm sure I can check into the local hotel. I don't want to put you to any trouble."

Mary Jo said, "Emile, I'm staying at the ranch, and I can assure you that you'll be no trouble."

"Well, I suppose I'm outnumbered. I'll be delighted to be your guest, Dr. Brooks, and to join you all for dinner. I did bring an overnight bag as a precaution, so I'll have to retrieve it from the plane."

"No problem," Alan replied. "How about you, Amy? Want to ride to Lester's with us?"

"No, but thanks anyway. I need to go home and tend to my dog. I'll just meet y'all out there."

"Okay," Pete said. "See y'all at Lester's at 7:00."

The group continued to work until close to 4:00, when they took Melissa back to the airport, picked up Emile's bag, and watched the Lear lift off into the fading light. Maria and Cesar were waiting at the ranch and helped Emile to his room. Once settled, Emile joined Alan and Mary Jo for drinks on the veranda.

Alan gave Emile a brief history of the Circle B, and the three of them watched as the sun set behind the distant mountains. Finally, Alan suggested that they start for Lester's. Alan decided to take one of the Jeep Wagoneers, rather than his pickup, just for the sake of comfort. When they left the ranch road, they turned away from town and headed due south. Soon, they turned back to the west and drove down a gravel road, which was quietly sheltered by live oaks.

The gravel ended in a parking lot that faced a rambling rustic structure that was topped with a rusty tin roof. There were no signs on the building, but the parking area was well lit and nearly full of cars and pickups. Alan saw Corelli's car in a reserved parking spot as they went through the front door into a bustling kitchen. Alan led them past a substantial black cast-iron stove with an open oven, which glowed because of its high temperature. There were racks of steaks sizzling away on what appeared to be metal coal scoops, and the air was filled with the aroma of grilling beef.

The kitchen was charged with men and women making salads, frying potatoes, and cooking huge G.I.-sized pots of hot tamales. Alan led them to a door leading from the kitchen to a reservations desk, which was manned by a middle-aged lady who was an easy 300 pounds. She smiled when she saw Alan, grabbed him into a bear hug, and roared as his feet left the floor: "Alan Brooks, that scoundrel Corelli said you were coming! Hear you told those pricks at WTSU to bite your ass."

Alan, who was smothering in a hundred pounds of pulsating breast, managed a muffled, "Hey, Lucy! Let me out before I die in hooter heaven!"

Lucy Prescott set Alan back down on the floor, held him at arm's length, and purred, "I'm proud of you, young man. We need more folks willing to stand by their principles."

"Thank you, Lucy. I'm not sure how much principle was involved, but I did quit my job," he said with a crooked grin. "We're here to meet Corelli."

"Oh, he's already here. Y'all follow me." Lucy snaked and weaved through the crowded dining room to a table by the massive stone fireplace. Pete and Amy were deep in conversation and didn't see them approach, and Lucy slapped her hand down on the table top, causing both to nearly jump out of their seats. "Corelli, your guests are here," she growled and pulled Mary Jo's chair back. When everyone was seated, Lucy asked, "Y'all gonna need setups?"

Pete pointed to several bottles wrapped in brown paper bags and said, "Yeah, bring us ice, Cokes, soda, and a corkscrew, and try not to scare the hell out of your customers."

"I'm not worried about scaring Amy, and, as far as you go, we'll just drag you out back and let the coyotes tend to you. What y'all gonna have tonight?"

"Why don't you go and get our setups, and I'll try to explain your goofy menu to my friends."

"Corelli, sometimes you don't know if you're winding your ass or scratching your watch."

As Lucy walked away, Pete grinned and said, "Concerning the menu, Lester's requires some basic understanding. First of all, there isn't one. They serve four steaks: an 18-ounce filet and small, medium, and large porterhouses. You're gonna get hot tamales, salad, Texas toast, the best French fries you've ever tasted, and an Eskimo Pie for dessert. The only real choice you have to make is which steak you want, and how you want it cooked."

"If the filet is 18 ounces, I'm afraid to ask the sizes of the porterhouses," Mary Jo said.

Alan answered, "The small is 24 ounces, the medium is 32 ounces, and the large is 48 ounces. I usually order a medium and take some of it home."

Mary Jo asked with amusement, "Are you given any idea what it costs?"

"No, but we all know that the steaks are priced by multiplying what Lester paid for them by four, and all of the rest of the stuff comes with the steak. The system's been working since 1941. I can remember coming here with Dad and Granddad," added Alan.

When Lucy returned, everyone placed their orders. Pete passed the bottles of bourbon and scotch around, and everyone mixed a drink. Lucy brought some extra water glasses for the wine and handed the corkscrew to Pete. "Here you go, Pete; this is probably the only tool I'd trust you with."

While the diners awaited their steaks, Pete looked at Alan and asked, "You still being haunted by the ghost of Cochise?"

Alan smiled at Emile and replied, "We've seen an Apache warrior lurking about; in fact, he's left a sign that he'd like a meeting."

"I'd have thought y'all had taken care of the Apache problem some time ago," Emile said.

"This is big country, Emile. The Circle B has over 16,000 acres, most of which is totally empty of human habitation. The Apaches roam our land, and everyone else's at will. They do us no harm, and we give them free access. We're just grateful that we don't have to fight them anymore."

Emile looked interested and asked, "What do you think this fellow wants?"

"Haven't got a clue, but, as soon as we finish the beta test, I'm gonna find out. Mary Jo and I are going to meet with him."

Mary Jo looked surprised and said, "Oh really, and when were you going to tell me?"

"I just did. It'll be part of your security duties."

"We're gonna need to talk about this, Kemosabe."

The conversation turned to the upcoming beta test, and Amy remarked that it would be a sure thing that the NSA would pick up on the increased activity coming out of a remote part of West Texas. It would be better to just accept the fact rather than try to disguise it in some way.

Emile agreed and suggested that it might be better to route the trading activity through one of the world's financial centers, where it would just blend in to the normal activities.

Alan said, "The more we talk, the more complicated it gets, doesn't it? If the system works on Friday, then I'll try to find a way to amp it up. Emile, if I could increase the amount we collect, what would it take to meet your minimum requirements?"

"Assuming everything else met our standards, we would be comfortable with an annual contribution of $10,000,000 or more."

"I think we're going to need your firm to make this work. Let me see how Friday goes, and we'll work from there."

Emile agreed, and the conversation moved over to what Alan hoped to accomplish if the system could be made to work. Amy brought up a State Department white paper she had recently seen, discussing the major issues facing the world in the next 50 years, and pointed out that clean water led the list of worldwide needs. The paper suggested that access to water would replace crude oil as the world's strategic issue.

"Yep," Alan agreed. "Those of us who live in a water-deprived part of the world can appreciate the truth in this. Wars will be fought over water sources, and nations blessed with water will become world powers. I'm very interested in developing new sources of it, and I just hope my system will generate enough to fund that effort."

It was Emile's turn to agree, and he made the observation that the economic benefits of developing a new water source could produce enormous economic growth and huge profit margins. Not only was this good from an altruistic standpoint, but it could generate great wealth, as well.

While Pete had little to say, he listened intently and silently, his entrepreneurial instincts perking up. They continued the conversation long after the steaks were gone and finally decided to call it a night as Lester's began to close for the evening.

On the way to the parking lot, Pete suggested that they meet at Alan's office on Thursday to discuss the water concept further. Alan agreed, with the proviso that they do it after lunch. He wanted to have the morning to meet with Emile's team and to do some fine-tuning of the system before Friday's test.

Later that evening, Alan, Mary Jo, and Emile sat on the veranda and watched the night skies, each sipping brandy. Alan shared tales about the early settlers and how they managed to carve a life out of an arid country, all the while fighting off Comanches and Apaches, not to mention any number of drifting outlaws and bandits. He pointed out that the justice system was pretty simple: catch 'em and hang 'em.

After one brandy, Alan suggested that they turn in for the night. The plane would be returning by 9:00 the next morning, and they had a big day ahead of them.

Just before he fell asleep, Alan jolted up in the bed. "Aw, shit! I gotta be interviewed by Ellen at 2:00 tomorrow!"

TWELVE

AFTER A QUICK BREAKFAST at the ranch, Alan, Mary Jo, and Emile took the Wagoneer to the Blister airport and met the incoming Lear. Melissa Green led a group of four people across the tarmac, where Emile greeted them.

"Good morning, Melissa. How was the flight?"

"Smooth and uneventful, thankfully," she replied.

"Good. Dr. Alan Brooks, I'd like to introduce our head of trading, Dr. Phil Andrews, and two of his traders, Bill Wysock, who trades financial futures, and Jane Williams, who trades derivatives. I believe you all know Mary Jo Thibodaux, who's serving as the security consultant to Dr. Brooks's new firm." When everyone had finished shaking hands, Emile added, "I'm going to suggest that the five of us rent a car and go check into the hotel. That'll give me a chance to brief y'all on what I want you to do; then, we'll meet Alan, Mary Jo, and Amy back at the office after lunch. Will that work for you, Alan?"

"Yes, that'll be fine, but I may have to step out for 30 minutes or so this afternoon. I have a reporter from the local newspaper coming by around 2:00 to interview me for an article for the Sunday business section."

"That shouldn't be a problem; we'll have plenty to do vetting the trading system."

Back at the office, Alan went straight to work on the system so that he could have it ready for Emile's team. Mary Jo went upstairs to her office and called Allie in Mobile, who answered on the first ring. "Good morning, Mary Jo. How's it going out on America's last frontier?"

"I've been here less than a week, and I'm already starting to appreciate its beauty. You have to see it to believe it."

"Yeah, I saw it was 106 degrees yesterday. I think I'll pass. What can I do for you?"

"Nothing. Just checking in. How're our projects going?"

"We've got the floating footings down on the Ono Island project, and Fred says they'll start pouring the dock next week, so we're basically on schedule. The first draft of the plans for the catfish operation came in yesterday, and I'll look them over and email them to you if you'd like."

"Yeah, send 'em on. I'll take a look, and we can discuss it later."

"Any idea when you'll be coming home?"

"Not yet. Emile and his team just got here, and we'll be working tomorrow. I may try to come back for the weekend, depending on what happens tomorrow. I'll let you know one way or the other."

"Okay. I'll be here if you need me. Just give me a call."

Mary Jo opened her email and found the plans for the catfish project and printed them out on the large-format printer Pete had insisted on. Mary Jo settled in and began going over the plans. Just before noon, Amy buzzed her to say she was running over to Shorty's to pick up a sandwich for lunch and wanted to know if Mary Jo wanted something. Mary Jo said a BLT would be nice and then worked until Amy dropped a Styrofoam container on her desk. Amy asked, "Want anything to drink? We've got Cokes, iced tea, and coffee."

"I'll grab a Coke, and thanks for the sandwich. How much do I owe you?"

"Alan made me the 'I'll buy if you fly' deal, so it's covered."

"I'll thank him later."

Mary Jo was just finishing the BLT and taking her trash downstairs when she heard Emile and his colleagues come in the back door. Mary Jo met them and guided them to the conference room. She and Emile left the trading people to set up their gear, and Mary Jo knocked on Alan's office door. Startled, he quickly responded, "Y'all come on in; I'm just winding up some tweaks on the system. I'll be ready in 10 minutes."

When everyone was seated around the conference table, Alan stood and said, "I'm much obliged to you and your team, Emile, for offering to assist me with the design of a credible trading system that will incorporate my proposed decimal-retrieval system. I know Emile has briefed all of you on my basic concept, and I've emailed each of you the latest iteration of my system. If you'll pull that up on your laptops, then I'll walk you through it."

Alan spent the next hour explaining the logic behind what he called his blended-options theory. He and the Dalhousie team were discussing some of the details when Amy came in and told him that Ellen was waiting in the lobby for her appointment. Alan excused himself and told the team that, hopefully, he'd be back in about an hour.

When Alan walked into the lobby, he smiled at Ellen, who was in deep conversation with Amy. When Ellen saw him come in, she said, "Brooks, you've made a serious move toward credibility by hiring Amy, but, for the life of me, I can't understand why she'd sign on as housemother for you and Corelli."

"I assure you, she's a great deal more than a housemother, but I should have made her responsible for media relations, as well. Then you'd have to deal with a lady who could make sense out of the post office."

"The post office will probably look pretty good after trying to herd cats around here," Ellen retorted. "Let's get on with this interview so I can do something more productive, like editing the obits."

Alan held open the door to his office and ushered Ellen to the wing chairs near the fireplace. She arched an eyebrow and said, "Well, I'm surprised; I thought surely you'd go to your desk. You know, preserve the barrier and put the opposition on the defensive."

"I might have if I thought you were the opposition and not the agent of our system of free press. I don't plan to let this become adversarial in spite of your acid tongue. How do you want to make this work?"

"Well, since it's an interview, suppose I ask you questions, and you give me straight, honest answers."

"That oughtta work. Fire away."

Ellen started with the usual stage-setting questions that were binary and entirely unprovocative. They sailed along, establishing the facts surrounding Alan's new venture, until Ellen shifted in her seat and changed her body language and facial expressions. She led with the following: "Dr. Brooks, tell me why you think someone with a background in Electrical Engineering can successfully trade securities?"

Alan paused and then replied, "Ellen, you'd be surprised at the percentage of successful securities traders who have a technical education. An analytical approach to understanding the financial markets requires the same skill sets as a scientist uses to understand the infinite universe. What appears on the surface to be random and disordered can be seen to work like a finely tuned machine, when approached scientifically."

"Are you suggesting that macroeconomics behaves in the same fashion as the universe?"

"Exactly. Once you see the underlying forces at work, then you can write algorithms to predict outcomes."

"Do you believe that you have written algorithms that will allow you to predict market moves?"

"It isn't necessary to predict anything. If your calculations are accurate, then you can position your trade to follow the natural order of the market, and, according to my theory, you'll be on the right side the majority of the time. You don't have to be 100% right. After all, you can get in the Hall of Fame by batting over 300."

"Can you be a little more specific regarding the underlying premise of your system, and how does it differ from existing trading systems?"

"Ellen, as I hope you can appreciate, the details of my system are proprietary, but I will tell you that the major difference between my system and the traditional trading systems is that mine is indifferent to interest rates, market trends, or economic conditions. It's based on the concept that the market is always right, and it allows me to float with it."

Ellen sighed and turned off her recorder. "Alan, that's just so much bullshit! I can't believe you expect me to begin to believe it, let alone print it under my byline. Why didn't you just claim to have invented perpetual motion or cold fusion?"

"I told you that I'd be frank with you, and, to the extent that I can, I have been."

"What you've just described is an economic impossibility; if it could be done, then the free market system would no longer work."

"Why? Just because someone has finally been able to see the order in the market, does it invalidate the whole market concept?"

"Exactly," Ellen replied.

"Okay, let's assume for the moment that you're right and I'm dead wrong. What will be the likely outcome of my system?"

Ellen snapped, "You'll go flat broke before you can say 'Corelli lost his ass!'"

"Well, I have to ask you to go along with me until I'm broke. Write your story without mentioning any particular strategy. Just say that I've started a securities trading firm, yadda, yadda, yadda. Make it a Sunday fluff piece for local consumption."

"And I'd do that because…?"

"If I'm still in business after I start trading, then there'll be a much bigger story to write, and I'll give you an exclusive."

"An exclusive, huh? Worldwide?"

"Worldwide. You'll be my conduit to the public."

"When do you plan to test this system?"

"Sometime next week," he lied.

"And I'll be there when you run the test?"

"Of course. I'll give you a call when we set it up — probably Tuesday or Wednesday."

"Okay, I have a gut feeling that you're playing me, in spite of knowing the consequences, but I'm going along with you anyway. I'll need to take a few photos before I go for, as you put it, Sunday's fluff piece. And, by the way, the offices are drop-dead beautiful."

"Yeah, Seth Thompson did a great job; you might want to give him a plug, as long as it's going to be a fluff piece anyway."

"Yeah, I can do that," Ellen said as Alan led her back into the main lobby. She took a couple of digital shots and was turning to leave when she saw the meeting that was under way in the conference room. She smiled and asked, "Who are your visitors?"

"They're accounting folks who're helping Amy set up our bookkeeping system."

"No kidding? All the way from Mobile, Alabama? Couldn't find anyone in Dallas or Fort Worth?"

"Why do you think they're from Mobile?" Alan asked this as innocently as he could.

"Got some hot scoop for you, Brooks. Lears have tail numbers, and I get a call when anything big or private lands at Blister. That includes your cute, little friend with the Cessna Mustang. I guess she's helping them with any Civil Engineering issues," Ellen said as she walked out the front door.

Alan was left standing in the middle of the lobby with his mouth wide open. He first thought, "Shit. She's gonna cause all manner of problems." Then, the dawn of realization hit him. Ellen had played him like a rainbow trout. She'd run a background check on the Dalhousies, as well as Mary Jo, and she knew that something unique was going on and that it was credible enough for one of the world's leading merchant banks to fly its CEO to Texas to be involved. She'd given him the opportunity to paint himself into a corner, and then let him off the hook with a promise to let her have an exclusive. He thought, "Masterfully done, Ellen. You're a hell of a lot smarter than I gave you credit for, and you led me into a classic ambush. I shouldn't have underestimated you. Now, I've got to decide what to do with you."

When Alan rejoined the meeting, Phil Andrews said, "Dr. Brooks, we've looked over your trading plans, and we believe we have a better option."

"I'd hoped that you would. I'm no trader, and I sure don't have a 'not invented here' problem. Tell me what you have."

"Well, let me start by saying that the key to our whole plan is your proposed decimal-retrieval system. If your system works, then you'll have something that to our knowledge is unique: a reliable cash-flow source that has no attendant cost or risk. When you add that to any trading system, you have a win-win situation. There are highly sophisticated systems for trading derivatives that have been able to quantify the outcomes within certain parameters. We propose to incorporate the cash flow generated by decimal scraping into this type of trading system and mitigate variable results. Thus, we'll have a constant flow of trading profits."

"I understand the concept of a reliable source of cash mitigating the outcome of any trading system, but it's my understanding that what I need is a system that can integrate the decimal-retrieval cash flow and create trading profits without revealing the underlying source of the cash. Does your proposed system accomplish that?"

"I believe we can, and let me show you graphically," Phil said, as he turned to the dry-erase board behind him and sketched out an x/y-axis. He continued, "If you were to graph our derivatives trading system, then the outcome net of trading cost would be neutral. Profits and losses, when charted, would create a perfect bell-shaped curve. The winning trades and the losing trades would be a perfect break-even situation," he said, as he added a perfectly even bell-shaped curve to the axis.

Alan asked, "Okay, are you saying that this is the system that y'all use to trade derivatives?"

"Yes, it's the basis for our trading."

"How do you make money using a break-even platform?"

"We don't. Jane and her team have to make sophisticated assumptions based on the performance of the cash flows from which the derivative was created."

"Doesn't that pose an element of risk?"

"Indeed, it does, and Jane's job is to understand and manage that risk."

Alan mused, "But, in our case, the decimal-retrieval system eliminates that risk, right?"

"That's the key to your situation. A perfectly balanced system that doesn't require risk-taking can create an electronic trail of trading activity that can be used to integrate the decimal-retrieval cash flows and create an overall profit, and the best part is that you can amp the system up or down to achieve any result that you choose."

"So, if I'm following you, I'd be able to control the outcome to produce the flow of profits."

"Yes, to the extent that you can control the decimal-retrieval system. We've designed the trading system to respond to the number of trades needed to mask the cash produced by decimal retrieval. You can control the decimal system, can't you?"

"Well, in theory I can. Two factors can determine the system's output: number of hours that the system runs in a given period, and the position of the decimal to be retrieved. I plan to run a beta test tomorrow using a one-hour run time but retrieving it after the fifth decimal digit."

"What do you think this will produce in cash?"

"If I'm correct, and the system works, a one-hour run should produce about $500."

"We'll design the system to balance the trades with the cash so that if you decide to lengthen the run time or adjust the decimal point, then the trading system will automatically respond."

Emile spoke up and added, "Alan, it'll take our folks some time to get their system in place, but we feel it will be ready to support tomorrow's test. The trial run will give us a beta test on the trading system, as well as the decimal retrieving."

"I have to admit to a certain bit of apprehension about tomorrow, so I think we could all use a break this evening. To that end, I'd like to invite everyone to a chuck-wagon dinner at the Circle B."

Emile looked at his people and arched his eyebrows in question. They all nodded in agreement, and Emile said, "Dinner under the stars sounds good. What time do you want us?"

"How about coming out about 6:00? If Amy doesn't mind, then she can ride with y'all and show you the way."

Amy smiled. "I'll be at the hotel at a quarter to six, and we can go in my car."

THIRTEEN

THE SUN WAS HOVERING over the distant mountains, and everyone was gathered on the veranda, watching as Cesar guided a sizable mule-drawn farm trailer into the parking area. The trailer had sides like a stake body truck, and bales of hay were placed around to form seating. The back gate was lowered to serve as steps.

Alan stood on the veranda and whistled for everyone's attention. Once the chatter had died down, he said, "As you can see, we're ready to start our 'desert at night' adventure. When the sun goes down, it'll get a little chilly, so be sure you have a jacket. It'll be about an hour's ride to join up with Maria and the chuck wagon, so freshen your drinks before we leave. There are Cokes and beer on the wagon, but no hard stuff. You might want to hit the head before we start too. There are porta-potties at our destination, but nothing on the way except mesquite and cactus. Anyone have any questions?" When no one spoke, he added, "Okay, grab a drink and let's load 'em up!"

Once the wagon had left the ranch buildings and their lights were left behind, the desert sky began to fill with stars. There was just the rosy glow of the setting sun behind the western horizon, and folks started reaching for their jackets. Alan sat on a bale of hay propped against the tailgate and talked about the history of the Circle B. Finally, a substantial bonfire could be seen ahead, and Alan changed from historical to useful information. He warned them of the need to be careful where they walked and encouraged them to try to stay within the circle of the fire.

It took another 15 minutes for the trailer to get close enough to see the chuck wagon that was parked alongside the bonfire. Cesar guided the cart to a spot just on the edge of the fire circle and lowered the tailgate. The porta-potties were on the other edge, and a rustic bar was set up on a large piece of plywood resting on sawhorses.

As soon as they descended from the wagon, a trio dressed in Mexican outfits, complete with sombreros, began playing traditional Latin favorites. Shortly, the group was joined by a young woman who sang with the voice of an angel. A couple of ranch hands moved the hay bales from the wagon and placed them around the fire. By the time everyone had used the porta-potties, fixed a fresh drink, and found a seat around the fire, complete darkness had surrounded them, and a slightly cool breeze stirred the scents of the high desert, mixed with the aroma of meat on the grill.

After about an hour of drinking and talking, Alan stood and walked over to the chuck wagon, rang the bell attached to its frame, and yelled, "Come and get it! Supper is served!"

Maria and Cesar had prepared their famous grilled chicken, along with center-cut pork chops and shish kabobs. Maria had also provided potato salad, baked beans, and biscuits cooked in a cast-iron Dutch oven over an open fire. Deep-dish apple pie, baking in another Dutch oven, filled the air with its sweet aroma. A gigantic pot of coffee was steeping over the cooking fire for later.

After everyone had eaten heartily, the trio switched from Latin music to the old campfire songs most everyone had learned as a child. Cesar, who proved to have an excellent tenor voice, led the singing, and, as everyone began to stretch and yawn, he did a near perfect version of "Danny Boy." As the last notes floated across the desert night, Alan stood on his bale of hay and said, "Well, folks, that's our signal to start back to the ranch. Get another cup of coffee and visit the potty, and we'll head for home."

As Alan was stepping down from the hay bale, his eyes caught a glimmer of light on a slight rise to the north. The image flickered like a small fire and then disappeared altogether. He was wondering just what he'd seen when Mary Jo eased up next to him and asked, "Did you see what I just saw?"

"I think I did, but I've lost it. Looked like a flame on the little rise to the north."

"Yeah, it was definitely out there, but I've lost it too."

"I'll just bet it's our Apache friend," Alan added. "Wish I had time to check it out, but I've got to get these folks home."

"You may not have time, but I do. Think I'll ease out there and see what he has on his mind."

"C'mon, Mary Jo. I can't allow you to go sneaking around by yourself."

"Oh really? It was okay for me to sneak out among a couple of hundred Afghan warriors who wanted us all dead, but you're worried about one, apparently peaceful, Apache?"

"Well, when you put it that way, I guess I see your point, and, besides, I don't think there's truly much risk. I'll go with the trailer and get everyone on their way. The chuck wagon can stay out here until I get back with horses. Then, I'll let Maria and the chuck wagon go home, and I'll keep the fire going."

"If I'm not back at the chuck wagon when you return, then just wait and I'll find you."

Alan looked at his watch and said, "It's 10:15 now, and it'll be at least two hours before I get back. If you can't find him, then just join Maria and head back. I'll meet y'all on the way. I don't guess you thought to bring a weapon, did you?"

"I don't usually bring heat to a picnic, but I do have my razor. Like American Express, I never leave home without it."

"Holy shit. I'm probably gonna get this poor guy's throat cut."

"Not if he plays nice."

"Oh well, he is an Apache, so he may cut yours…and, if he does, then I'll have to hire him as my new head of security."

"I wouldn't count on that if I were you. Just tell everyone I'm going to stay behind to give Maria a hand with the cleanup, and I'll see them in the morning. I don't want to miss the big test."

Alan agreed. "Hey, be careful. I don't want to have to explain to Emile Dalhousie how I got a big client killed."

"Don't worry; I'll probably be waiting for you when you get back to the wagon."

While the ranch hands reloaded the bales on the trailer, Mary Jo gave Emile a heads-up that she planned to stay behind to give Maria a hand but that she would see everyone in the morning. He smiled and said, "Does your need to help have anything to do with the little fire I saw on the ridge to the north?"

"You don't miss much, do you?"

"An infantry company commander either learns how to notice such things, or he goes home in a body bag. Be careful out there."

Once the wagon pulled away, Mary Jo checked her equipment. She had on jeans and a long-sleeved sweatshirt, and she wore the boots Alan had given her. She decided to put on the fleece-lined jean jacket as well, tied her hair in a ponytail to keep it out of her face, and then checked her back pocket and felt the comforting outline of her straight razor. She realized that she didn't have a compass, but, since the night was clear, she could navigate by the stars.

Mary Jo walked over to the dying campfire and found a charred piece of wood near the edge. She touched it and found that it was cool enough to use. She smeared the black ash all over her face and quietly stole into the desert night. When out of the dying light of the campfire, she oriented her position, using the stars as a guide. She tested the direction of the gentle breeze and found that it was coming out of the west. She assumed that an Apache warrior would have a keen sense of smell and hearing, which meant she'd have to circle back to the east to begin her recon. She'd estimated the distance from the campfire to the target to be about a half mile in a straight line, and she could move freely until she got within several hundred yards.

Mary Jo's stalking skills were honed in the swamps of the Atchafalaya Basin, and, early on, she'd learned to place herself in the mind of her quarry. Even though she didn't think the mystery warrior posed a serious threat to her, she would proceed as if he did; if nothing else, it gave her a chance to practice her tradecraft.

Mary Jo moved slowly, but steadily, in smooth motion. She knew that the primal eye was trained to pick out unusual movements, and she didn't intend to give it any. She regularly checked her position by using the stars and eased to her knees when she felt that she was nearing her target. Her decision to come in downwind had given her the advantage of smell, and she began to pick up the faint odor of an open fire. She could smell it, but she couldn't see it.

Mary Jo began to move forward in a low crawl, easing up a slight rise. When she reached the crest of the rise and looked into the little draw, she saw a lone figure wrapped in a blanket, sitting in front of a small campfire. The man seemed to be asleep. Mary Jo stayed on her belly and watched the sleeping figure, trying to decide her next move, when she felt a tap on her shoulder. A soft voice said, "Why don't we move in closer to the fire where it's a little warmer?"

To her credit, Mary Jo didn't jump entirely out of her skin but said, "That would probably be a lot more comfortable," and rose to her feet. She followed a tall, thin man, wearing an olive drab jumpsuit, in closer to the flickering fire. He tossed a couple of new logs on the fire, and it sprang to life, providing enough light for her to see the man's features. He had a tanned, chiseled face, with deep lines around his eyes and well-groomed jet-black hair, held in place by a red bandanna.

When the fire was growing brighter, the man looked at her and said, "Your approach was well planned and skillfully executed. My guess is that you've had some military training."

"Yeah, it was skillful enough to get my throat cut. I never saw, smelled, or sensed your presence."

The man smiled, held out his hand, and said, "I'm Carson Black."

Mary Jo took his hand, shook it, and replied, "Good to finally meet you, Carson. We've been wondering when you'd decide to clue us in. By the way, I'm Mary Jo Thibodaux, and I'd like to know how you managed to sneak up on me."

"Well, to begin with, I had the advantage of knowing you were coming, and then you fell for the oldest trick in the book. You allowed yourself to believe what your eyes saw."

"Okay, I can't argue with the results, but tell me what I fell for."

Black walked over to the sleeping warrior and nudged it with the toe of his boot. The figure collapsed into a pile of sticks, covered with a blanket. Black stirred the fire and said, "I gave you a fire to focus your senses and a decoy to disarm your instincts. This provided me with the opportunity to pierce your defenses. An Apache, faced with the same situation, would have diverted all of his attention away from the bait and on to the area behind him."

"Damn, now that you explained it, makes perfect sense."

"Yes, but you have to remember, when under stress, we all act by muscle memory. We Apaches have been trained in these skills since childhood, and we can react in a way that is counterintuitive to most non-Apaches, and I include most of our tribal rivals in this. It goes a long way in explaining how a couple of small bands of Apaches have made peoples like the feared Comanches bend to our will."

Mary Jo thought for a moment and said, "Carson Black, I have no idea what your day job is, but, when all of this is over, I want you to become my sensei."

"Be patient, Cricket. As you say, when all of this is over." Black said the words and placed his hands together, making a slight bow. He then continued, "In the meantime, why don't we begin to deal with all of this?"

"It's here where you give me some idea *what* we need to deal with, right?"

"Since I saw you riding with Dr. Brooks, and you came out here tonight, may I assume you have his confidence? By the way, you made it up that rocky hill pretty good. I think he ought to let you ride Lucifer."

"Yes, I believe I have his confidence. I'm also his security consultant, and I hope you'll tell him your opinion about Lucifer."

"Again, patience, Cricket. You mentioned my day job so let me start there. I'm a Texas Ranger, working undercover on an ongoing investigation of trouble on the Apache reservation that borders the northern boundary of the Circle B. I've been tracking the man who had to shoot his snakebit horse a couple of weeks ago."

As Carson spoke, he took out his badge and credentials and showed them to her. Mary Jo replied, "Alan mentioned the dead horse, but what does this have to do with the Circle B?"

"I'm getting to that. Remember, Cricket, be patient."

Mary Jo placed her hands together, bowed her head, and said, "Sensei."

Black continued with his monologue. "As I said, I've been tracking the rider since he left the reservation. When his horse went down, he kept moving on foot until he reached the highway to El Paso. He was picked up by a black SUV, and, of course, I lost him. I wanted to take a closer look at his dead horse, but Dr. Brooks and his foreman found him before I got back. They brought out a backhoe and buried him that morning."

"Why do you need to see the dead horse?"

"It's just a hunch, but I think I know where the rider has been, and maybe what he's up to. Do you think you could convince Dr. Brooks to dig up the horse and let me have a look?"

"I don't see why not. When would you like to do it?"

"The sooner, the better."

"Well, today is out of the question. We've got too much going on in town, but we might be able to arrange it for Saturday morning."

"That'll work for me."

"Okay, how do I get back in touch with you, smoke signals?"

"That would probably work, but why don't I just give you my cell number?"

"Aw darn. I've always wanted to use smoke signals, but I guess I can give you a ring. I'll discuss this with Alan later and give you a call. If Alan agrees, then we can pin down a time on Saturday."

"I hope he agrees. I don't want to try to explain to some judge why I need a warrant to search a dead horse," Carson chuckled.

"I don't think it'll come to that," Mary Jo replied. "I guess I'd better head back to the wagon."

"You've got a beautiful night to stroll in but let me hear from you as soon as you can."

"Why don't you just come in with me and spend the night at the Circle B?"

"Me no like white man's ways. Besides, it's not often that I get a chance to sleep under the stars. Thanks, but I'll just bunk in here. Tell Brooks I'll say hello to his Uncle Lloyd."

Mary Jo told Carson good night and headed for the fire in the distance.

FOURTEEN

SLIGHTLY AFTER MIDNIGHT, Mary Jo got close enough to see Alan squatting by the fire, two horses grazing nearby. When she stepped into the fire's circle, he said, "Well, Shiva, how'd it go?"

"Shiva got her ass handed to her by a middle-aged Texas Ranger. I've been back to escape and evade school."

"I guess he was sneakier than Shiva the Destroyer, huh?" Alan asked this as he kicked dirt onto the dying campfire. He handed Mary Jo the reins to Janie, and he got on Streak. They turned toward the Circle B.

"Yeah, and you really didn't do justice to an Apache's warrior skills. They aren't trained; they're bred. He knew exactly where I was from the moment I left the campfire."

"Well, at least he didn't cut your throat; that's something."

"It wasn't because he couldn't have, but it turns out he's a pretty nice guy. His name is Carson Black, and he said something about your Uncle Lloyd, whoever that is."

"It's my Dad's brother, Lloyd. He's high up in the Rangers; might even be this guy's boss."

"Why doesn't that surprise me? After all, we're in a land where the cows outnumber the people."

"Now don't start in on Texas. If Alabama were out here, it'd be one of our smaller counties."

"Yeah, maybe, but it's probably double the population of the whole state."

"While he was taking you to sneak school, did he happen to mention what's on his mind?"

"He did. He wants you to dig up the horse you buried and let him take a look at it."

"You're kidding, right?"

"No, that's what he said."

"Did he say why?"

"Just that he had a hunch he needed to check out. I told him we couldn't do it tomorrow, but maybe on Saturday."

"Tomorrow is already here, but I suppose we can do it on Saturday. What time did you suggest?"

"I told him I had to check with you and would get back to him with a time."

"How you gonna do that — leave a lance on the ridge?"

"No, he gave me his cell-phone number."

"Well, give him a buzz and set it up for 10:00 a.m. on Saturday."

Mary Jo dialed Black's cell number. When he answered, she said, "Hope I didn't wake you. We're on for 10:00 a.m. Saturday morning."

"Apache sleeps with one ear open. Thanks, Cricket. See you on Saturday."

While Mary Jo and Alan rode through the chilly night, she broke the silence and said, "Oh, by the way, he said to tell you that I'm a good rider, and you oughtta let me ride Lucifer."

"Did he now? We'll just have to see. Have patience, Cricket."

Mary Jo shook her head and thought, "Damn, I seem to be one step behind everyone in the whole damn state of Texas."

On Friday morning, the friends got up early, ate a quick breakfast, and even beat Amy to the office. They were just fixing their first cup of coffee when she came bustling through the back door. She reached for a mug and said, "Sorry I'm late, but I met Emile and his team at the hotel for breakfast. They'll be here in a minute."

Alan shook his head and said, "Amy, you're hardly late; it's only 7:45."

Amy smiled at him and said, "That's late, for me."

Pete came in just as Emile and his team arrived, and everyone took their places around the conference table. Alan said, "I'm going to connect my computer screen to the overhead projector so that everyone can see what's happening. The purpose of today's test is twofold: first, to confirm that my decimal-retrieval system will actually work, and, second, to be sure that the Dalhousie trading system is in sync with it. I'm planning to set the system to retrieve, starting with the seventh decimal point. I don't expect this setting to produce my projected $4,000 per day objective, but it should give us sufficient data to check out the two systems. Anyone got any questions?"

Phil Andrews raised his hand and asked, "Alan, how long do you intend to allow the system to run?"

"I plan to run it at least 15 minutes. Even at a seventh-decimal setting, this should give us enough to work with. Do you have any suggestions, Phil?"

"Not really. Bill and Jane and I were talking at breakfast, and we agree that if our trading system integrates with your system properly, then a short run should give us the data we need to confirm it."

"How about you, Pete? You've got a sizable investment in our results."

"No, most of this is over my head technically, so I'll just sit back and watch the movie."

"Anyone else?"

Amy placed her coffee mug on a coaster and quietly asked, "I hate to bring this up, but, for a moment, let's say that the system, as configured, doesn't work this morning. Can it be fixed?"

Alan thought for a moment and then replied, "That's the elephant in the living room, isn't it? Sadly, I'm afraid the basic concept found in Dr. Wu's paper is binary; either it works, or it doesn't. If the problem is there, then we can put out the fire and call in the dogs. This hunt's over. If the problem is in my programming of the application of Wu's theory, then, yes, I can probably find it and fix it."

"Well, good enough," Pete said. "Let's crank this baby up and watch you get rich."

Alan nodded, and, with a knot in his stomach, began tapping codes into the master control computer. He stopped, looked at everyone, said, "Here goes nothing," and pressed the start key.

The group watched intently as the three screens projected on the overhead. For about 60 seconds, nothing happened. Then, the telemetry screen lit up, and code began to flash across the monitor. Alan said, "Well, at least we've penetrated the systems; this is a good start."

The screen showing the balance in the holding account suddenly sprang to life. The number was racing so rapidly that they couldn't read a total. Clearly small amounts were hitting the system in a flood.

Alan said, "It's moving so fast that I can't get a reading on the running total. I'll have to tweak some programming to let us know when we reach, say, $100.00. I'm going to shut the system down until I get that done, and we can crank it up again. It's been running for six and a half minutes, so we should have enough data to see if the integrated trading system worked."

Alan hit the keys to bring the test to an end. They watched as the numbers slowed down, and they could finally read the amount that had been deposited. The screen flashed $1,238,786.22.

There it was, flashing over and over again: $1,238,786.22. Everyone in the room just stared at the computer screen. Finally, Alan exclaimed, "Holy shit!"

"It appears that you may have made a bit of a miscalculation on the setting, but I'd say that you can rest easy on whether or not it works," Pete replied.

Phil Andrews asked, "Good heavens! Do you have any idea what this would total in 24 hours?"

"Let's do the math," Bill Wysock suggested.

"You ran for about six minutes before you turned it off, so, in an hour, you should have had 10 times $1,238,786.22 or close to $13,000,000. In 24 hours, that would add up to a little over $300,000,000.00. This could make you as rich as I am over time, say in about an hour or two," Pete said.

"Holy shit," repeated Alan.

Pete said with a wide grin, "Is that all you can say? Sometime this month you could be the richest man in history. That oughtta deserve more than a couple of 'holy shits,' don't ya think? How about something along the lines of 'one giant step for Alan Brooks,' or something equally as profound?"

"Pete, we need to have a 'come to Jesus' right this moment. In the first place, I don't have any intention of using this system to amass wads of money, and, in the second place, I want to keep under the radar of all of the regulatory agencies. Turning up with a billion dollars next month will have every three- and four-letter outfit in D.C. camped out in Pecos Springs. I'll have to make considerable adjustments to tone the system down. All I want is enough cash to fund my research work, and it seems that I can do that with a lot less production."

Pete continued grinning and said, "This may come as a surprise to you, but, I actually agree. You can't just show up with billions of dollars and expect to remain unknown; it just doesn't work that way. Wall Street will go nuts trying to figure out how you did it; the politicians will want to tax it; and the establishment will want to steal it. Pecos Springs is not so remote that nobody will notice. What can you do to slow this thing down?"

Alan began to list the adjustments he could make to tone the system down a notch or two. The first item on the list was to move the decimal point pickup from seven places; this should substantially reduce the amount retrieved. He could reset the system to collect a certain amount each day and then automatically shut down. That amount could vary, depending on his actual needs for a particular period. Pete listened and finally said, "How long will it take you to make these changes?"

"Changing the decimal point is just a matter of resetting the system. That'll take less than a minute. I'll have to write a short program to shut down after a certain production, and that may take me an hour or two. I'd like to think the whole thing over."

"I agree that this type of wealth would send flags up in every system out there," said Emile. "It's probably a good idea to think about it over the weekend. You may have a tiger by the tail, and there's something I want to do before we all leave this room."

Emile asked Melissa to hand him two files, which she slid across the table. He picked up the first file and said, "I'm going to pass around a Confidentiality and Nondisclosure Agreement. There is a copy prepared for everyone in the room. I also feel compelled to add that in spite of what you may have heard about the enforceability of NDAs, this one is ironclad and has stood the test of time. Many people take the position that the protected party will not, or could not, absorb the legal fees that would be incurred to enforce it." He waited until everyone had read through the agreement and asked, "Does anyone have a problem with the agreement?"

No one said a thing, and Emile continued, "Then, let's all sign it." He pulled his pen out, signed his name, looked up, and said,

"Melissa, will you collect everyone's agreement, make a copy for each person, and bring the originals home with us?"

Again, Emile paused, glanced around the table, and then continued, "After what you have just witnessed, there should be no question in your mind about Dr. Brooks's ability to pay legal fees. At the worst, it might even require an extra minute or two of run time."

Emile paused and pushed the second file across to Alan and began again: "This brings me to my last item. Dr. Brooks, I have just handed you the necessary paperwork to become an official client of the Dalhousie Merchant Bank, if you so choose."

Alan picked up the file and was silent for a moment before he replied, choking back a catch in his throat: "Emile, I can't tell you how much I appreciate this vote of confidence."

Emile smiled and said, "The next point I want to make — and this is the last thing I'm going to say on this subject — is this. Don't think that just because you've known Alan Brooks all of your lives that he'll allow you to slide if you let something about this morning slip. I assure you that, while Alan might be understanding, the firm managing his assets will not. Now, I believe it's time to celebrate. Before the meeting, I asked Pete where I could take everyone for a festive lunch, and he recommended a charming local establishment called the Choke and Puke."

***

When everyone returned to the office after lunch, Phil Andrews and his team took over the conference room to be sure their trading system synced with Alan's system. Melissa Green took over a spare office and began setting up Alan's account. Everyone else gathered in Alan's office. Amy broke the silence and said, "Last night, I re-read the State Department white paper on the strategic issues facing the world in the next 50 years, and one thing is obvious. The biggest issue is going to be water. The paper suggested a variety of ways to address this, scientifically, before it becomes the cause of future wars. The bottom line is that there are no current technologies that can produce water at a cost that society can bear."

Alan asked, "What about desalinization?"

"The only desalinization method that is cost-effective is nuclear power, and, at present, the risks are too high."

Emile asked, "So, the desalinization technology is workable, but the energy costs are prohibitive?"

"Yes, that's about it," replied Amy.

"It seems to me that the real issue isn't the cost of energy but the consequences of using fossil fuels. If solar or geothermic sources of energy could be expanded, then desalinization would be a practical source of water," mused Alan.

"That would certainly be true in areas near the ocean, but it wouldn't help much out here in West Texas," added Mary Jo.

"True. Out here we'd have to have a system that extracted water from the atmosphere. The earth's atmosphere and oceans are a perfectly balanced continuous source of water. Rain falls and either evaporates back into the atmosphere or runs into rivers back to the oceans. Nature provided a continuous source of clean water; it just never anticipated the enormous needs of a world with over seven-billion people," Alan said.

Emile asked, "Alan, you and Mary Jo are engineers. Is there a known way to extract the water from the atmosphere?"

"I can't speak to the physics or chemistry of such a system, but I can say that, if the technology were found, we could build it," Mary Jo answered.

Alan sat staring at the wall and finally replied, "The physics and chemistry are pretty simple, but it all comes back to an acceptable energy source. With sufficient energy we could extract unlimited water at any point on the earth, but the energy would have to be at no cost and unlimited, and I'm afraid that as of today that is an impossibility."

It was Mary Jo's turn to sit quietly and then respond: "Maybe it's not impossible. I just recalled a conversation I had with Will Ransom a couple of years ago. Will was telling me about a professor at Mississippi State University who was working on such a system. Will seemed to be pretty enthusiastic about it."

"Well, hell, let's get Will on the phone and check it out," Alan said.

Alan looked up Will's number and dialed it. There was a pause, and then a female voice answered, "Good afternoon. Cumberland Plantation. How may I direct your call?"

"May I speak to Will Ransom, please?"

"May I tell Mr. Ransom who is calling?"

"This is Alan Brooks."

"Thank you, Mr. Brooks. I'll connect you to Mr. Ransom's office."

After several clicking and connecting sounds, Will said, "Alan, I can't imagine why you've finally decided to give me a call, but I'm glad to hear from you. What's up?"

"Hello to you too. I'm sitting in my new office, along with some other folks you might remember. I've got you on speaker. Say hello to Emile Dalhousie and Mary Jo."

"No kidding? Now there's a combination I'd never have guessed. What in the hell are y'all up to?"

"We're plotting the future of the world's water supply. What are you doing lounging around the office when crops are ready to harvest?"

"Actually, I'm standing in a field checking on the millet I planted for dove hunting. The call was forwarded from my office to my cell. Tell me about the water deal."

"Mary Jo brought up a conversation y'all had about some professor at Mississippi State who was working on an unlimited energy system. Do you remember?"

"Yeah, in fact, I visited with him on two occasions, but it's been over a year since we talked. What's y'all's interest in that project?"

"You might not be able to relate since you sit on a huge aquifer, but we're water-starved out here. We were discussing solutions when your guy's name came up."

"Okay, Alan, I'll buy into that for the time being. It must be a hot topic to have the head of a major merchant bank and a snake-eating civil engineer sitting in. Just for grins, what can I do to help?"

"Will, I'll explain the whole thing, but, for now, can you tell us, in general, what you know about this guy?"

"The short version is this; his name is Vassily Volanov, a professor of physics, who defected from the USSR in the sixties. He was a top scientist for the Red Army and an expert in optics. The boys in Langley arranged his escape and set him up at Mississippi State. He works on a variety of projects, all funded by DARPA, and mostly military-related. Just for fun, he dabbles in arcane areas of science. For instance, he adapted the work done in the 1930s by an eccentric scientist in California, using a technique known as dark-field microscopy, and came up with an instrument that would allow a researcher to see the interworking of an individual cell. Not only did he build and test it, but he also wrote the peer-reviewed explanation of its physics. Another of his personal projects is an adaptation of Tesla's 'tower of power.' You may not be aware of Tesla's work, but he was Thomas Edison's chief rival at the turn of the 20th century."

"C'mon on, Will...I've got a Ph.D. in Electrical Engineering. Of course I'm familiar with Tesla, and, in fact, I think he was a far superior scientist compared to Edison, but he lost the contest for funding when Edison's alternating current won J.P. Morgan's backing. I seem to remember an experiment Tesla did on one of his ideas that blew the entire power grid out in Colorado Springs."

"Yeah, well, Volanov contends that with all of the improvements in modern equipment, Tesla's tower would work today. He was seeking funding to build a test tower."

"Did he build it?"

"I don't know. In fact, I need to check up on him anyway. Suppose I give him a call and find out?"

"Would you do that and get back to me?"

"Sure, but I can't tell you how curious I am about your little get-together. My feelings are hurt that I wasn't included."

"Get us the information about Volanov, and we'll make it up to you."

"I'll hold you to that. I'll call you as soon as I speak to him."

FIFTEEN

WHEN WILL LEFT THE LINE, Emile suggested that they check with his folks in the conference room to see if the trading system kept pace. When they came through the door, Phil and his team were unhooking their computers and gathering up their papers. Emile asked, "Well, did it do what you thought it would?"

Phil smiled and said, "Yeah, boss — we did a few minor adjustments to compensate for the increased volume, but it's ready to roll now. Anyone checking it out would never know that it was being underpinned by a steady stream of cash. There is one change that we made. Rather than using the local bank as the initial depository, we've switched it to our bank in Montreal. Large deposits won't be unusual there, and we'll let today's deposit go to the local bank to form the basis for a petty cash account. Dr. Brooks, we'll be ready whenever you decide to crank up the system."

Alan said, "I'll have to do some tweaking on the minimum/maximum settings, but I'll come in this weekend and get that done. What do y'all think about a short run, say a couple of million early next week? This should give us some seed money in our Dalhousie account, and we can get more as the need arises. Also, I may want to withdraw a little to cover some improvements at the Circle B."

"You can have a wire transfer to your local account with an hour's notice," replied Melissa.

Emile said, "Well, it seems that our work here is complete. Let's gather up and head to the airport. Mary Jo, are you flying back tonight?"

"No, Alan and I have something to attend to in the morning, and I'll probably head back late tomorrow afternoon."

Amy stuck her head in and said, "Alan, it's Will Ransom on the line for you."

"Thanks, Amy. I'll take the call on the speakerphone."

Alan reached across the table and connected Will to the phone. "Hey, Will, I've got you on speaker. What'd you find out?"

"I spoke with Volanov, and he said that he'd been too busy to do anything with the Tesla project, but, if he can find the funding, he'd like to build a test tower and check out his theory. I told him I might know someone with an interest and that I'd get back with him."

"Great! Give us the weekend to put a plan together, and we'll get back to you on Monday or sooner. If it works out that we want to meet Volanov, then could you make the introductions next week?"

"Yeah, I can do that. All we're doing is watching the cotton and beans to know when to start the harvest, and no hunting season is open, so I'm free all next week."

"Thanks, man. I appreciate it. We'll get back to you and let you know."

"Okay. Look forward to hearing from you. Have a good weekend."

Alan smiled and asked, "Well, what do y'all think about that?"

Mary Jo answered, "Next week works for me. How about you, Emile?"

"I've got meetings scheduled with our French people the first part of the week, but, if you set up a meeting, I'd like to include one of our in-house lawyers to go along to make sure we do it right. Which reminds me, Alan, Melissa will be emailing you a consulting agreement for you to sign regarding Mary Jo's work as your security consultant. I have to watch her, or she'll work for free. Now that I know you can afford her standard rate, it's time to paper it."

"No problem with Mary Jo's agreement. Just send it, and I'll sign it. We'll let you know if and when we want to meet with Will and Volanov. You folks have a safe trip back to Alabama. I'm excited and honored that we'll be working together."

After another round of good-byes, the Dalhousie team left for the airport. Alan sank back in one of the conference room chairs and sighed, "Man, that was enough action for one day. Let's have a light dinner and call it a week."

"Don't forget that we have to meet Carson Black in the morning," Mary Jo added.

"Oh yeah. I need to let Cesar know we'll need the backhoe at the site in the morning. We better stop by Home Depot and pick up some painter's masks. Digging up a horse that's been buried three weeks is gonna smell to high heaven."

"I'm gonna be really interested in what Black's looking for. So far, none of this makes any sense."

"Well, I suppose it'll all be revealed in the morning."

The two made the side trip to Home Depot, and, back at the ranch, they ate a sandwich on the veranda and visited until it was dark. Then, they both turned in for the night.

***

Saturday morning, Alan and Mary Jo were sitting on the veranda having a second cup of coffee when Cesar drove up in the ranch's John Deere Gator and said, "Señor, the backhoe is in place. Do you want me to leave the gator for you?"

"Yeah, that's good. Do you need a ride back out there?"

"No, I'll take one of the pickups; I want to bring a couple of shovels just in case."

"Good idea. We'll be out as soon as our guest arrives."

Cesar walked away, and Mary Jo reminded Alan to bring the masks, so he went inside to get them. Before he returned, a dark-green Jeep came into view at the top of the hill, kicking up a trail of dust. Alan came back out as Carson Black stepped out of the vehicle and climbed the steps. He was wearing faded jeans, a plaid shirt, and dusty cowboy boots. His long black hair was in a ponytail, tucked beneath a sweat-stained Stetson. He smiled and extended his hand saying, "Good morning, Cricket, and this must be Dr. Brooks. I'm Carson Black."

Alan shook his hand and replied, "Good to finally meet you, Officer Black. Cricket has extolled your skills. Praise from Shiva is praise indeed, and I mean that."

"Okay, let's get something straight. I'm standing right here, and my name is Mary Jo. The two of you can lose the Cricket and Shiva crap right now."

Alan grinned and said, "I guess we better listen. She may not be able to slip up on you and cut your throat, but I'm only an ex-Navy SEAL, not an Apache, and I want to be able to sleep at night."

Carson smiled and said, "And I don't want her pissed at me either, so Mary Jo it is."

Mary Jo said, "Okay, now that we've got that worked out, let's go dig up that damn horse."

Alan drove the gator out to the little meadow where the backhoe stood waiting. When the trio climbed out of the gator, Alan gave Cesar the go-ahead to begin digging. Alan handed masks to Mary Jo and Black, and they stood upwind and watched.

The backhoe operator worked his shovel carefully, removing one layer of soil at a time until the rib cage of the little animal was exposed. He stopped and asked, "Señor, do you want me to lift the carcass out of the hole?"

Alan looked at Black for an answer, and Black replied, "All I want to see is one of his hooves. If you can do that without pulling him out, then he can stay in the ground."

The operator moved the bucket skillfully and uncovered one of the animal's back legs. Black jumped down in the hole, held the hoof up, and stared at it. He pulled out his pocket knife and scraped something into a small plastic bag, sealed it, and climbed out. He walked over to Alan, who asked, "Can you share what exactly you removed from the hoof?"

"Let's get back to the house, and I'll tell y'all what I think I found."

When they all arrived back at the ranch, Alan pulled the gator up near the hitching post, and the three of them climbed up onto the porch. Alan said, "Why don't y'all have a seat, and I'll get Maria to make us a fresh pot of coffee." Shortly, he came back out and sat on the porch rail facing Carson and Mary Jo. "Okay, the coffee will be ready in a sec. Now, Carson, give me some idea of what's going on."

Carson held up the plastic bag and said, "If this is what I think it is, then we may have a big problem."

Alan took the bag and saw a small, black pebble inside and then passed it to Mary Jo, who asked, "What's so sinister about a little, black rock?"

"I won't know for sure until I get it to our lab in Fort Worth, but I'm betting that it's pitchblende."

"Uranium ore?" Alan asked, "Where in the hell do you think that horse stepped in pitchblende?"

"If it is pitchblende, then I know exactly where it came from, and it's on your land," Carson replied.

"Oh c'mon. I don't know of any deposits of pitchblende on the Circle B," said Alan.

"Alan, may I call you Alan?"

"Yeah, Alan's fine."

"Well, Alan, how long has your family owned this land?"

"We came out here in 1846, just after Texas Statehood, so that's over 150 years that we've owned it."

"We Apache have made this our home for a thousand years, and we probably know it far better than you. Do you own all of your mineral rights?"

"Yes, we refused to allow any oil exploration because there isn't a well anywhere near us."

"You may not realize it, but the far northwest corner of the Circle B contains one of the Apache's holiest sites. In fact, it borders the southern boundary of our reservation and should have been included on the res."

"Yeah, I knew that we owned part of an ancient burial site, and I've made sure we left it in peace."

"Well, if this sample does turn out to be pitchblende, then we may both have to reconsider our attitudes about that little piece of land."

Alan asked, "Why is that?"

"I've ridden all across the burial site, and there's a huge outcropping of this mineral right in the middle of your portion, and, if it is pitchblende, then it could be worth millions."

"Carson, may I call you Carson?"

"Yep."

"Carson, if you had told me this last week, then I might have reacted differently, but today I want to ask you a question."

"Okay, shoot," Black replied.

"If this is pitchblende and if it were entirely on Apache-owned land, what would your people do? Would they exploit the mineral value or protect the sacred site?"

"That's a question way above my tribal pay grade, but I would guess that in spite of the need for schools, health care, and relieving the poverty level, our elders would very likely choose to protect our heritage."

"Well, there you go. We'll just leave things as they are and forget this ever happened."

Carson paused before speaking and then said, "I wish it were that simple, but I'm afraid it won't be. The man I followed is working for somebody, and they'll know about the deposit. I can't see them just walking away."

"Yeah, but what can they do? I own the land, and I have no interest in selling it. In fact, I'd be willing to cede it to the Jicarillas, with the understanding that they'd never allow mining on it."

"I find it hard to believe that you'd be willing to walk away from millions of dollars just to protect our holy site, but, even if you were, it might be better if you retained title. If you give it to the tribe, then it becomes only a matter of breaking an Indian treaty to put it back on the market. Remember, the Bureau of Indian Affairs has a sad history of screwing over those it's supposed to protect."

"What if I gave the land to the tribe with the understanding that the tribe could allow closely supervised mining if it could be done while respecting the burial sites? It would provide some much-needed capital to the tribe — might even be better than a casino."

"And you'd do this because…?"

"For two reasons: first, I truly respect the tribal traditions, and, second, because I don't need the money."

"Maybe I'm missing something, but the Circle B doesn't look all that prosperous to me."

"Let's just say I have a source of private income that's providing all I'll ever need."

"What are you doing, robbing convenience stores?"

"No, I trade securities, and, as a matter of fact, I just resigned my teaching position to do it full time. What do you think the tribe's reaction would be if I made them that offer?"

"As I said, this is above my tribal pay grade, but I can see if there's any interest."

"I'd appreciate it if you would," Alan replied.

Mary Jo spoke up and said, "Do you have any idea who was scouting the site out?"

"No, but I'll hang around for a while and keep my eyes open. I'll visit the tribal leaders and get back to you when I know something. I just want to say that you're a stand-up guy to make that offer. You've made some friends, no matter what happens. Mary Jo, I'll get back to you if I feel there's any threat from our visitors. Maybe you and I can deal with it, if there is one."

"Carson, I have complete trust in your hanging-around abilities; just keep me in the loop."

"Okay, guys, let me head over to the res and see what they think. Thanks for digging up our smelly friend over there."

"He's headed back under as soon as we leave."

When they got back to the ranch, Mary Jo said, "I think I'm gonna take a shower before I go to the airport. I can still smell the horse."

Alan asked, "When do you plan to return?"

"I guess that depends on what you decide to do about Will's project in Mississippi. You said you'd come up with a plan over the weekend, and, if it's a go, we'll need to travel to Starkville early next week."

"I'm going to meet with Amy and Pete and decide how to handle that, and I also need to make another test run sometime next week. I'll give you a call and let you know."

Later, after lunch, Alan dropped Mary Jo at the airport, and she was wheels up by 1:30. Alan watched as the little jet disappeared to the east, and then he drove to his office to work on making the adjustments to the system. He worked until well after dark and then called Amy and Pete and asked them to meet him on Sunday after church. Both agreed, and Alan locked up for the evening.

**

Mary Jo set the Mustang down in Mobile just after 7:00 and drove straight home. She checked her messages and gave Allie a call, asking her to come in Sunday afternoon. Mary Jo checked on the progress of the Ono Island project and looked over the proposal for building the catfish facility before turning in for the evening. She went to sleep watching *Saturday Night Live*.

On Sunday morning, Mary Jo rode her bike to the Cathedral for Mass and then across the park to A Spot of Tea for breakfast. Then, she headed home to *The New York Times* crossword puzzle. Mary Jo was finishing the local paper when Allie came through the kitchen door.

SIXTEEN

ON SUNDAY MORNING, Alan opened the *Pecos Springs Clarion* and turned to the business section, and, as expected, there was the fluff piece Ellen had written about Brooks Capital. All in all, he was pleased. After lunch, Alan was in his office putting the final touches on the software fix to limit the amount of money produced by the system when he heard the back door open. Amy walked into the main lobby and spotted him. She came to his door and said, "Good afternoon, Alan. I see that I beat Pete here. I'll make a pot of coffee and bring it to the conference room."

"That's fine. I'm almost finished. See you in there."

Amy and Alan were pouring cups of coffee when Pete came in wearing tennis shorts, revealing his artificial leg. Alan said, "Pulled you off the court, I see."

"Not a problem. I'd played earlier this morning, and Ellen and I had lunch at the club."

Alan knew that in spite of his injury, Pete was a formidable tennis player, and he and Ellen were the reigning mixed-doubles club champs. After Pete poured his coffee, he sat down and said, "Okay, chief, you called this meeting. Let's get it going. I'm taking Ellen to dinner tonight."

"Still trying to win her hand, I take it?"

"Yeah, and I think she's wearing down. She was almost civil during lunch. Now, what's on our agenda?"

"First, I've adjusted the system to automatically stop after a fixed production, so we should be able to control things much better. Second, I want to fill the two of you in on the little problem at the ranch. Finally, we need to talk about Will Ransom's 'tower of power.'"

Amy looked at Alan and said, "Why don't we discuss the next test run of the system? You mentioned that you wanted to do that early next week."

"Yeah, and that's still the plan. The guys from Dalhousie assured me that they can monitor a test run remotely, so they won't need to fly back out here. I'm ready to go, and I think I'll do it tomorrow."

Pete asked, "If it works as it should, then how much will you allow it to yield?"

"I'd like to let it run long enough to be able to meet the Dalhousie minimum of 10 million."

"How long will that take?"

"Using a setting at the seventh decimal, less than an hour."

"Damn, that's just amazing; you're taking all of the mystique out of making money. I'll have to get another hobby."

"Maybe we can find something constructive for you to do around here. You may have a talent for making money, but you have a greater talent for spending it."

"Yeah, if you're looking for a Chief Disbursements Officer, then I'm your huckleberry. What's going on at the ranch?"

"Mary Jo and I had a meeting with our Apache, and he turned out to be an undercover Texas Ranger named Carson Black. He's been working on a case up at the reservation that borders the Circle B to the north. He discovered that some outside party sent a man onto my property to do a little prospecting."

Pete asked, "Prospecting for what? Cactus and sagebrush?"

"No, apparently he found pitchblende."

"Pitchblende? Isn't that uranium ore?"

"Yes, indeed."

"Damn, Brooks, when you're hot you're hot. I suppose next you'll find a diamond pipe."

"Yeah, that's the good news. The bad news is that it's on an Apache burial ground."

"Oh shit, that is bad news. Are you going to be able to mine it?"

"Don't intend to try. I'm thinking about deeding the land to the reservation and letting the tribe work out whether or not to mine it."

Amy, who had been taking it all in, said, "Alan, are you aware of the value of pitchblende, or, as it's known in the trade, uraninite?"

"Only because I just googled it. It's currently selling for close to $10,000 per pound, depending on its specific gravity."

"Are you aware that pitchblende is a strategic material, and, as such, is tightly controlled by the Nuclear Regulatory Commission?"

"Again, only because I googled it. None of the above will be my problem if I give it to the tribe."

"No, but there may be some restrictions concerning the gifting of strategic materials to a foreign entity."

"C'mon, Amy, I'd be giving it to Native Americans, for God's sake. The Apaches are hardly a foreign power."

"No, but they're considered a sovereign political unit, subject to some but not all U.S. laws. I only bring this up because it may be a factor in what you're thinking about doing."

"Oh, crap! No good deed goes unpunished!"

"I'm just suggesting that we get a clean legal opinion before we act. Did the Ranger know who'd been checking the site out?"

"No, but he's working on it. He's also running my idea by the tribal council to see if they're even interested."

"Just to be sure of our standing, let's write up a memo for the Dalhousie's legal department and see what advice they have."

"Good, will you take care of that for me?"

"Of course. Now, let's talk about Colonel Ransom's Russian professor."

"At least I didn't have to google Tesla. He's a legend in Electrical Engineering, and I'm familiar with his premise that the earth's atmosphere contains massive amounts of electrical energy — at times it's made itself known through natural events, such as lightning and the Northern Lights. He attempted to capture this energy at his lab in Colorado Springs at the turn of the 20th Century, but he couldn't control the results and destroyed the whole electrical grid in the city."

Alan continued, "Apparently, the professor in Mississippi has been researching this subject, and he believes that, with today's technology, we could harness this source of power. Frankly, I'm skeptical. Although the concept has been studied before, no one has come up with a working prototype. It would be akin to perfecting perpetual motion."

Amy said, "Or maybe akin to picking millions of dollars from cyberspace."

A strange look swept across Alan's face, and he replied, "Yeah, something like that too. I see your point, and we'll give this a thorough hearing. Amy, why don't you contact Will and see when we can go to Mississippi and meet with this guy. Be sure to include Mary Jo and Emile Dalhousie on our team. How about you, Pete. Want to go?"

"No, I'll stay here; having me on a tech trip makes no sense whatsoever. I'll stick around in case Ellen needs me."

"Okay, I think that covers everything I had on my mind. Amy, you can take care of the Mississippi meeting and the memo to the Dalhousies in the morning, and, Pete, you can resume your pursuit of Ellen while the band in your head plays 'The Impossible Dream.'"

Pete turned as he headed for the door and replied, "Bite my ass."

***

While Alan, Amy, and Pete were just getting started with their meeting, Allie came through the back door of Mary Jo's home. Allie took the elevator to the office, looking for Mary Jo, and found her sitting in the conference room with a beer in her hand. Smiling, Mary Jo said, "Sorry for the Sunday meeting but I might have to leave again, and I wanted us to have a chance to catch up. There's more beer in my office fridge if you want to grab one."

"No, I'm fine. I just finished lunch, and I'm stuffed."

"I want to bring you up to speed on our gig in West Texas. We've been engaged as security consultants by Brooks Capital, LLC. Emile has a copy of our engagement agreement, and I'll get him to send you over a copy. There's a retainer and a monthly fee, and, to be honest, I didn't even look at them, but, knowing Emile, they'll be substantial."

Mary Jo continued, "Brooks Capital is a new client for the Dalhousies, and their primary business is trading securities. I'll help set up the security procedures and then turn the day-to-day operations over to a yet-to-be-hired professional, but, in the meantime, I'll be traveling back and forth between home and Texas. There's a lady named Amy Wilson, who'll be handling all of the administrative affairs for Brooks, and you'll be coordinating our work through her.

By the way, she's a spook for the navy and is a close friend of General Litton's."

Mary Jo added, "You may hear from Amy about a meeting this week in Starkville, Mississippi, and, if you do, set it up for me to attend. You may need to touch base with Melissa Green at Dalhousie, as well. I had a chance to look over the progress reports on our two current projects, and I see that Ono Island is winding down to be handed over to the client on schedule in September, and I also saw that Auburn had signed off on our design for the catfish project. Is there anything I need to know from the engineering side?"

"No, that takes care of me. How about you?"

"No, I'm good, so I guess you can take off. Thanks again for coming over and breaking up your Sunday. I'll let you know when I plan to go back to Texas. See you in the morning."

Mary Jo dialed General Litton's home phone, and Karen Litton answered, "Good afternoon, Mary Jo. It's good to hear from you."

"Hi, Karen. Is the General available?"

"No, dear, I'm afraid he's taking his after-lunch nap. He should be coming down soon though. We usually have tea and a snack about this time on Sunday. Can I have him call you?"

"Please. I recently met one of his admirers, and I want to tell him about it."

"Oh, that will please him; I'll have him give you a ring."

Mary Jo took the back stairs to the kitchen and rummaged through the fridge, looking for a snack. She remembered the biscuits that Laurie had baked and frozen. Mary Jo found them and was just about to thaw them in the microwave when her phone rang. The caller ID read "Litton." Mary Jo propped the phone under her chin and began to soften the biscuits while she spoke. "Good evening, General. Thanks for calling me back."

"Of course. Karen tells me that you've met someone I should know."

"I have. Do you remember Captain Amy Wilson?"

"Indeed, I do. Amy's a good friend, and, in fact, you may have met her in Washington when I got the medal."

"I do remember seeing her there, but last week we found that we'll be working together out in West Texas."

"Yes, until just recently, Amy was postmistress somewhere on the frontier. She's also a skilled intelligence officer, as I suspect you've discovered. She called me checking up on you."

"We traded information last week, and I wanted to thank you for the kind things you said about me."

"All true. You'll enjoy working with Amy. She'll give you good advice, so be sure to pay attention to what she says."

"You know I will. Amy tells me she's up for flag rank soon, so she'll really outrank me then."

"She deserves it as much as anyone I know. Give her my regards, will you?"

"Of course. I'll probably be back out there later this coming week. You take care of yourself and listen to Karen."

"You say that like I've got a choice. She has me under lock and key."

"Good! Keep well."

The microwave dinged, indicating that the biscuits were thawed. Mary Jo split them, put in a pat of butter and a small piece of cheddar cheese, and then she put the tray into her toaster oven and set the timer. When the biscuits turned a golden brown, she removed the tray and took it to the breakfast nook, along with a jar of Laurie's fig preserves and a cold glass of milk. After she devoured the biscuits, Mary Jo moved into the living room and turned on PBS to watch *Masterpiece Theater*.

***

Alan was sitting on the front veranda of his ranch house watching the desert night descend when his cell phone rang, and the caller ID read, "Unknown Caller." Typically, he would have let it ring through to voicemail, but he answered it out of a combination of boredom and curiosity. He said, "Alan Brooks."

"Good evening, Dr. Brooks," a refined voice replied. "I must apologize for calling you at home on Sunday evening."

"What can I do for you?"

"It's more a matter of what I can do for you," the voice continued. "I would like to visit with you as soon as we can meet."

Alan asked, "Who is this?"

"Oh, I'm sorry. My name is Lester Fellows. I'm a partner at Fellows & Johns. We're attorneys in Los Angeles."

"I see, Mr. Fellows, and what would we be meeting about?"

"I have a client who is interested in buying your ranch and is prepared to offer you a very attractive price."

"I see, and do you have any reason to assume the Circle B is for sale?"

"None. But it has been my experience that for the right price, everything is for sale."

"Mr. Fellows, I have to take another call. Do you have a number where I can reach you in, say, 15 minutes?"

"Of course. I'm at my office, and my private number is 310-445-9897. I hope you'll call me back."

"Oh, I'll call; just give me time to get off this other line."

When he had broken the connection, Alan put his foot back on the porch rail and thought, "I need to buy some time to think. I know I'm not interested in selling the ranch, but I am interested in knowing who is so interested in buying it and if it has anything to do with Carson Black's revelation. I think I'll take the meeting, just to find out."

Alan sat watching the dark for a few more minutes and then dialed the number Fellows had left. After the first ring, Fellows said, "Hello, Dr. Brooks. I appreciate your calling back. As I mentioned, I'd like to meet with you as soon as possible."

"I'm in the process of starting a new business, so your call may be timely, but I'll be tied up the first part of the week. How would Thursday work for you?"

"I can be there as early as you wish. We'll be flying into the local airport, which I believe is in Blister, Texas."

"It is, and I assume you're flying private."

"Yes, my client has a Lear, so it's only a couple of hours from LAX."

"Okay, let's make it 10:00 on Thursday morning — and by 'we' am I to assume your client will be with you?"

"Not the client personally, but one of his top financial aides will be along."

"That'll be fine; I'll expect you on Thursday."

"Yes, and thank you, Dr. Brooks. You won't regret this; I can assure you of that."

When Fellows had left the line, Alan said under his breath, "No, I'm sure I won't."

SEVENTEEN

WHEN HE CROSSED THE PARKING LOT and opened the office door, Alan could smell the coffee brewing. He stepped into the little kitchen, poured a cup, and headed to his office. He could see Amy hammering away on her computer, and, as he walked by, she looked up and mouthed, "Good morning."

Sitting down at his desk, Alan saw that Amy had placed a copy of the day's *Wall Street Journal* on his credenza, which reminded him to get her to stop delivery of it to his old office at WTSU. He booted up his computer and entered the codes to get on the company's cloud provider. When the dashboard appeared on the screen, he chose "main system," and the screen filled with the controls for the decimal-scraping program. Alan entered "settings" and began to check his adjustments.

There was a gentle rapping on his doorframe, and Alan looked up and saw Amy holding a file folder. She asked, "May I come in?"

Alan turned away from the screen and replied, "Of course! Have a seat."

Amy sat down in one of the wingbacks and said, "I hate to interrupt, but I need you to read this memo to the Dalhousie legal department before I email it." She handed the file to Alan.

Alan opened it and began to read. After he finished, he said, "Perfect. You've laid out our legal questions just as we discussed. I'll be interested in their advice."

"When do you plan to meet with Officer Black again?"

"Don't really know…the ball's in his court, but I really want to hear from this memo before we do."

"Okay, I think that's a wise idea. As soon as it's 9:00 a.m. in Mississippi, I'm going to call Will Ransom and set up the meeting at Mississippi State. When do you want to do it?"

"I plan to run the next test of the system this morning; then, I'm free until Thursday. I have a morning appointment with a lawyer from L.A. who wants to buy the Circle B."

"Oh, I didn't realize the ranch was for sale."

"It's not, but I want to hear him out. Somehow this has got to be connected to the pitchblende."

"What's the name of the law firm? I'll try to check them out."

Alan looked in his shirt pocket and pulled out the note from the previous night. "His name is Lester Fellows, with Fellows & Johns."

"Okay, I'll see what I can find out about him."

After Amy returned to her office, Alan finished checking out the system and then sent an email to the team at Dalhousie, also copying Mary Jo. Alan let them know that, if everyone would be ready, he'd run a test of the system at 10:00 a.m. Mountain Time. He called Pete and left a message, giving him the same information. While Alan waited for replies, he decided to call Ellen and thank her for the piece.

When Ellen came on the line, she said, "Don't think you're off the hook, Brooks. You still owe me an exclusive."

"Good morning to you too, Ellen. What's got you in such a foul mood?"

"If you think this is a foul mood, just wait until I find out you and Corelli have been jacking me around."

"I have no responsibility for Corelli's fawning over you like a schoolboy. In fact, I've been encouraging him to try to get a life."

"Now I understand his problem. He's been going to you for advice about his love life. Not only are you unemployed, but nobody remembers the last time you had a date. Rumors are spreading about your sexual preferences."

"Yeah, I'm beginning to wonder about that myself. How'd you like to remedy my problem?"

"And break Corelli's heart? No, you're just gonna have to handle that by yourself, but, remember, it may cause blindness."

"You remember that I offered you the chance, and you turned it down, but, seriously, thanks for the piece — it was well done."

"You're welcome. Now, when do I get the real story?"

"There are a few loose ends I need to clean up, but it'll be soon."

"I'm holding you to that. Don't make me ask again."

"I called you today, didn't I?"

"Yeah, but you're probably trying to pacify me. Don't even think about playing me. I'll cut your nuts off and stick 'em up your nose."

"Just the thought of that turns me on. I'll keep in touch."

Alan was grinning after the exchange with Ellen, when Amy came in and said, "You look like a jackass eating briars. What's so funny?"

"Just another round with the acid-tongued Miss Sikes."

"I read her article on us in the paper yesterday. She seemed kind enough to me."

"Yeah, but I'm waiting for the other shoe to drop. Did you talk to Will?"

"I did, and we're on for tomorrow or Wednesday, if it works for you."

"Okay. Check to see if Mary Jo and the Dalhousie lawyer can be there, and y'all pick the day and time. I'd like for you to accompany me to the meeting, so make some airline reservations for us, if you would."

"I've been meaning to bring up an idea that Pete and I've been discussing. He's willing to co-opt a new plane with us. He has an older turboprop, and he'd like to move up to a Citation."

"I have a hard time thinking like that, but I suspect we'll need a plane in the near future. Why don't you do some research on a Citation and get back to me."

"On the possibility that you might be interested, Pete and I already did some research, and here it is in a nutshell. The Citation X seats eight in executive configuration, with a crew of two. It has a range of 3,100 miles and a cruising speed of 600 MPH. You can fly nonstop anywhere in the U.S., including Hawaii and Alaska."

"What are we talking about in cost?"

"Just at $23,000,000, or less than a day's income."

"Amy, do you think we can afford to do this?"

"Yes — not only can we afford it, but we actually need to do it."

"Alright. You get with Pete and work out the details but give me some time to come up with our share."

"Pete and I have already come up with a plan. He'll foot the initial layout, and we can come in later with our share. If you approve, then I'll give Pete the go-ahead."

"Good. Just let me know, but, in the meantime, we'll still need reservations."

"Not really. Pete ordered the plane last week, and it was delivered over the weekend. That's what he's been up to. His pilots were checked out, and we can use it this week."

"I see, and what would y'all have done if I'd nixed the idea?"

"We'd have talked you into it anyway."

Alan smiled. "Well, I guess you can make whatever arrangements we'll need to use it. Like I said, just let me know."

When Amy left, Alan looked at his email and saw that Mary Jo and the Dalhousie team were okay with 10:00 a.m., so he buzzed Amy to come back in for the test run. She and Alan moved into the conference room and got everyone on the speaker. When they all were on the network, Alan hit "execute," and the screen sprang into life. It took close to 45 minutes to reach the goal of $10 million, and the system automatically shut down.

Alan gave it a minute to sink in and then said, "Okay, everything looks good from my end. How'd the trading system handle it?"

Bill Wysock replied, "Everything worked perfectly. It shows that you bought and sold derivatives contracts all across the globe, resulting in profits of close to $10 million. I'd say we're ready to do some serious trading, and, by the way, the proceeds have been received by our bank in Montreal and have posted to your account."

"Excellent. Now, can you get the attorney Emile mentioned in the office?"

"Hello, Dr. Brooks. I'm already sitting in. My name is Earl Lipscomb, the firm's in-house counsel."

"Good to meet you, Earl. I suppose you know Mary Jo."

"Yes, I've met Miss Thibodaux."

"Okay. Amy Wilson is here with me, and she wants to settle on the timing of our visit to Mississippi State University."

Amy spoke up and added, "Thanks, Alan. I have two possible days for us to meet: tomorrow or Wednesday of this week. Does anyone have a preference?"

"Not me," replied Mary Jo. "Either works for me."

"If it's no problem for anyone else, I'd prefer to go on Wednesday," said Lipscomb. "By the way, I received your memo asking for advice on gifting land to the Apaches, and I've already got some of my people working on it. I should have an answer when we meet in Mississippi."

"Thanks for giving it priority treatment," answered Amy. "I guess if there's no objection, we'll all meet in Starkville on Wednesday morning," she added. "I'll get with Will Ransom and set up a meeting for 9:00 a.m. Does that suit everyone?"

Mary Jo replied, "Yeah. It's only a little over an hour's flight for those of us coming from Mobile. I'll bring Earl with me, and we'll land at the Raspet Flight Center at Mississippi State by 9:00 a.m. Central Time. I talked to Will last night, and he tells me that the center can accommodate anything up to a 737. He'll be coming in a King Air turboprop. Alan, if you and Amy are flying commercial, then you'll want to come into the Golden Triangle Airport, which is less than 20 miles from the campus. We'll have someone meet you, but you may have to arrive the night before."

"No, we'll come directly into the flight center. We'll be using Pete Corelli's new Citation X, and it's only a two-hour flight."

Mary Jo stifled a giggle and said, "Gee, Alan, it didn't take long for you to embrace private aviation."

"You know what they say; time is money. See y'all in Starkville Wednesday."

After the conference call, Alan returned to his office and sat thinking. The little voice in his head that always warned him of danger was nagging at the back of his mind. "I need to clear my head of all of the collateral crap that's going on and concentrate on the chief objective, which is how to use my newfound wealth to fund my research. If I listen to almost all of the government and private think-tanks, then the critical issues for the next 50 years revolve around energy, water, and food. There is concern about global warming, but it's tied to greenhouse gases and the depletion of the ozone layer. If we were able to come up with clean, cheap energy and eliminate the use of all fossil fuels, then we could solve global warming, clean up

147

the air, and encourage economic development in the third world. If something like what this guy at Mississippi State is working on proved viable, then we'd take a big step on the energy problem. With abundant energy, we could tackle the water problem, both for human consumption and for agriculture; this would kill two birds with one stone."

Alan had a final thought: "If this were a SEAL operation, then we'd do a risk analysis to try to anticipate the unexpected consequences of our actions, and I need to do just that. I'll ask Amy and Mary Jo to work with me on it after the meeting in Mississippi."

Once Alan had made the decision, the little voice eased up; it didn't go away completely, but it backed off a notch or two. He met Pete for lunch at Shorty's to give Pete an update and promised to give him another heads-up when they returned from Mississippi. As he was leaving, Alan told Pete that he agreed that the Citation was a good idea. Then, Alan and Amy spent the rest of the day preparing for their trip.

The Citation lifted off just after 6:00 a.m. MDT the next morning, and the travelers pulled into the tie-down area at the Raspet Flight Center at 9:15 a.m. CDT. Alan and Amy descended the stairs to the tarmac to find Mary Jo waiting for them. She took them to the small waiting lounge, where Will Ransom and Earl Lipscomb were having a cup of coffee.

When the newcomers got coffee themselves and sat down, Will said, "There's a van coming to pick us up and take us to our meeting. Volanov's office is in the university's research park on the other side of the campus. In fact, I see them pulling up now."

The ride from the airport took the group through the center of the shady, well-landscaped campus, and Will thought just how much it reminded him of WTSU, only with a lot more vegetation. The van entered the grounds of the Thad Cochran Research Park and wound its way to a three-story building, where it pulled under a covered entrance.

The visitors were met by a lady in a lab coat who introduced herself as Dr. Golda Petranov. She explained that she was Dr. Volanov's assistant and asked that they follow her. She led them to an elevator, and Mary Jo noticed that she pressed the down button.

They descended to the basement level, where Petranov opened a door to a large conference room and held it for them to enter.

The three people seated at the table rose and indicated that the Brooks collaborative should be seated on the opposite side of the table. Petranov took a chair beside a tall, dark man who was a dead ringer for Abraham Lincoln — right down to the sagging face and bushy eyebrows. Petranov smiled and said, "Dr. Volanov wishes to welcome you to our laboratory; we hope you had a pleasant journey. I'd like to introduce Dr. Norman Story," she said, as she turned her hand toward one of the seated figures.

Petranov continued, "Dr. Story is a professor in our Electrical Engineering department and has agreed to be available to try to explain any technical questions regarding Dr. Volanov's inventions."

Alan thought, "I guess my engineering creds didn't impress the guys at MSU, but I'll keep my mouth shut."

Story acknowledged the intro, and Petranov turned to the third guy and said, "And this is Jan Thornton from our Office of Technology Transfer. She will be available to advise on issues of agreements and intellectual property."

It was Will's turn, and he made the introductions for the Brooks group, making a point to reference Alan's Ph.D. When Will completed the introductions, he continued: "I want to thank Dr. Volanov and his staff for meeting with us this morning. I've met with Dr. Volanov on several occasions to discuss a technology that he's developed that might improve on some of the work previously done by Nikola Tesla a hundred years ago. Alan, would you like to start the meeting?"

Alan stood and said, "As we all know, Tesla built a tower in Colorado to test his theory that usable electric power could be extracted from the atmosphere surrounding thunderstorms. The experiment failed and did severe damage to the electrical grid serving Colorado Springs. Since then, no one has been able to improve on Tesla's technology. It is widely assumed that, while Tesla's ideas were technically sound, there is no practical method of exploiting them. Is that about the gist of it, Dr. Volanov?"

The lanky Russian came to his feet and said, "Yes, Dr. Brooks, that is the current thinking, but I'm afraid that I have to suggest that Tesla's work was flawed, and his system cannot possibly produce usable electric current."

Alan was stunned and thought, "If the damn system cannot work, then what in the hell are we doing here?"

Volanov saw Alan's surprise and quickly added, "No, Dr. Brooks, Tesla's system will not work, but mine will work perfectly."

EIGHTEEN

VASSILY VOLANOV PAUSED to let what he had just said register around the table, and then he continued: "Nikola Tesla's work was based on capturing the power generated by thunderstorms, and I believe it will never be feasible to do this. The enormous surges of raw electricity generated by storms will overwhelm today's transmission technology and, in my opinion, any future improvements. Not only did the initial surge wreck his device, but there was, and is, also no method to distribute this great surge of energy to any end user."

Alan thought for a moment and then said, "If I hear you correctly, then you reject Tesla's work completely?"

"Not all of Tesla's work, but certainly his efforts in Colorado Springs."

"But you think you have a workable system?"

"Yes, I believe I do. We have built and tested a small prototype machine, and it works perfectly. I'll be surprised if it does not work on a fully scaled-up machine, but that has yet to be built."

"If I may, and I defer to Dr. Story on this, I assume you've seen something that escaped Tesla and the entire academic community. I'd like a little more information," said Alan.

Norman Story shook his head and replied, "I'll have to confess that I have no clue. As far as I know, the Department of Electrical Engineering has never seen Dr. Volanov's work, and I too would like to know more."

At that point, Jan Thornton interrupted and said, "I'm afraid that I will have to ask everyone to sign a nondisclosure agreement before we go any further. Dr. Volanov's work cannot be released into the public domain at this point."

As Jan began to pass around a two-page legal document, Alan said, "Earl, I think this falls into your bailiwick, and we'll follow your advice."

Lipscomb took the document, pulled out his reading glasses, and began to examine the material. Finally, he looked up and said, "I have no problem with signing this; it's pretty standard, and it does provide the university protection against the misuse of Dr. Volanov's work."

Everyone signed a copy and passed the executed documents across the table to Thornton, who said, "Dr. Volanov, you may proceed."

"As I said, I believe the problems that resulted in the disaster in Colorado Springs were caused by Tesla's attempt to harness energy from the storms. I believe, and I think we have proven, that the better the weather, the better chance one has to extract ambient electricity from the atmosphere. Tesla employed what was essentially a lightning rod. My system uses an extractor-converter to provide a steady, dependable flow of power that can be controlled on an as-needed basis."

Alan asked, "How does your extractor-converter work?"

Jan Thornton answered the question. "Dr. Volanov's invention of this device is the heart of the system. We have yet to decide if we will apply for a patent or not, but we are unable to provide technical details at this time. We have filed for a provisional patent to establish the date of discovery."

Alan was confused. "May I ask why the university is hesitating to apply for a full patent?"

"We may decide to apply later, but for now we feel it is in our best interest to keep the 'how to' information private."

"I guess you do understand that this makes a potential licensee's due diligence much more difficult?"

"We do, and we suggest that a demonstration of the system's workability would be the first step, and, with that in mind, why don't we let Dr. Volanov show us his invention?"

"Of course," replied Alan.

Volanov signaled to Petranov, and she left the room. Volanov then suggested that everyone follow him to the parking lot. While they were making their way through the lot, Mary Jo leaned over and whispered in Alan's ear, "Does all of this sound just a little too good to be true?"

"Yeah, but, as Amy reminded me, whoever thought you could pull money out of cyberspace?"

"Good point. I guess we'll see what he's got."

Once they all were assembled, the door to the building opened, and Petranov and two students wheeled in a small cart with equipment mounted on top. They placed it where everyone could see it and left. Volanov walked to the cart and said, "What you are about to watch is the first public demonstration of our technology. First, I'd like for Dr. Brooks and Dr. Story to examine the prototype and be satisfied that there are no electrical connections."

Alan and Dr. Story walked around the cart, looking carefully for wires or transmitters, and nodded to Volanov that they were satisfied. Volanov continued, "When we first tested our prototype, we did it inside our labs, and it worked just fine. Then, it occurred to me that what we might be picking up was not ambient atmospheric power, but rather reflected charges from the lighting and other electrical systems in the building. As you will see, the system works even better in the open air." When he reached over and flipped a toggle switch, there was a slight humming sound, and the meters mounted on the cart began to come to life. After there was sufficient current flowing, Volanov flipped a second switch, and a small electric fan began to whirr. There was only the slight humming sound and the slightest smell of ozone to indicate that it was in use. Volanov turned a rheostat, and the current increased or decreased at his direction, at which point he turned to the group. "There you have it. We are extracting ambient electricity from the atmosphere and using it to power a small motor. I can build a larger extractor-converter that will be able to produce enormous amounts of power."

"Give us an example regarding megawatts," suggested Thornton.

"Entergy's nuclear plant at Grand Gulf Mississippi is a medium-sized generating plant. It produces a little over 1,300 MW, and that would easily be within our reach. I would like to scale up to 10 MW in a beta system to allow us to get a commercial-size test without the expense of major league transmission lines."

Alan asked, "What do you think such a prototype would cost?"

"I'd want Dr. Story to verify my figures, but I think we could build the whole thing for a little less than $3 million."

Alan continued, "If my quick calculations are correct, then that would be enough to power a town of 15,000 people?"

"Yes, I'd say 10 MW could easily do that if the town were not an industrial center. The problem that concerns me is having to sell excess power back into the grid. The local power company does not welcome privately generated power. They want to be able to justify building additional plants that they own and control."

Alan said, "Dr. Volanov, I'm impressed with your system, and, to that end, I'd like to discuss licensing the commercial applications. I propose that Mr. Lipscomb prepare an option agreement to present to your Office of Technology Transfer. The provisions of the option will spell out the terms of the license and give my company 60 days to complete our due diligence. If we're satisfied that we have what we need from that process, then I'll pay the university $500,000 upon the signing of the option."

Alan continued, "That will be nonrefundable if we decide to pass; if we decide to close, then I would expect that a patent application is pursued immediately. Upon signing the licensing agreement, I'll pay the university $1,000,000 and another $2,000,000 if the 10 MW scale-up works. Once the system is in commercial use, I'll pay a 5% royalty for the life of the patent. Once the licensing agreement is signed, we'll begin construction of the beta plant."

Alan looked at Thornton and asked, "Is this a reasonable approach from your point of view?"

"I believe it is. Of course, the devil is always in the details, but I'm willing to start as you suggest."

Alan asked, "Earl, how long will it take you to prepare the option agreement?"

"Even with the attendant licensing agreement, I can have a draft back to Jan by this Friday."

"Okay, it looks like we're about to embark upon a pretty exciting endeavor," Alan said as he walked over to Volanov and took his hand.

"Vassily, this may be the start of an interesting relationship. I'm looking forward to working with you."

Volanov nodded and asked, "Tell me, Dr. Brooks, what your plans for developing this technology are?"

"I plan to use it to change people's lives: first with affordable energy, then clean and plentiful water, and ultimately the elimination of fossil fuels."

"I see. I was certainly hoping there was more to it than just making money. I have some ideas about producing water and eliminating fossil fuels that we should discuss, but first things first, as you Americans like to say."

***

On the way back to the airport, Will Ransom said, "Alan, where are you thinking about building the beta unit?"

"Don't really know. I'd like to do it where there's the least likelihood of publicity. Why'd you ask?"

"While I was listening about the ability to power a small city on 10 MWs, it dawned on me that Cumberland plantation, my place over in the Delta, probably uses close to that much power. Maybe we could be your test site."

"Damn, Will, are you sure you use that much power?"

"Yeah, pretty sure, but I can check it out easily enough. We have over 800 acres of catfish ponds, which use large amounts of electricity to keep aerated. We have gins, a catfish processing plant, and irrigation equipment a gogo. Power is one of our biggest expenses."

"How would you deal with the local power company?"

"That's the most interesting part. I get my power from the local REA, Central Delta Power, and they buy their power from TVA. I believe they'd welcome a competitive, reliable second source."

"Do you know anyone to talk to at the REA?"

"I'm chairman of the board and the largest customer they have."

"Well, that's convenient. Check it out and get back to me as soon as you can."

"I'll get on it as soon as I get home."

When the group arrived at the Raspet Center, they sat in the little lounge and ate a sandwich, and Mary Jo told Alan that she planned to be back in Pecos Springs tomorrow after lunch. Everyone said goodbye and went to their respective aircrafts. Mary Jo and Earl Lipscomb were the first to take off, and they were back in Mobile by 2:30 in the afternoon.

Alan and Amy were last to leave, and, as the Citation reached cruising altitude, Amy opened her briefcase and said, "Before we took off, Earl handed me this folder." She opened the folder and gave a document to Alan. "Here are copies of the answer to our memo asking for guidance on the gifting of land to the Apaches."

Alan took the document, and they both began to read. Amy was the first to finish, and she looked out the cabin window while Alan read it carefully. When he finished, he said, "If I'm reading this correctly, then there doesn't seem to be any legal reason I can't deed the land over to the tribe, and then the issue of commercial mining of the property will be their decision entirely. Is that the way you read it?"

"Yes. If the tribe can get comfortable with the mining of any or all of the land, then it'll be entirely up to them."

"As soon as I hear back from Carson that the tribe has agreed, I'll get Earl started on the paperwork."

"Do you think the lawyer from L.A. will still be interested in buying the Circle B?"

"We'll just have to wait and see."

The two set down at the Blister airport in mid-afternoon and stopped by the office to check to see if there were any calls or emails. There weren't, and both went home for the evening.

When Alan topped the ridge and could see the ranch house, he noticed Carson Black's Jeep parked in front. Carson was sitting with his feet propped up on the porch rail. As Alan walked up, Carson stood and said, "Maria told me you were on your way home, so I made myself comfortable."

Alan shook his hand and said, "Glad to see you. Did you talk to the elders?"

"I did."

"And what did they think of my idea?"

"When I convinced them that you weren't totally loco, they gave it serious consideration."

"Okay, so what do they want to do?"

"They want to speak with you. They've invited you to a meeting of the tribal council."

"Did you explain that I was willing to deed the property over to them legally?"

"Yeah, but you have to accept that Native Americans don't have a lot of faith in written agreements with whites. They're a lot more interested in looking into your eyes than reading what's on a piece of paper."

"Yeah, I can see that. When's the meeting?"

"They'll schedule it at your convenience."

"Well, I want to get this done. Think we could have the meeting tomorrow?"

"I'm sure we can; just let me call the chief and check it out."

Carson stood, pulled his cell phone from his back pocket, and walked out into the parking area while it rang. Alan could see him talking to someone and then hang up. Carson climbed back on the porch and reported the answer. "We're on for tomorrow evening at 7:00 at the cultural center on the reservation. I'll meet you there."

"I'll probably want to bring Mary Jo with me. Will that be a problem?"

"No, I'll take care of it."

"Good. I'd like to get this done as soon as possible. Now, where do you intend to spend the night?"

"I was planning on getting a motel room in town."

"Nonsense. We have plenty of room out here, and you can join me for dinner. I'm sure Maria has plenty prepared."

"Okay, I'll take you up on the room and board, and I've already checked — we're having chicken and dumplings for dinner. Maria asked me what my favorite dish was."

"Damn, I see what the Arabs mean about not letting the camel get his nose under your tent. Camels and Apaches seem to have a lot in common."

"The thought occurred to me that since you seem intent on giving away your land, I might be available for a couple of sections. Then I wondered what I'd do with desert land with no water."

"Grow cactus, just like the rest of us, and wish for a source of water."

After dinner, the men sat on the porch and swapped stories. Black talked about his life as a Ranger, and Alan told him about being a SEAL, including the tale about Shiva's night patrol against the Taliban. After breakfast the next morning, they took a ride, and, before Alan left for the office, they agreed to meet at the Apache Cultural Center that evening.

When Alan walked into the office, Amy was waiting with a cup of coffee and another file folder. Alan smiled and said, "I'm beginning to expect a new file folder every time we meet."

"This was waiting for me when I checked my email this morning. You remember I offered to check out the lawyer you're meeting with tomorrow?"

"Yeah. Did you find anything?"

"Just read the file, and we'll need to discuss it."

Alan took the file, sat at his desk, and began to read. When he'd read it through a couple of times, he set it down and called Amy to join him. She sat in one of the wingbacks, and Alan said, "You've read this whole thing?"

"I have, and I found it both interesting and disturbing."

"Yeah, so did I. It seems that Lester Fellows of Fellows & Johns has only one client, New China Industries of Los Angeles."

Amy asked, "Yes, and did you read the info on New China?"

"I did, and they sound like a front for the Chinese military."

"My friend at the agency asked why I wanted the information and warned me that the Peoples Liberation Front, which is what they call their military establishment, would not hesitate to move aggressively to meet their strategic needs."

"What'd you tell him about wanting the info?"

"I told him I was just following up on some background concerning another matter."

"Don't ask, don't tell, huh?"

"Something like that. The real question is what do you plan to do?"

"Oh, I'll still take the meeting. If the Chinese want the Circle B, then I better try to find out why."

"Are you worried about telling them no?"

"Not really. I'll do it firmly, but politely."

"I can see nothing good coming from this, Alan. You be careful."

"Carson Black was waiting for me when I got home last night. The Apache elders want to meet with me tonight at the reservation to check me out. Mary Jo is coming in this afternoon, and she's going with me. Want to come along?"

"Do you need me?"

"Not especially, but you're welcome to join us."

"If you don't really need me, then I think I'll take a pass. I've got some navy work that needs to be done, and tonight's a good time to do it."

Alan was waiting as Mary Jo parked her plane at the Blister airport. Once the aircraft was secured and they were in the truck headed to the ranch, Alan said, "You and I are going to join Carson Black at a meeting of the tribal council this evening."

"Okay. Were they interested in the land?"

"Yeah," Alan answered and filled Mary Jo in on his conversation with Black. When he was done, he added, "Amy called someone at the CIA and checked on the background of the lawyer we're meeting with tomorrow, the one who has a client interested in buying the Circle B."

"Did she find anything?"

"His only client is a large holding company based in Los Angeles, which serves as a front for the Chinese military in their search for strategic materials."

"No kidding. This just keeps getting weirder and weirder."

Alan agreed. "Yeah, don't it just?"

NINETEEN

ALAN AND MARY JO left a little earlier than necessary to attend the tribal meeting. After asking several people, they located the tribal council center and found a parking spot on the backside of the lot. Carson Black was waiting for them near the entrance. When they reached him, he said, "The council follows tribal tradition and has little need for Robert's Rules of Order. Alan, you are a guest, so you'll be included in the circle of elders. Cricket and I will be seated in the visitors' section. You will be expected to speak freely, so don't worry."

Mary Jo frowned at Carson and whispered, "Don't give me any more incentive to try you on again. I may get lucky the next time."

"Maybe in your Shiva dreams," Carson replied.

"Don't forget — I can always shoot your smart ass."

"You cannot shoot that which you cannot see. Apaches move like spirits on the wind."

"Okay, children, play nice. Carson, I'll try not to embarrass you, and thanks for setting this up."

"You'll do just fine."

Everyone took their seats, and the tribal chief opened the meeting. "Brothers and sisters, we are gathered here tonight in a special session of the tribal council, and there is only one item of business on our agenda. We have as our guest, Dr. Alan Brooks, our neighbor to the south. Mr. Brooks has a request to bring before the council. Dr. Brooks, you may state your request."

"Thank you, Chief. I come before you tonight in the spirit of peace and solidarity. For nearly 200 years, our people have lived in peace, and I feel a close kinship with the tribe. As you know, one of your holiest sites lies on the northern border of my ranch, and I have always treated this site with respect and reverence. Rather than a sense of ownership, I've felt a sense of obligation. The tribe has had unfettered access to the site, and others have been kept out. This arrangement has been in place for many years. It has become necessary that we alter the terms and conditions regarding this land. We have reason to believe that there is a large outcropping of pitchblende, or uranium ore, on the site, and there will be efforts to mine it."

A spattering of conversation swept through the crowd, and many of the elders spoke to their companions. The chief waved his hand and said, "Please, allow Dr. Brooks to continue."

The muttering died down, and Alan continued: "It is my opinion that, as a private landholder, I could be compelled to allow this mining to take place, but I do not want to see outsiders desecrating the holy sites and stealing the minerals that rightfully belong to the tribe. Therefore, I am proposing to gift the property in question to the tribe, with the understanding that the tribal council has the authority to allow limited mining, if they so choose."

Alan sat down, and a loud murmur swept through the room. Once order had been restored, the chief opened the floor for questions from the elders. A grizzled man of at least 80, dressed in traditional Apache attire, stood and said, "I am an old man, and, since I was a boy, we have had cordial relations with the Brooks family, and they have always respected our traditions, so I'm not surprised to hear Dr. Brooks make this proposal, but I do have a question. Is there any estimate of the value of this mineral?"

Alan stood again and answered, "There has been no formal survey, but, from what is visible, I feel it is safe to say that we're talking about millions of dollars."

"I see," the old man replied. "And exactly why are you giving up such a fortune?"

"There are two answers to the question. First, I do not need additional wealth. The second reason is that I've always felt the Apache got a raw deal and were consigned to the backwaters of our society. If the tribal council should see fit to allow carefully controlled mining, then the millions of dollars that would come to the tribe could provide a better standard of living for a people that I hold in the highest respect."

Several more of the elders had similar questions and one asked, "How would you feel if the council decided not to allow mining on the land?"

Alan stood and replied, "I'll not have a problem with such a decision. Once I deed the land to the tribe, there will be no strings attached. If the council decides to preserve the site as a tribal holy place, then so be it."

A murmur of approval swept the room until, finally, the chief said, "I believe Dr. Brooks has made his case, and the council will consider his request. Our session is adjourned."

Alan walked over to Carson and Mary Jo and said, "So that's all there is?"

"Yep, that's it. They'll let me know their decision before the next full moon."

"Should I have my lawyers start on the agreement?"

"I have no idea what their decision will be, but I'd hold off for a bit. I do know that you impressed them, and, regardless of the outcome, you've made many new friends."

"Then I guess the trip was well worth it. Thanks again, Carson."

"Sure, and, by the way, I think I know who killed the little horse, and you'd never guess in a hundred tries."

"That would be an agent of New China Industries out of L.A., right?"

"You're beginning to behave like an Apache, and, believe me, that's a compliment. What do you think that's all about?"

"Don't know for sure, but Mary Jo and I are meeting with their lawyer tomorrow. It seems they want to buy the Circle B."

"Hmm," muttered Carson. "I'll bet pitchblende is behind all of this."

"We'll know more tomorrow, and I'll keep you in the loop. Call me when you hear something from the elders."

On the drive back to the ranch, Mary Jo rode in silence until they were almost there, and then she said, "Alan, I'd like to ask you a philosophical question."

Alan smiled and said, "Oh shit, that usually comes just before the discussion about commitment in a relationship."

"I guess that may apply here. My question is this: If the Chinese decide to start playing rough, what are we going to do?"

"We'll do everything we can to avoid it, but, if it happens, then we'll take them down."

"Okay, that gives me some direction. I can work with that."

"If it comes to that, we'll kick their asses all over West Texas. Hell, we faced down the Comanches," he said smiling, "so a bunch of L.A. thugs will be easy. We'll take them down and eat their livers. I plan to call a risk-analysis meeting with you and Amy after our meeting with the lawyer."

"Good plan. We can deal with them, if they force us to," Mary Jo answered.

On Thursday morning, Alan and Mary Jo took a ride before breakfast and arrived at the office before 7:00 a.m. They took some coffee into the conference room and filled Amy in on the meeting with the Apaches. Alan mentioned the risk-analysis meeting later in the morning. They each went to their individual offices while waiting for Lester Fellows to show up.

When Alan's phone rang, Amy told him that Will Ransom was holding. Alan picked up and said, "Good morning, Will. What'd you find with the REA?"

"Just as I thought, we have an open-ended agreement with TVA to supply our power. We can draw down as much power as we need, and we pay a floating price based on their generating cost. I talked to our contact at TVA and asked if it would cause them any heartburn if we cut back on our usage, and he assured me that it wouldn't. In fact, he said they'd welcome it. They're running near capacity and would actually like to buy anything we could provide."

"Did you tell him where we might be getting extra power?"

"Only that I was looking at some wind and solar alternatives and that I might be cutting back on my usage from the REA and might even be selling some excess power back to them. His reply was that they stood ready to continue to supply our REA with a reliable source of power, but they'd welcome any relief we could give them."

"Sounds like this might be a win-win situation. Can the REA buy any of our excess production?"

"Yeah. They've agreed to buy it for the price they pay TVA. I wanted to suggest that we give them a much better price to help offset the loss of my business. I'd like to see the association at least break even."

"Off the top of my head, I don't see a problem with that. In fact, it might help the association grow. If you're willing to allow us to build the beta plant on your place, then we'll provide you all of your power needs for free and sell the excess to the REA at a discount to TVA's pricing."

"Okay, we've got a deal; just let me know when we need to get started."

"I will, just as soon as we paper the agreement with Mississippi State."

When Alan's conversation with Will ended, Amy came to his door and said that Fellows and two other men were waiting to see him. Alan asked her to take them to the conference room and to round up Mary Jo and meet him there.

Alan and Mary Jo came into the conference room, and Alan greeted the guests. "Good morning, gentlemen. I'm Alan Brooks, owner of the Circle B Ranch. This is Miss Wilson, our office manager, and Miss Thibodaux, our head of security."

A smiling man with a perfect tan, gleaming white teeth, and a thousand-dollar suit, held out his hand and shook Alan's. "I'm Lester Fellows of Fellows & Johns, Dr. Brooks. I'd like to introduce you and the ladies to Mr. Gerald Bass, CFO of New China Industries, and Bill Clark, our chief operating officer."

Alan immediately noticed that they were all Caucasian, not Asian. Bass looked just like an accountant — wispy blond hair and steel-rimmed glasses — while Clark looked like a sumo wrestler jammed in a suit. His neck and shoulders ran together, and both seemed like they might rip his coat apart if he made a sudden move. Clark apparently spent a lot of time in the company gym.

When everyone was seated, Alan said, "Well, Mr. Fellows, you asked for a face-to-face meeting, so I guess you have the floor."

"Thank you, Dr. Brooks. As I told you on the phone, our client, New China Industries, has an interest in acquiring ownership of your ranch. We have done our due diligence, and we're prepared to make you a generous offer this morning."

"I've just got to ask why in the world a California-based company would have an interest in desert land in West Texas."

"I'm not at liberty to discuss our corporate strategies, but just let me say that we feel your ranch would be part of our long-term beef production plans. I'm assuming that you have an interest in selling, or you wouldn't have agreed to meet with us."

"I believe I mentioned that I was starting a new business, so a discussion about selling the ranch might be timely, and that's still the case. The only caveat I have is that I'm considering deeding over to the Jicarilla Apaches a small, less than 200-acre parcel that adjoins their reservation on our northern border. This parcel contains one of the Apache's holiest burial grounds, and I believe they should have it."

A look of surprise crossed Fellows face but was quickly gone as he replied, "I'm afraid that might be a problem. Our offer is based on acquiring all of the Circle B. It does not allow for any portion to be carved out."

"I agree then that this will be a problem. I've given my word to the Apaches that the land is theirs, if they want it."

"So it's not a done deal yet?"

"No, but, as I say, I've given my word, and any sale would have to be contingent on that offer and their willingness to accept."

Fellows was about to respond when Bill Clark said, "I think Mr. Fellows has made our position clear. We intend to buy all of your land. We will not allow any deviation."

"Mr. Clark, of course, you can structure your offer any way you choose, but I won't go back on my word to the tribe. If that's your position, then I don't see any need for further discussion."

Clark stood up, adjusted his bulging coat, and growled, "We'll decide when this meeting is over, so here's what's going to happen. Mr. Bass is about to hand you a formal offer to buy your entire ranch for $1,500 per acre. That's three times the market value of the property, and he'll attach a check for $24,000,000 to the offer. Our offer is good for one week, and, after that, it will drop to $8,000,000. I expect to receive your signed agreement before next Thursday."

"I understand your terms and conditions, and I have to agree that it's a very generous offer. I'll take it into consideration and reply before next Thursday."

"Dr. Brooks," Clark glared, "I'd advise you to accept our offer. I don't have time to come back to talk to you again."

Alan smiled, looked Clark dead in the eye, and said, "No, *Mister* Clark, I doubt you will enjoy coming here again. In fact, I can almost guarantee it. I'll have an answer to your offer in the allotted time."

Clark turned to his companions and said, "This meeting is done. Get your stuff together and let's get the hell out of here."

The three men filed out of the building without saying another word.

When they were gone, Amy said, "Well, that was forceful."

Mary Jo added, "Did y'all see that vein pulsing on the side of Clark's neck? It looked like a garden hose."

Alan grinned and said, "I guess we must have upset Mr. Clark. I get the impression he's used to getting his way."

"Yes," Amy replied. "I'm sure he is. I wonder if he caught your challenge concerning another visit."

Mary Jo shook her head and said, "Oh, yeah, he caught it, and we can expect to see him again. I think we're okay until next Thursday, but he'll be back around shortly after the deadline, and, by then, we'll be sufficiently ready for him."

"Good," Alan said. "Security is your department, so just let me know what you need from me, and you can consider your budget unlimited."

"Unlimited should be adequate."

"Well, that's settled. Let's get back to work. I'd like to get right into our risk analysis. Let's take a quick look at what we're doing that might trigger unexpected consequences."

Everyone turned to the yellow legal pads in front of them and began to make notes. When everybody had looked up, Alan said, "I'd like to hear from you first, Amy."

"Well, the first thing on my list is simple; we're starting to trade serious positions in the market to mask our decimal-skimming operation. This is bound to trigger notice, and soon we should start hearing from other traders."

"I suspect we all had this on our list," Alan responded and looked over at Mary Jo, who nodded in agreement.

"I thought so. Let's take this first. The Dalhousie team has integrated our trading volume into their own trading stream, and, as such, it will only show up as increased volume for them and cannot be traced back to us. Since we're only running our system when we actually need cash, this shouldn't raise any eyebrows in the market."

Amy thought for a moment and then replied, "Okay, let's assume we're safe, at least for the time being. We're only sending money to Pete's bank when we want to do something locally. Otherwise, all cash reserves will be in our Dalhousie account in Montreal. There should be no problems from that quarter. The only other issue from an operational aspect is our relationship with the U.S. government. We'll be visible on some of their intelligence systems, and questions will be asked. This is especially true if we begin to tamper with the balance of electrical power on the grid. This is considered a high point of national vulnerability. They'll come snooping."

"I agree that we have serious exposure in that area," Alan added. "What do you suggest?"

Mary Jo broke in and said, "Of course, this is much more in Amy's wheelhouse, but let me mention that, when rape is inevitable, one strategy is to pretend to enjoy it. There may be a proactive approach that can allow us some flexibility in any future relationship with the snoopers."

"I agree with Mary Jo. It may make sense to reach out to some trusted people in the intelligence community from the very beginning. We'll have a much stronger hand when we're offering something than we'll have once they're on the trail," Amy added.

"Amy, Mary Jo's right. This is in your area. Would you be willing to prepare a plan to provide preemptive coordination with selected members of the community? This would be a major project and would have to be managed carefully."

"Yes, I'll begin working on an overall plan right away, and, Mary Jo, we might want to get some advice from Jack Litton in this area. Do you want to approach him or should I?"

Mary Jo thought for a moment and then replied, "If I approach him with the idea and he rejects it, then it's only between friends, and he won't have to take a position professionally. We can agree to forget the whole business — no harm, no foul. If he's willing, then I can get you involved."

Alan asked, "Okay, why don't y'all work on this?"

"Consider it under way," Mary Jo replied.

"That's really all I have on my list," Amy said.

Alan thanked Amy and turned to Mary Jo. "Okay, what's on your mind?"

"Several things...first are the routine security issues that any business faces, and I plan to have some suggestions for setting up a permanent department to deal with all of it. I have some folks in mind that I've seen in action, and I'll have a plan for the two of you to review in the next week. The more impending issue that I'm concerned with is the possibility that we may have a problem with New China Industries that'll have to be met with an extraordinary response."

Amy asked, "By extraordinary, do you mean operational rather than theoretical?"

"Yes, operational and potentially volatile. I want to be prepared for a worst-case situation, and I'm going to need good solid intelligence to do it."

Amy followed up: "What sort of intelligence are you talking about?"

"I'd like background information on our potential adversary, and human intel from inside their camp. I want to know when Clark plans to make his move and what to expect when he does."

Amy sat for a moment and then said, "I'll see if I can find someone inside New China. I can't guarantee it but let me check it out. I know I can get all of the background on the company and its leadership, and I can have it pretty quickly."

Mary Jo said, "That'll be great. I'm going to be concentrating all of my efforts on this until I feel they're no longer a threat."

Alan glanced around the table waiting for additional comments, and, when there were none, he said, "Okay, I think we have a pretty good plan. Let's proceed with it."

TWENTY

A FTER THE MEETING, Alan asked Amy to email a copy of the New China offer to Earl Lipscomb at Dalhousie, with a note requesting that he call when he had a chance. Then, Alan dialed Pete's cell phone. When Pete picked up, Alan said, "Good morning. Thought I'd give you an update."

"Great. How was the trip to Mississippi?"

"Good. It seems like the power-source technology might actually work, and, by the way, I'm gonna love our new toy."

"You liked the Citation, huh?"

"Man, having an airplane has got to be one of life's great pleasures. I love it."

"Kinda thought you would. So the power thing is real?"

"I believe it is. Earl Lipscomb at Dalhousie is working on a licensing agreement with Mississippi State, and we plan to build a test site as soon as we can."

"Sounds good to me. Where are we going to build it?"

"Will Ransom has offered his place in Mississippi; it can be worked into the local grid without raising any eyebrows."

"What's in it for Will?"

"Free power for his whole operation."

"Okay, that makes sense, if the test site works out. What's next?"

"I don't really know. We'll have to decide when we have a scalable technology."

"Damn, Brooks. You've only been on your own for a month, and you've developed a source of unlimited cash and free electricity. I shudder to think what you'll come up with when you have some free time."

"All kidding aside — the real goal of all of this is clean and affordable water; that's the end game," Alan replied.

"I'm sure you'll figure it out. Any developments on the Apache front?"

"Yeah. Mary Jo, Carson Black, and I met with the Jicarilla tribal council last night, and I presented my plan to cede them the property."

"Oh, and how'd they react?"

"In typical Apache fashion…indecipherable to the white man but cordial."

"No shit? It isn't every day someone offers them a source of millions of dollars for tribal development. I'm glad they were cordial. Did you meet with the lawyer from Los Angeles?"

"We did, and they've made an offer to buy the Circle B for $24,000,000, about three times what it's worth."

"Are you tempted?"

"Not in the least. They, however, were less than amicable when I told them that it couldn't include the Apache burial site."

"Deal killer, huh?"

"They left in a huff and made some veiled threats regarding the consequences of turning down their offer."

"Are you taking the threats seriously?"

"Oh yeah. I've got Mary Jo working on how we'll handle that if it comes."

"You know, Alan; we could just go to L.A. and confront them first. In Fallujah, we found that the best defense was a good offense."

"Amy's working on getting some intel about New China; then, we can decide how to handle them, but, I agree, I'd rather act than react."

"Well, keep me in the loop. You going to need the plane this week?"

"Not that I know of, but, if I do, I'll get Mary Jo to fly me. Where are you going?"

"I'm taking Ellen to New York to meet with some of her Wall Street buddies."

"What's she up to?"

"Who knows, but we've got a suite at the Plaza, and I have high hopes."

"One or two bedrooms?"

"Two, but, still, you never know."

"When y'all get back, I need to meet with her and fill her in."

"Yeah, she mentioned that just last night. I'll see if I can soften her up for you."

"I won't be depending on that. So far, she's played you like a trout."

"I'm lulling her into a false sense of security."

"Well, that part of your plan is working. See y'all when you get back."

It wasn't long before Earl Lipscomb called and told Alan to be looking for an emailed copy of the tech-transfer agreement with Mississippi State. He suggested that Alan and Amy check it over, and, if there were no changes, he'd email it to MSU's Office of Technology Transfer. Alan thanked him and went over the deal points for an agreement with Will Ransom regarding the beta-test site.

Earl took notes as Alan spoke and then said, "Okay, I'll start on an agreement with Ransom as soon as Mississippi State signs the licensing agreement. Where are we on the land deal with the Apaches?"

Alan said, "I haven't heard anything yet. I'll give you a call when I do."

Earl asked, "Have you looked over the offer from New China?"

Alan said, "No, but I did agree to an answer by their deadline, so work me up a formal refusal."

Earl asked, "You want it now?"

Alan responded, "No. I intend to wait until the last minute to send it. I want to buy some time before stirring up their reaction."

Earl asked, "What are you expecting them to do, raise the price?"

"No, but I do believe it won't be the end of their efforts."

Earl said, "Well, I'll get it ready, and you can send it when you want to. Let me know when you hear from the tribe. Can you think of anything else I need to be working on?"

"Not at the moment, but I'll call if anything comes up. Thanks, Earl. We'll talk later."

Alan and Mary Jo walked over to Shorty's for lunch, while Amy manned the office. The friends sat at a table for two near the kitchen and ordered the special. When the drinks arrived, Mary Jo said, "I hate to be a nudge, but I have a really uncomfortable feeling about New China. All of my alarms are going off, and I can't shake it."

"Yeah, it's bugging me too. Clark's reaction was a clear-cut threat."

"Oh, he threatened you, no doubt about it. What we're going to do in response is what's nagging me."

"Pete and I were talking about it, and he's in favor of a preemptive strike, but I don't know that we need to declare war on the People's Republic. What are your thoughts?"

Before Mary Jo could answer, Carson Black came in the front door and quickly spotted them. He walked over to their table and said, "Amy thought I might catch the two of you here. Is it okay to join you?"

"Absolutely," Alan said and motioned to the waitress to come over.

Carson placed his order and then reached into his briefcase and pulled out a buckskin package wrapped with rawhide thongs. He handed it to Alan. Alan took it and said, "What do we have here?"

"It's the tribal council's answer to your request," Carson replied. "Why don't you open it?"

Alan untied the rawhide and opened the buckskin, placing it on the table. It was covered with brightly colored pictograms. Alan studied the hide for a moment and asked, "Carson, can you read this?"

"I can. It seems you have been invited to become a member of the Jicarilla Apaches."

"No kidding? I'm flattered to be considered for honorary membership."

"No, not honorary — full tribal membership, and I've never heard of a white man being invited. That's the good news; the maybe not so good news is that, if you accept the invitation, it comes with some serious obligations and duties."

"Such as?"

"Most are ceremonial and traditional, but two are not to be taken lightly. First, as a member of the tribe, you agree to assume the welfare of the tribe as a whole, and you agree that you will protect the tribe with your life."

"Wow, I've already sworn to protect the Constitution of the United States. What if the tribe went on the warpath?"

"You'd be expected to paint your face and saddle up."

"Is this contingent on the ceding of the land?"

"No, they've voted to accept your offer. See?" Carson pointed to a series of drawings. "It says so right here."

"I can't wait to send this to Lipscomb for his review," Alan chuckled.

"Oh, don't worry — they've given me this to deliver, as well," and he handed Alan a brown envelope.

Alan took his pocket knife, slit the letter, and found a legal document prepared by the Apache's tribal lawyers, laying out the terms and conditions of the transfer. Alan read it through and said, "Well, that seems to cover everything. I'll get it off to Lipscomb as soon as we get back to the office. As far as the offer of tribal membership, I'd like some time to think it over. When are they expecting my reply?"

"If you choose to accept the invitation, then there'll be an overnight ceremony this Friday evening. If you don't accept, just don't show. The tribe will not be insulted but will appreciate that you gave serious consideration to their invitation."

"Carson, tell me what would you do if you were me?"

"It's difficult for me to say. I understand fully the honor that you've been offered and also the obligations that come with it. I can only say this. If you accept the invitation, then you'll never again be alone in this world. You will be part of an extended family that will lay down their lives for you and yours."

"That's an awesome responsibility, and one that I would take seriously."

"Know this. In Apache culture, there are no written contracts. A man enters into an agreement with another man voluntarily, and his individual code of ethics is his only guideline. If you accept, then it'll be up to you to figure out your obligations."

"That seems to be an effective way to put the responsibility squarely on the individual involved."

"Yes, it does do that. I suggest that you take a long ride and think all of this through — then either come to the ceremony or not. In the meantime, what did the lawyer from Los Angeles have to say?"

"He and his boss made me an offer to buy the Circle B, but, when I told him about my agreement with the tribe, he informed me that it was an all or nothing offer and that I'd better take it."

"Or what?"

"Didn't go into the details, but he made it clear that I didn't want to have them come back to see me."

"How'd you respond?"

"I agreed that I didn't want to see them again."

"What are you going to do if they come back?"

"Make them see the error of their ways."

"You'll make a good Apache, Fighting Otter."

"Fighting Otter?"

"Yeah, that's as near as we could come to 'Killer Seal.'"

Mary Jo choked back a giggle and said, "Oh, Carson, I can't tell you how much I'm going to get a kick out of dealing with Fighting Otter. He just loves naming people."

"Yes, Cricket, I know you are. I suppose *you'll* be putting a plan together to respond to the boys from Beijing?"

"Yes, and I'll keep you in the loop."

"If things go well Friday night, then you have additional resources to consider," Carson said. "Got to be moving on," he added and left a ten-dollar bill on the table before he walked out.

Mary Jo watched Carson leave and said, "You interested in my opinion?"

"Always. On anything in particular?"

Mary Jo said, "I think you should accept the tribal invitation."

"Oh, yeah? Why?"

"Two reasons. First, you don't have any immediate family other than your uncle, and I think you'd enjoy the relationship. Second, the Apaches need someone as an advocate, someone with a sense of duty, and I believe you'd protect and support them."

"Thanks for your thoughts. You know that if all of this technology works out, we could really change the lives of a bunch of people, and, God knows, the Jicarilla need help."

"I hope you do it. I'll give you all the support that I can, beginning with handling New China. You can relax on that score; I've got your back."

Alan paid the check, and they walked back to the office. When they came in, Amy met them and said, "I looked over the tech-transfer agreement, and I think it's ready to go. I also received the intelligence file on New China and put it on Mary Jo's desk. Earl Lipscomb sent a draft of the beta-test site agreement for you, Alan. It's on your desk. And, now, I'm going to lunch."

"Have a good one, and, when you get back, I want you to send Lipscomb this draft of the land transaction prepared by the tribal council. I'll read over the MSU agreement and have it ready to go after you return."

"Great. See you in an hour or so."

"Take your time, Captain. I've got the helm."

"Very well, Commander. Try to stay between the buoys while I'm off the bridge."

"Aye aye, ma'am."

Mary Jo walked into her office and closed the door. She sat at her desk, opened a drawer, propped her feet up, and began to think. "I just assured Alan that I'd take care of the Chinese, and I will. I just have to figure out exactly how. I also need to get some help in here with the run of the mill security stuff, and I might as well get on with it, which brings me to Maurice."

Maurice Lebeaux headed up security for the Dalhousie firm, and he and Mary Jo had worked together during the investigation into the disappearance of Jake Broussard. Maurice was a retired member of the French Foreign Legion, and he and Mary Jo had developed a mutual attraction, that, so far, had resulted in a couple of dates and a chaste good-night kiss. Mary Jo thought, "Maurice and I have been hesitant to let our relationship move to the next level, and, for now, I'm okay with that. The fact is, he has all of the knowledge I need to set up Alan's security office, and I'm going to ask for his help."

Mary Jo picked up her office phone and dialed Maurice's number in Mobile. A male voice answered, "Security. This is Joe Phelps. How may I help you?"

"Joe, this is Mary Jo Thibodaux. May I speak with Maurice?"

"Hello, Miss Thibodaux. Maurice isn't in the office, but I can patch you through to his cell."

"Yes, I'd appreciate that."

There were some switching sounds and then Maurice said, "Mon Cherie, it's good to hear from you. How are things going?"

"Everything's falling into place, but I need your help."

"Of course you do. What do you need?"

"I've got to recruit a full-time head of security for Alan's new business. Has Emile briefed you on what we're doing?"

"Only to the extent that Dr. Brooks is a new client."

"I see. Well, I think I better give Emile a call and let him know that I want to talk to you. Let me do that, and I'll call you right back."

"That's a good idea. Call me on my cell. I'm taking a day off. I'm fishing on the Gulf."

"Sorry to bother you. This can wait until you're back in the office."

"Not a problem. We're headed in…in fact, we just entered Mobile Bay at Fort Morgan. Call me when you've talked to Emile."

Mary Jo dialed the Dalhousie number, and Melissa Green answered. "Hello, Mary Jo. Can I get Emile for you?"

"Hi, Melissa. Yes, please."

Emile came on the line and said, "Good afternoon, Mary Jo. You've been a busy girl."

"Yeah, I guess Earl Lipscomb is keeping you up to date."

"He is. What can I do for you?"

"I'd like to use Maurice as a resource as I set up the security system out here, but I wanted to clear it with you first."

"That won't be a problem; as you know, Maurice is very skilled."

"Great, I'll give him a call. Has Earl told you that Alan received an offer to buy the ranch?"

"Yes. I've seen all of the documents that are being prepared, including the New China offer."

"Are you aware that New China is a front for the Chinese military?"

"Earl mentioned that, and he said that they were really after the Apache's burial site and the pitchblende."

Mary Jo paused for a moment and then decided to tell Emile about the threats. When she finished, she said, "I'm working on a plan of action based on their intimidations, and I need to offload the day-to-day security issues."

"Mary Jo, you know we have some highly trained young men on staff, and Maurice may be able to help with your response to the Chinese, as well as the day-to-day security."

"Thanks, Emile. I'll be speaking with Maurice, and I'm sure he'll keep you up to date."

"I'm sure he will; call me if you need me."

"Will do," replied Mary Jo as she broke the connection.

Mary Jo called Maurice right back and said, "Emile is fine with your involvement, and I want to get started as soon as possible. In addition to the routine security issues, I need your help with a more pressing problem."

"I'm at your disposal. When do you want to fill me in?"

"I'd like to do it face to face. Let's plan on meeting late Friday afternoon."

"I've got a better idea," replied Maurice. "Let's have dinner Friday night."

"I'd like that," Mary Jo said with a smile.

"Good. I'll pick you up at 7:00."

"I'll be looking forward to seeing you."

Mary Jo went to Alan's office and tapped on the window; he looked up and motioned for her to come in. She sat in one of the wingbacked chairs and said, "I'm assuming that you'll be visiting the Jicarilla tomorrow night, and at least part of Saturday."

"Yeah. I'm going to accept the tribe's invitation. I think it's the right thing for me to do."

"I do too, so I'm going to run back to Mobile and meet the head of Dalhousie's security. I've asked him to help me get your system set up."

"Will you mention the Chinese?"

"Yeah. This guy is ex-Foreign Legion and pretty darn good in special ops."

"Alright. I trust your judgment. Well, I'd say we've accomplished quite a lot this week. Earl Lipscomb is amazing. All of the agreements are either completed or under way. Mississippi State has signed the licensing agreement, and Will has signed the test-site agreement. I'll take the signed agreement deeding the property over to the tribe with me tomorrow, and I have the letter turning down the New China offer ready to send when you tell me to do so."

"Yes, it has been an unusual week. I hope you pass the Apache initiation rites."

"Damn, I made it through SEAL training without ringing the bell. It can't be worse than that, can it?"

Mary Jo smiled. "No, probably not, and I'm sure you'll do fine. I'll tell Amy what I'm up to, and I'll plan on seeing you sometime late Monday."

"Okay, have a nice weekend. See you Monday."

TWENTY-ONE

WHEN SHE RETURNED TO HER OFFICE, Mary Jo began packing her briefcase for the trip to Mobile, but she decided to leave all of her clothes and personal gear at the ranch. She asked Amy to take her to the airport, and Mary Jo was wheels up by 3:00 and landing at Carson Air Service a little after 8:00. When Mary Jo arrived at her house, she could see the lights on in the upstairs office, where she found Allie at her desk. Mary Jo asked, "Working a little late, aren't we?"

"Yeah, I'm still trying to get the final approval for the catfish project from the Alabama environmental people. It seems you have to have an environmental permit to build anything these days."

"Any problems I can help with?"

"No, I've got it figured out; just getting it into the proper forms is all that's left. Are you home for a while?"

"I'm flying back on Monday, but I'll be here until then. Is there anything I need to do?"

"No, I'll just wind up this permit application, and I'm outta here. See you in the morning."

Mary Jo told Allie good night and headed into her own office. Mary Jo set her briefcase on the coffee table and pulled out Amy's intelligence report on New China. She put it in the center of her desk, intending to give it a good once-over. She thought, "I need a shower and something to eat before I get into this report. I think I'll start on it after I eat."

After a shower and putting on some clean jeans and a fresh t-shirt, Mary Jo rode her ten-speed the half-dozen blocks to Wentzel's Oyster House. She sat at the bar and ordered a dozen on the half shell, a dozen broiled, and an icy mug of draft beer. While she watched them shuck the oysters, she remembered her first time at Wentzel's.

Mary Jo had just left the army and planned to move to New Orleans. She was in Mobile to visit with the Dalhousie firm, and Emile asked if she liked seafood. She replied that she loved oysters in any presentation, from raw to broiled, and he had suggested Wentzel's for lunch. Wentzel's proved to be the mother church of oysters, and now she came in at least once a week.

After stuffing herself with bivalves and a couple of drafts, Mary Jo rode back to St. Louis Street and dug into the intelligence report on the Chinese. Amy's source provided not only hard intelligence but also personal assessments. New China Industries had been formed following Nixon's opening of relations with the People's Republic. It wasn't until the post-Vietnam era that they became active in seeking U.S. technology to license on the mainland. In the late sixties and the early seventies, the company concentrated on securing western technology to fuel China's emergence as a world economic powerhouse.

In 1998, the company had reorganized as a U.S. corporation, and the Chinese executives were replaced by a team of American executives recruited from top U.S. companies. The current CEO, Louis Holland III, was a 43-year-old veteran of Silicon Valley, with an MBA from Harvard. He was currently in the process of converting the corporate mission from technology acquisitions to securing essential raw materials.

The second in command was an old-school labor warrior from Detroit who ran all of the company's operating business. His name was Bill Clark, the guy who came to the meeting. In 2001, the company had floated an Initial Public Offering, and, while still majority-owned in Beijing, operated as an American publicly held company. Trading on NASDAQ under the symbol NCIEX, the corporation had a market cap of less than $500,000,000.

Mary Jo read on and found that the company currently had over 500 employees, all in California. The Board of Directors totaled six members, four of whom were U.S. citizens and two from mainland China. Both of the Chinese members were connected to the military.

Mary Jo pulled up the personal resumes of Holland and Clark and read them carefully. Holland's family had been prominent in financial, social, and governmental affairs in New Jersey. He had attended Lawrenceville for prep school and Brown for college. He was a top student and a superb athlete. He accepted an ROTC commission in the army and finished jump school and Ranger training before applying for Delta Force. He commanded a special ops team during the invasion of Grenada, and later in Africa and Bosnia. He had been awarded two Silver Stars and the Purple Heart. He was honorably discharged and completed graduate school at Harvard.

After Mary Jo finished reading Holland's file, she leaned back and thought, "Damn, this dude has been there and has all of the t-shirts. I'm surprised the Chinese would employ someone with Holland's military background. Depending on the level of training of their security force, New China could be tough nuts to crack. Let's see about Clark."

Mary Jo pulled up Clark's file and began reading. Clark was the polar opposite of Holland. He had dropped out of school after the tenth grade and soon ran afoul of the law. He spent two years in juvie. He was in and out of jail during his twenties for charges ranging from assault to robbery. He joined Ford as a labor specialist, where he quickly established himself as a union buster. Included was a psych evaluation from his juvie days, and he was suspected to be a sociopath.

When Mary Jo had finished the files, she leaned back and thought, "One guy's a well-trained soldier, and the other is a self-made thug. One is a businessman; the other is pure muscle. Together, they make formidable opponents. Which one would we rather deal with?" When she finished the report, she turned off the office lights and headed to bed, still thinking about it.

It rained overnight, but the sky had cleared by dawn, and Friday promised to be a beautiful late-August day; in fact, the front had brought cooler temps and taken the hard, hot edge off summer. Mary Jo slept until 7:00 and then made herself a cup of coffee and walked out into the courtyard. Her home was a three-story brick town house, built as a family home in the 1840s after a fire had destroyed the original 18th-century structure. The old house had seen many renovations and commercial uses since the original family sold it in

1953. Mary Jo bought the building from the estate of an attorney, and she had completely restored it, along with adding many modern conveniences, such as an elevator.

The courtyard had been sorely neglected before she purchased the property, but a local lady who specialized in New Orleans-style landscaping had been hired, and the cool, shady space had been completely redone. There were fountains, brick pathways, and fragrant and blooming plants wherever the eye turned. Mary Jo spent as much time as she could on her chaise lounge, reading and napping.

This morning, Mary Jo sat at a table with an umbrella that blocked the morning sun, sipped on her coffee, and thought about New China. All of her military training urged her to hit them where they lived and do it without warning. The only problem was that the Chinese government would not take kindly to such business. Also, she didn't think Alan would be well served by an international incident with a nation of over a billion folks.

The other course of action was to refuse their offer and wait for their response. There was always the possibility that cooler heads, such as Louis Holland, would prevail, and a confrontation might be avoided. The other possibility was that Clark would make the decision, and there was no doubt in Mary Jo's mind that he would mount an aggressive response. He couldn't ignore the challenge.

There was another option, and that was to meet with Louis Holland to see if a peaceful solution could be arranged. It would be better to negotiate than challenge them head-on, so Mary Jo decided to talk it over with Maurice at dinner tonight. She was finishing her coffee when Laurie asked, "Do you want eggs for breakfast?"

"Thank you, Laurie — an omelet would be great."

Mary Jo ate the omelet and then spent the rest of the morning working with Allie and Fred Ansley, her construction foreman, on the Ono Island sea-wall project. Fred had been overseeing the completion of a sea wall and boat dock large enough to handle a 90-foot fishing boat. They were putting the last touches on it and were scheduled to turn it over to the owner just after Labor Day.

During lunch, Allie left to run some errands, and Laurie made Mary Jo a turkey sandwich and a glass of iced tea. Mary Jo ate in the courtyard and thought about her dinner date with Maurice. She'd been out with him on a couple of occasions since the shootout at John Henry Litton's office in late May. They had enjoyed each other's company, but neither had seemed ready to take the relationship much further yet. She mused, "Maurice and I seem destined to work together, and I guess that'll always be a problem for us. I find him very attractive, and I respect his skills, and it sure would be nice to have a man in my bed. I think I need to create the opportunity for a closer look at this relationship. In fact, I think I should do that right now."

Mary Jo picked up her cell and dialed Maurice's phone. When he answered, she said, "Hey, it's me; do you have any particular plan for this evening?"

"Not really. I figured we'd go someplace where we can discuss the situation in Texas and also get something to eat."

"Could you be gone until tomorrow morning?"

"I can be gone until Monday morning; I have the weekend off."

"Good. I'm going to suggest that we go down to my beach house in Gulf Shores and eat dinner at a little diner nearby. I've got three bedrooms, and a night at the beach sounds like fun. We can talk about Texas in complete privacy."

"I like this plan. When do you want to go?"

"We should be able to get away by 5:00."

Maurice asked, "Want to take my car?" He had a fully restored 1964 Porsche 356 sports coupe, and it was his pride and joy.

"I'd love to take the Porsche, but tonight let's take my helicopter. We can be there in 15 minutes and have the rest of the time together."

"Okay, you've talked me out of the Porsche. Want me to meet you at Carson about 5:00?"

"Yeah. I may be a minute or two late but don't leave without me, and, hey, be sure to bring your swimming trunks."

"Will do; see you at 5:00."

Mary Jo went upstairs and stuck her head into Allie's office and said, "Now, I've got to get ready. I'm heading to the beach for the evening."

"Going by yourself or is Maurice coming along?"

Mary Jo smiled. "Yes, he is. Tonight might just be the night."

TWENTY-TWO

MARY JO TOOK THE ELEVATOR to her bedroom on the third floor and began packing for the trip to the beach. She'd just about finished when she came to deciding on a swimsuit. She could go from a thong number that left nothing to the imagination to a two-piece that completely covered everything. She chose a bikini.

Mary Jo stuck her head in and told Allie goodbye and then told Laurie she'd be gone until Sunday. Mary Jo drove the Ford 150 to the airport and parked in the Carson parking lot. When she walked into the lobby, she found Maurice reading a golf magazine, and, as she approached, he stood and gave her a buzz on the cheek. He looked at the small overnight bag she was carrying and said, "Good. I packed pretty light too, mostly shorts and t-shirts."

"Alright then, let's see if Doug has the helicopter ready."

In addition to the small Cessna jet, Mary Jo owned a Bell Jet Ranger. She used the helicopter on any flight that was less than two hundred miles, and she loved flying it. She managed to keep her flying skills honed between the two. Today, the Bell was parked and serviced just outside the hanger. She did a quick pre-flight check, and they loaded their bags.

Mary Jo lifted off and turned to the southeast across Mobile Bay. When she reached 2,000 feet, Fort Morgan came into view on the horizon. Fort Morgan was built before the Civil War as one of a string of brick forts guarding U.S. seaports.

Mary Jo circled the fort and sat down on a small airstrip, just behind the primary structure. There were two small single-engine planes tied down, and she parked the helicopter between them. She and Maurice tied the ship down and carried their bags over to a Jeep CJ-5, where Mary Jo removed the Jeep's top and stowed it in the back seat. When they were driving through the fort's entrance,

Maurice said, "I knew you owned a beach house, but I didn't know you could fly over here."

"Yeah, the airstrip dates back to WWII, so it's not in the best condition. Those of us who use it chip in to keep it operational, and it's great for me because it's only two miles from my house."

Mary Jo turned toward the Gulf at the entrance to the Dunes development and pulled up to her house on West Dunes Drive, which, of course, faced the Gulf. Mary Jo had designed the house to be as hurricane-proof as possible. Rather than using treated wooden pilings, she had sunk large steel pilings, and she'd used steel framing rather than wood. The house was built 15 feet above the dunes, so she pulled the Jeep underneath.

The couple took the outside steps to the deck surrounding the house and unlocked the side door. They hauled their bags up and turned on the lights, and Mary Jo decided to open some windows and turn on the attic fan. The day was too pleasant to bottle up in the air-conditioning. They walked onto the screened-in front porch and looked across the dunes to the Gulf. The sun was hanging just above the western horizon, and they could hear the rhythmic sound of breaking waves.

Maurice stood on the deck facing the Gulf and said, "You know, I've always marveled at the soothing effect of the seashore. You can feel the tension melting away."

"Yeah, I don't get over here as much as I'd like, but you're right; as soon as I get here, I feel at peace. What do you say to some wine before we leave for dinner?"

"Wine would be good; show me where it is, and I'll open a bottle."

Mary Jo led Maurice to a pantry door and showed him the small wine cooler. While he chose a bottle, she took two long-stemmed wine glasses from a cabinet. They carried their wine out to the deck and sat, propping their feet up on the rail, talking while they watched the sunset. Mary Jo avoided the subject of New China Industries, not wanting to break the spell.

As darkness set in, the two drove the Jeep down Hwy. 180 and turned into the Sassy Bass Grill. The little café shared space with a small market and a pizza place. Mary Jo ordered a dozen oysters on the half shell and the seafood gumbo, and Maurice dug into a broiled redfish.

On the way back to the beach house, Mary Jo said, "I know we need to talk about my problem with the Chinese, but let's keep tonight for ourselves. We'll have plenty of time to work on business before we leave on Sunday."

"I agree," replied Maurice. "When we get back, let's take a long walk on the beach. It's a beautiful night, and we can walk off some of the Sassy Bass."

When the couple got back, they grabbed jackets and strolled across the line of sand dunes to the beach. They started walking east toward Gulf Shores, whose lights glowed in the distance. The two strolled on the hardpan just above the surf line and took off their shoes to let the breaking waves caress their feet.

There were lights on in many of the houses, as people moved in for the weekend. All of the homes on this end of the island were privately owned, and the nearest public beach access was close to four miles down the beach. They passed several other groups of walkers, some couples and some families. The sky overhead was twinkling with a zillion stars, and the breeze from the Gulf was warm and comfortable.

Soon, Mary Jo and Maurice were on an entirely undeveloped part of the beach, which bordered the Federal Wildlife Refuge. Far in the distance, they could see the flickering light of a bonfire, where someone was having a beach party. They shared stories of past experiences they had each had at the beach, and, some of the time, they just walked in silence.

The two were a half mile or so from the bonfire when they picked up the clashing sound of rap music. As they got closer to the party, they could see four dune buggies and could hear the laughter of beer-enhanced male voices. They could see maybe a half-dozen guys standing around the bonfire. As the couple drew abreast of the party, one of the guys saw them and shouted, "Hey, come on up and join the party!"

Maurice waved in response, as he and Mary Jo continued walking. The man who had called out started jogging toward them and stopped directly in front of them, blocking their way. He appeared to be maybe in his mid-twenties, tan, with sun-bleached hair, and wearing only shorts and no shirt or shoes. He had the well-defined body of a gym rat and smiled a crooked grin. "Hey, man," he said. "Didn't you hear me? I invited you and your girlfriend to join our party."

Maurice looked back down the beach and saw the other five guys coming up behind them, blocking any thought of retreat. Maurice looked at Mary Jo and said, "You up for this?"

Mary Jo smiled. "By all means…let the games begin."

Maurice waited until the other five took up their blocking positions before he said, "Look, guys, we don't want any trouble. Just let us pass and we'll be on our way."

"Oh really," the blond guy said. "Just like that, you turn down our invitation and insult us and then ask to be on your way. Why? You think we're a bunch of pussies?"

Maurice looked dead into the eyes of the blond guy and said, "Son, you are close to getting into something that is way outside of your skill set, and you'd best back off while you can."

"I'm not your son, and you have no idea what my skill sets are. But we're reasonable people, and we'll be happy to let you pass, right after your girlfriend and I go over there behind that dune and work out a little compromise."

Maurice looked at Mary Jo and raised an eyebrow. She smiled and said, "Honey, if they'll let us go, just let me go along with what he asked. Please, don't get into a fight with them."

The blond guy moved closer to Mary Jo. "Hi. My name's Sonny. I thought you'd see it our way, sweet thing."

Mary Jo looked at the other five and said, "Okay, let's get it over with, but, please, don't hurt my boyfriend while we're gone."

Sonny grinned and said, "I'm sure he'll be just fine. These guys don't want to get all sweaty and tired out. They might want a turn behind the dunes with you themselves."

"Look, I said I'd go with you, so let's get to it."

Sonny reached out and took Mary Jo's hand and began leading her behind the dune line. As they disappeared into the night, one of the men looked at Maurice and said, "Dude, you don't seem too upset that your chick is about to get it on with another guy."

"Hell, she's a grown woman. I can't worry about it. What's the chance of getting one of those beers?"

Mary Jo followed Sonny into the dunes and, when they were out of sight from the beach, he stopped and said, "Okay, let's see what you've got. Get your clothes off."

Mary Jo slipped out of her shorts, pulled off her t-shirt, and stood in her panties and bra. She smiled and said, "Okay, honey, I showed you mine. Now, you show me yours."

Sonny began to breathe heavily and stepped out of his shorts. Just as he placed them on the ground, Mary Jo kicked him squarely between his legs and then head-butted him in the face. He fell to his knees, holding his testicles, when she gave him a full pivot and hit his head with the side of her foot. He crumpled into the sand, softly sobbing.

Mary Jo climbed to the top of the dune in her panties and bra and said, "Okay, who's next?"

One of the guys called out, "Is Sonny done?"

"I guess he is," Mary Jo replied. "He seems to have lost his erection at any rate."

The second guy trotted toward her yelling, "Don't worry; I'll bring you another one!"

After the third guy had gone behind the dunes with Mary Jo, Maurice crushed his beer can and slammed it into the face of one of the remaining two guys. He kneed him in the nuts and smashed his nose with the edge of his hand. The guy fell to the sand, and the other one took off running. He never saw Mary Jo waiting in the shadows. She tripped him, and, using her heel, she broke his nose and then kicked him between the legs. He lay quietly moaning as she rejoined Maurice near the fire. The guy that Maurice had worked on was regaining his composure, and Mary Jo grabbed him by the hair and pulled his face up close to hers. "I'm only going to say this once. Go up there and scrape your buddies out of the sand, and all of you get your crap together and get off this island. If I ever see any of you again, I'll cut your acorns off and stuff them down your throat."

Mary Jo held him by his hair and asked, "Do you understand me?"

"Yes, ma'am," he whimpered. "I understand."

Mary Jo tossed him back into the sand, looked at Maurice, and said, "C'mon, honey. Let's finish our moonlight stroll."

The hour's walk back to Mary Jo's beach house gave them time to absorb some of their extra adrenaline and a chance to talk about their mutual propensity for violence. They agreed that they would always prefer to choose fight over flight because, deep down, they enjoyed kicking some smart-mouthed bully's ass.

The confrontation had sidetracked any romantic feelings that might have developed though, and, without discussing it, they went to their separate bedrooms and fell asleep almost immediately.

On Saturday morning, Mary Jo awoke to the smell of freshly brewing coffee. She pulled on her shorts and a tee and walked out onto the deck. Maurice was sitting in a deck chair holding a steaming cup of coffee. She smiled at him and said, "Good morning. Let me grab a coffee, and I'll join you."

"Good morning to you," Maurice replied and looked back out to sea.

Mary Jo poured the coffee, came back out, and sat down beside Maurice. "Thanks for making the coffee. I'm afraid there's not much in the way of breakfast stuff on hand. I usually take a run down to the little country store just outside of Fort Morgan and grab something there."

"A run sounds good; I'm still a little pumped from last night."

"Yeah, so am I. It's about two miles to Fort Morgan and back, nothing too difficult but enough to get the old blood pumping. We can get started on a plan for dealing with the Chinese when we get back."

The two put on their running gear and started at an easy jog down the oyster-shell road toward Hwy. 180. There was no sign of life in the Dunes development, as it was too early for the average beach-goer. When they reached the store, they each picked up a biscuit and sausage and a cup of coffee, and took their food onto the back deck overlooking Mobile Bay, where they ate in silence.

When the two returned to the beach house, they both showered and put on fresh shorts and t-shirts. They returned to the deck chairs and Mary Jo said, "Since we first talked about this, I've read over an intelligence report on New China, so let me give you the Cliffs Notes version. I brought the reports with me, and you can read over them later."

Mary Jo spent the next 30 minutes briefing Maurice on the entire situation and ended by saying, "The way I see it, we've got three possible courses of action. We can hit them first; we can send in the refusal and wait to see if they react, or we can try to reason with them. Louis Holland might be a total psychopath, or he may be a reasonable businessman and a loyal American. What do you think?"

"I agree that we could hit them first and take out the leadership, and I agree that such a move would result in all manner of complications for Brooks Capital. We would quickly emerge from below the Fed's radar."

"Yeah. I think we agree that, as tempting as it is, we can discard that option," Mary Jo replied.

"The second option of waiting for their reaction is just as unacceptable. Doing so would give them the strategic advantage, and they could hit us at a time and place of their choosing. I guess that leaves us with meeting them in L.A."

"You know," Mary Jo mused, "I've been thinking about doing just that and trying to anticipate their possible reactions. I'd be interested in your thoughts. Why don't you read over the intelligence reports, while I run into town and get us some food for tonight?"

"Sounds good. What'd you plan to get?"

"I know how much you like your steaks, so I thought you could fire up the grill and cook a surf and turf. I'll get some rib-eyes and jumbo shrimp, and we can have the best of both worlds."

"That sounds perfect. Grab a bottle of Dale's Steak Sauce while you're at it."

"There's a bottle in the fridge. Anything else?"

"Yeah, get something for breakfast; I hate to run on Sunday."

"Okay, I'll be gone for an hour or so, and you should be able to finish the intel by then."

When Mary Jo returned from the Winn-Dixie, Maurice had moved inside the house and was sitting at the breakfast-nook table with the reports spread out in front of him. He looked up when he heard her and yelled out, "Need any help?"

"No, I've got it," Mary Jo yelled back.

Mary Jo put the food away, slipped into the seat opposite Maurice, and asked, "Well, what do you think?"

"I think you have access to some high-grade intelligence sources. Dare I ask?"

"Dare away; one of our associates is a highly placed officer in naval intelligence, with connections at the puzzle farm in Langley."

"Can't have too much intel — particularly professional grade. I feel like I know Louis Holland and Bill Clark."

"And what do you think?"

"I'd be willing to bet that Holland doesn't want adverse publicity. He's trying to reposition New China as an acquirer of raw material rather than technology, and, once he realizes that the Apaches own the pitchblende, he'll back off and move on. Clark, on the other hand, would be as aggressive as need be to convince Alan to change his plans. I guess meeting with Holland is our best plan of action."

"Well, since we agree, let's see if we can set up a meeting."

"Do you think you'll be able to find Holland on the weekend?"

Mary Jo said, "I bet they work 24/7. I'll give it a shot. Let me grab my laptop and go online. I can get the number for New China from our files, and we'll see if anyone's there."

Mary Jo got the number and dialed it on her cell phone. She set the phone on the table and hit speaker. After ringing several times, a professional sounding, young woman answered. "Good afternoon. New China Industries. How may I direct your call?"

"My name is Mary Jo Thibodaux with Brooks Capital. I'd like to speak to Mr. Holland, please."

"Might I ask the nature of your call, Miss Thibodaux?"

"You can tell Mr. Holland that it pertains to his offer to buy a ranch in West Texas."

"Thank you. I'll see if Mr. Holland is available."

In about a minute, Holland came on the line and said, "This is Louis Holland. How can I help you, Mrs. Thibodaux?"

"It's Miss, and I'd like to make an appointment to visit with you early next week regarding your offer to buy the Circle B Ranch."

"Interesting…why me? I believe our Mr. Clark made the offer."

"If I have my facts straight, you and Mr. Clark have different responsibilities at New China, and the purpose of my visit falls more into your area."

"I see, and just what is your area of responsibility at Brooks?"

"I'm acting head of security, but, in this matter, I have full authority to negotiate."

"I see. Well, Bill and I will be glad to meet with you, and Monday would be best for us. We want to conclude these negotiations before the deadline on Thursday."

"Monday will work for us too, and I'll bring along one of my guys, if you don't mind."

"Not at all. The more, the merrier. We'll have a lunch sent in, so why not make it about 11:00 Monday morning?"

"Thank you, Mr. Holland. We'll be at your office at 11:00 on Monday."

After the line went dead, Mary Jo looked at Maurice and raised her eyebrow. He grinned and said, "Okay, Shiva, we have our date. Let's go for a swim."

After the two changed into their bathing suits, Mary Jo and Maurice opened the storage closet under the house and pulled out two beach chairs and an umbrella. Mary Jo carried the chairs, and Maurice took the umbrella and a cooler. Once they got set up, Mary Jo raced toward the surf yelling, "Last one in is a loser!"

Mary Jo hit the surf line at full speed and dove headfirst into the incoming breaker. When she surfaced, Maurice was treading water next to her, with water running down his face. The surf was up a little, and Maurice started toward the open Gulf with long, smooth strokes.

Mary Jo was a strong swimmer, but she had trouble keeping up with Maurice. Finally, he stopped, treading water again while she caught up. "Damn," she said. "You're pretty good in the water."

"Thanks. Let's catch the next big one and body-surf in."

The two spent the next hour catching wave after wave, until Mary Jo said, "Okay, Danno, I've had enough. Let's take a break on the beach."

The swimmers dried off, sat in the beach chairs, and watched the surfbirds skim back and forth. Mary Jo opened the cooler and pulled two cold beers out. She popped the tops, handing one beer to Maurice, and they drank in silence. They both drifted off after a while, and, when they awoke, it was well after noon.

TWENTY-THREE

AFTER LUNCH, MARY JO turned on the sound system and dialed up *James Taylor Radio* on Pandora. The couple sat on the side porch with the overhead fan blowing, and both of them were soon back asleep. When they woke up, it was almost 4:00, and the afternoon was beginning to cool off.

Mary Jo asked Maurice to bring in the stuff they'd left on the beach, and she began making a salad for dinner. After stowing the gear back into the closet, Maurice pulled the grill out and emptied a bag of self-starting charcoal onto the grate. Soon, the fire was lapping at the top of the grill, and Maurice came in and looked through the wine cooler for a bottle of red.

The couple sipped the wine, while Maurice grilled the rib eyes and shrimp. Then, they ate dinner on the deck. When the meal was over, and the kitchen was cleaned, they took snifters of brandy back outside. They sat watching the lights of the freighters that were leaving Mobile Bay enter the Gulf at Fort Morgan. Mary Jo and Maurice were quiet and seemingly lost in their thoughts. Finally, Maurice reached over, turned Mary Jo's face toward his, and said, "I want you to know something. In spite of my best efforts, I'm falling in love with you. I think you have those same feelings about me, and I also think we should acknowledge them. But as much as I'd like to make love to you, I want that to happen when there are no work-related issues distracting us. I want it to be completely our time, and I don't want to share it with anyone else."

Mary Jo took his hand and looked into his eyes. "Of course I have those feelings." She took a deep breath, smiled at him, and said, "I have to confess. I had every intention of making love to you this weekend, but I agree with you. There's a real possibility for something good to develop between us, but I'd much rather let it simmer and not cram it into one weekend. Let's get this problem with the Chinese settled, take some time off, and go somewhere for a week or so, maybe even somewhere romantic, like…Paris."

"Willing to do this on my home turf, are you?" Maurice asked this with a smile, and, after a brief pause, he added, "Yes! Paris sounds great! We could even fly down to Corsica to visit my family."

"I just realized that I know absolutely nothing about your life before the Legion, so I'd like to meet your family, and I've never been to Corsica."

"You'd love the island and the people, and my *family* is a pretty interesting group. My mother died some years back, and my father, Don Ernesto Capriati, is head of Corsica's leading mafia families." Maurice paused to let Mary Jo process this shocking revelation about himself.

After what seemed like an eternity, Mary Jo said, "Wow…well, there's no doubt that you had an interesting upbringing, but what made you decide to join the Legion?"

Maurice gave her a sheepish grin and said, "I had a 'misunderstanding' with the Italian Navy regarding some import business. The Don arranged for safe passage to Marseilles and a quick enlistment. I was 17 at the time, and Lebeaux is my Legion name. My real name is Maurice Alfonso Capriati. As young as I was, I soon grew to love the Legion."

"Do you go back?"

"Oh sure, at least once a year. The Don is getting along in years, and my brothers and I all arrange to get together to be with him."

"How many siblings do you have?"

"Six: three brothers and three sisters. All of my sisters are married and live near our village, but my brothers are scattered all over the place. The oldest is a general in the French Army, the middle one a Merchant Marine Captain, and my youngest is Chief Inspector with the French police."

"Sounds like a family of overachievers to me," Mary Jo mused.

"I'm the only one without a formal education, but my problems with the navy and the police made it necessary to forgo university."

"Well, alright! I'm captivated. I can't wait to meet them all."

"Okay then. Let's put this Chinese thing to bed, and we'll head for France."

On Sunday morning, the couple did a quick cleanup and took the helicopter back to Mobile. As soon as they landed, Maurice left to go pack for their trip to Texas, and Mary Jo made arrangements to have the Cessna ready to leave by noon.

Mary Jo drove the pickup back to St. Louis Street and packed a few things she'd need to augment what she had already at the ranch. Then, she stuck the intel report into her briefcase and drove out to Carson Aviation. Maurice was waiting in the lobby, and they were airborne by 1:00.

Mary Jo had just begun her descent into the Blister airport, when Maurice commented, "It looks just like Algeria from the air; I'm expecting to see camels and nomads."

"Yeah, looks like Afghanistan too. I suppose mountain deserts look the same all over."

The two landed, taxied to the private aviation terminal, and followed the instructions from the ground crew. As Mary Jo and Maurice deplaned, the team began the tie-down, while the couple headed into the terminal. Mary Jo gave the lady at the desk instructions for the Cessna and then gave Alan a call. He said he'd head right out to get them.

When she hung up, Mary Jo turned to Maurice and said, "Alan's on his way to pick us up. I told him that we'd be in the coffee shop."

"Cool, I could use a hot cup."

The travelers got two cups of coffee and sat at a table with a view of the door. Maurice took a couple of sips and then said, "Could Dr. Brooks drop me off at a hotel on your way to the ranch?"

"I don't think so. Alan has plenty of room at the Circle B, and we'll need to leave for Los Angeles early in the morning. It'll be a lot easier for you to bunk in at the ranch."

"That's okay with me, as long as it works for Dr. Brooks."

"I'm sure Alan will be delighted to have you," Mary Jo replied.

As the two finished their coffee, Alan came through the door and looked around the room before spotting them. He signaled that he was going to get a cup of coffee and come over.

When Alan approached the table, Maurice stood and extended his hand saying, "Dr. Brooks, I'm Maurice Lebeaux. I'm glad to meet you."

"Hey, Maurice, and please call me Alan. Mary Jo's told me all about you, and I really appreciate your assistance with our security issues."

"Not a problem. Glad to help," Maurice replied.

Alan turned to Mary Jo and asked, "How was your flight?"

"Routine, just like I like them. I've invited Maurice to bunk in at the ranch."

"I assumed that he would, and Maria's fixing dinner for all of us. I've invited Pete and Amy to join us, as well."

"Good. Maurice and I plan to fly to L.A. in the morning, and dinner will give me a chance to fill everyone in on the plan for the Chinese. I assume you're now a full-fledged member of the Jicarilla Apaches. How'd it go?"

"It was one of the most moving experiences of my life. The only things that could rival it would be receiving my Eagle Scout badge and my SEAL Budweiser. I can't begin to describe the emotional impact."

"I guess we'll have to call you 'Fighting Otter' from now on."

"Oh, I think Alan will still work unless you're willing to be called Shiva."

"Touché," Mary Jo replied.

After everyone had finished their coffee, Alan suggested that they drop by the office to show Maurice around, before going to the ranch. They parked behind the building and went in the back door. They gave Maurice a quick tour and showed him the office he and Mary Jo would be sharing. Then, they returned to Alan's truck and drove out to the Circle B. As they turned into the ranch from the highway, Alan noticed Maurice taking in the lay of the land and the approaches to the main ranch house. Alan smiled to himself and thought, "This guy is a professional; he's already working on a defensive plan if we're attacked from the highway."

Alan showed Maurice to his room, while Mary Jo freshened up from the flight. When she came out, the men were sitting on the porch with drinks in hand. Mary Jo said, "Those things come like dead men? One to the box?"

Alan smiled and said, "If you'll look on the rail, there's a bourbon on the rocks waiting for you."

Mary Jo took the drink and sat beside them. Alan said, "Maurice and I've been admiring the scenery; he tells me it reminds him of his home on Corsica."

Mary Jo said, "Yeah, I think we all agree that this land has its own kind of beauty."

"Pete and Amy will be here about 6:00, so why don't y'all give me a quick rundown on your plans?"

Maurice turned to Mary Jo and raised his eyebrow. She nodded and began, "We spent most of this weekend reading the intel reports on New China and discussing our options. We finally decided to fly out to the coast tomorrow to have a try at settling the whole thing amicably. We'll meet with Clark and his boss, Louis Holland. Holland's an ex-Delta Force officer, with an MBA from Harvard. We hope he'll be open to reason."

Alan asked, "Do you think he'll be interested?"

"One would hope so. He really doesn't have an attractive alternative. Clark, on the other hand, might be prone to using intimidation."

"So what are we going to do?"

"Hope for the best and prepare for the worst," said Mary Jo.

"I've always preferred preparation to hope."

"Yeah. We'll get more into that part when Pete and Amy get here."

The trio sat nursing their drinks and watching the sun go down behind the mountains to the west. There was still a little light left when Pete and Amy drove up in Pete's black Jag convertible. The newcomers climbed the steps to the porch, and Amy said, "I think I can really get into running around with Corelli. He's got some awesome toys." She smiled at Maurice and continued, "You must be Sgt. Major Lebeaux. I'm Amy Wilson. I try to provide the adult supervision to this outfit."

Maurice clicked his heels and bent to kiss Amy's outstretched hand. He said, "I'm honored to meet you, Captain Wilson; I've read your intel reports with great interest and admiration."

"Damn, Mary Jo, you better keep a close tab on this one. I'm a fool for someone kissing my hand."

Mary Jo laughed and said, "We're both lucky to work with a trio of eligible bachelors; it's truly a target-rich environment."

"It certainly is," replied Amy.

Alan suggested that Pete and Amy fix a drink and join them, while Maria was putting dinner on the table.

After dinner, Maria served flan, coffee, and brandy, and the group settled in around the table. Amy broke the ice and said, "Have the two of you decided how to handle the Chinese?"

Mary Jo spent the next 15 minutes in a play-by-play account of their weekend's work, and, when she finished, Pete said, "I have to agree that it's better to try to talk it out, but I'm skeptical that it will work."

"I think we all share Pete's skepticism, and I fully expect there to be trouble — probably out here," Amy added.

Mary Jo said, "Maurice and I came to the same conclusion — try to make peace but prepare for other options. We'll go ahead and fly out there tomorrow to talk with Holland and Clark though. We should have a pretty good idea about their intentions when we get back."

Maurice added, "We should be back late tomorrow afternoon. Let's plan on a meeting here tomorrow evening."

"That sounds good," Alan answered.

"I'd also like to include Carson Black in that meeting."

Mary Jo looked around the table and asked, "Anyone have something else?"

No one had anything to add, and, after they'd finished their brandy, Pete and Amy left, and everyone went to bed.

After an early breakfast, Mary Jo and Maurice began getting ready to go. He stopped her and asked, "Are we going armed?"

"I suspect we'll be checked pretty thoroughly before we meet the brass, so I can't see carrying a piece. I have a plastic straight razor with a ceramic blade that's like my American Express card; I never leave home without it."

"Ditto. I have a set of ceramic knuckles that I carry for the same reason. I guess we go into the lion's den with minimum armament."

Alan dropped Mary Jo and Maurice at the airport, and they were clearing Blister by 7:00 Mountain Time. The flight plan called for a three-hour flight to Riverside Airport, the FBO nearest New China's office building. After working her way through the tangle of military and civilian air traffic blanketing the Los Angeles area, Mary Jo touched down at 9:00 Pacific Time, and, by the time they had dealt with the plane and rented a car, it was close to 10:00.

Mary Jo set the GPS in the rental to use the surface streets in order to stay off the freeways, and it took them half an hour to find New China's office building. They saw a guard shack at the entrance to the outdoor parking lot, and Mary Jo rolled down the window, smiled at the burly guard, and greeted him politely. "Good morning. I'm Mary Jo Thibodaux. We have an appointment with Mr. Holland."

The guard grinned. "Mr. Holland is expecting you. Park over there in one of those visitors' spaces, and go through the double doors over there," he said, pointing to a set of doors that led into the building.

The visitors entered the building into a formal lobby that had a receptionist desk in the center. There was a pretty Latino girl sitting at it, and Mary Jo introduced herself and Maurice, stating their business. The girl checked a clipboard and said, "Si, they are expecting you. Would you please go to the security station by the elevators?" The girl said this as she pointed to a TSA-like screening arch.

There were two guys dressed in jeans and golf shirts, which had New China Security embroidered on them, manning the arch, and one of them asked, "Are either of you carrying?"

Both indicated that they weren't, and the biggest guy said, "Walk through the arch and wait on the other side."

The couple walked through and stood waiting for the inevitable examination. The other guy used an electronic wand and gave them the standard search. When nothing was found, they were directed to a bank of elevators and told to go to the sixth floor, where someone would meet them.

The two rode up in silence, fully aware that everything was being filmed and recorded. The doors opened to a small waiting area with another receptionist. The visitors stated their business again, were offered water or coffee, and asked to take a seat. They passed on the drinks and sat, quietly waiting.

In less than a minute, a young man in a well-tailored suit came out and said, "Please, follow me." He led them to an empty conference room, and, again, offered something to drink, and this time they both accepted coffee. After the coffee was served, the young man said that Mr. Holland and Mr. Clark would be with them in a moment and left.

Clark and Holland came in together, and Clark said, "Miss Thibodaux, I remember you from the meeting in Texas, but who is this guy?"

"Good to see you again too, Bill. This is Maurice Lebeaux, a consultant to me. Maurice, this mannerless clod is Bill Clark."

The tall, well-built man standing beside Clark had a grin from ear to ear. He said, "Hello, I'm Louis Holland, and I agree. Bill is a mannerless clod, as you so aptly put it, but he's also our director of security, and we depend heavily on his advice."

They shook hands all around, and everyone took a seat. Holland said, "I see that Tim has fetched the coffee, so let's cut to the chase. Why did you want to see us this morning?"

Mary Jo said, "I anticipate that you'll be receiving our reply to your offer in the next day or so, and I also anticipate it to be a rejection. Bill made some thinly veiled threats during our last visit, and I want to make an effort to avert any unpleasantness."

Holland said, "What you're really saying is that you're here to gauge our reaction to turning down our very generous offer."

"Not so much gauge it, as an attempt to be sure that the situation doesn't get out of control," Mary Jo replied.

"You referred to Bill's making threats. It's been my experience that Bill makes promises, not threats, and as far as ensuring that the situation doesn't escalate, the answer is very simple. Accept our offer as submitted."

"Mr. Holland, I can tell you that will not happen. First, Dr. Brooks has deeded the land containing the pitchblende outcropping to the Jicarilla Apaches, and that deal is done. Also, he doesn't have any desire to sell the balance of his ranch."

"Well, I'd say that we have our answer without waiting for Thursday. I don't see the point of further discussion. Bill, let's let these folks get back to Texas and get on with our business."

Clark was red in the face and looked like he might explode. He stood and sputtered, "I don't think you know exactly who you're dealing with. This ain't some candy-assed Wall Street firm. I can promise you that you haven't heard the last of this. We'd settle this right now if I had my way."

Mary Jo looked at Maurice, as his hand slipped into his pocket and gripped the ceramic knuckles. She gave him a "cool it" look and replied, "I guess we're fortunate that you can't have your way then, aren't we? Mr. Holland, I appreciate your time, and I hope that your sensible nature will be able to prevent Bill from doing something stupid. In the meantime, we'll be getting back to Texas."

Without another word, Mary Jo and Maurice walked to the elevator and left the building. When they cleared the guard house and turned on to the city street, Maurice said, "Well, I think we know what's coming next."

Mary Jo gripped the steering wheel and replied, "Yeah, now if we only knew when, where, and how."

"I wish we had someone on the inside at New China, so we could at least know how many were coming, and when."

"I've got a funny feeling that we may already have someone on the inside. I doubt that Holland is willing to let Clark start a war. I might try to talk to him in private, so let's wait and see. Let's get back and start making our plans for *whatever* comes our way."

TWENTY-FOUR

WHEN MARY JO AND MAURICE RETURNED, Amy told them that Alan had moved the evening meeting to the office, and he planned to take everyone to Lester's for steaks afterward. Amy added that Alan had just left to meet with Ellen and would be back in time for the meeting.

Mary Jo asked Amy and Maurice to join her in the conference room, and, when everyone was seated and had a coffee, she began. "Maurice and I met with Clark and Holland this morning, and, just as we expected, Clark is really pissed. He'll try to get Alan to stop the deal with the Apaches. We have no way of knowing where or when, but we've got to prepare for it. I think we should put together a broad outline of our response before the others get here."

Amy immediately replied. "I agree. We need to think carefully through our options. We'll be hindered by considerations of legality and liabilities, while Clark can let it all hang out."

Maurice thought for a moment and then said, "In the Legion, we would have done what we had to do and then let God and France sort it all out, but, in this case, we must anticipate the aftermath and the consequences of what we do. We can't just take down a corporation because we think they're a threat. First, let's review our assets."

Mary Jo tapped her finger on the table top and said, "At the very least, we have four people with some knowledge of confrontation. Amy, I don't think you signed up for a corporate shootout, so you may want to sit this one out."

"And miss all the fun?" Amy laughed and said, "No, I'll be looking forward to taking part, and it won't be my first fight."

"Okay. I don't think that there will be a physical confrontation. Clark might want to try one, but I'm betting Holland won't allow it. Clark might try to intimidate one of us, but I doubt he'll risk inflicting physical damage; however, we have to be alert to the possibility."

Amy asked, "What do you expect them to do?"

"My guess is that they'll try to exert political or economic pressure on us. Holland is smart as hell, and he'd much rather work behind the scenes to gain his objectives. I got the sense that Holland is trying to reposition the company, and Clark is opposing the changes. They may not be as buddy-buddy as they appear. Clark, on the other hand, is more likely to want to try something physical. We'll have to prepare for both possibilities."

Amy returned to her office, and Mary Jo and Maurice poured another cup of coffee each and sat back down at the conference table. Mary Jo said, "Let's talk about security on the long-term basis. You and I have to leave Alan with a first-class setup, and I'm hoping you have some ideas on that."

"I do. I talked it over with Emile before I left Mobile, and he's agreed to let Brooks Capital hire my number-two guy, Daniel Cannon. Dan's an ex-MP officer with a wealth of experience, good instincts, and proven organizational abilities. I hate to lose him, but he deserves to move up."

"Yeah, I met him during the cleanup after the gunfight at the cannery. He seemed very capable."

"He is, and he's from Texas, so there'll be less culture shock. He'll come in understanding the local dynamic."

"That'll be a big advantage. When can he start?"

"It's up to you. He can come out tomorrow and help with the Chinese, or he can wait until the dust settles."

"Let's wait and see how tonight's meeting goes and decide then."

Maurice and Mary Jo were gathering up their empty cups to return to their offices, when Mary Jo's cell phone rang. She looked at the screen, and it said New China Industries. She motioned to Maurice to sit back down. "This is from New China; I'll put it on speaker."

Mary Jo hit the speaker button and answered, "This is Mary Jo."

"Hello, Miss Thibodaux. This is Louis Holland. I hope your flight back was pleasant."

"It was. How can I help you, Louis?"

"Well, Mary Jo, I'm glad we're on an informal basis now, and the question is…how can I help you?"

Mary Jo paused for a second and then responded, "I can think of several ways you could be of assistance to me."

"I was thinking of a possible quid pro quo."

"That sounds fair. What do you have in mind?"

"As you pointed out, I'm in the process of redeploying New China's assets in a new strategic direction. For the most part, I have the support of our officers and non-Chinese board members, but there are some who'll always want to keep to the old ways."

"Let me guess. That faction is led by Bill Clark."

"Yes. Bill just can't wrap his head around the new concept."

"Am I safe in assuming you'd like to see him gone?"

"More than safe. I've offered Bill the opportunity to take his guys and form their own security business. He refused, and I know he's planning to mount a palace coup. I can win if he does try something, but it'll cause me some heartburn, and it'll slow down my plans. I'd much rather you guys take him out for me."

"Look, Louis. I see your logic, but we aren't in the 'take him out' business."

"Of course you aren't, but I suspect you are making plans to defend yourselves when he and his boys come calling."

"Now, that's something you can depend on."

"I thought so. It also occurred to me that it might be helpful if you knew his plans ahead of time."

"Yes, that would indeed be very helpful. You mentioned a quid pro quo. What's in it for you?"

"I'll need your assurance that any official heat will fall on Clark, and I'm prepared to supply some cover for you that will deflect the whole business away from Brooks Capital and New China."

"I take it that you've abandoned plans to acquire the pitchblende deposits?"

"Of course. Once the Apaches got title, it became irrelevant, and there'd be no way I'd let a strategic material fall into foreign hands. There are too many other businesses looking for capital and management skills."

"Then, I've got to ask why you allowed Bill to make an offer?"

"Clark is tight with the Chinese, and he convinced them that no one knew about the pitchblende. He figures the Chinese could find a way to sneak it out of the country. Not very realistic, but Bill's not a realistic kind of guy."

"I got the feeling during our visit to your office that you might be having second thoughts about the whole idea of helping China. Was I right?"

"Very perceptive on your part. I hope I'm not that transparent, but, yes, I plan to seek other employment, and getting rid of Clark will allow me to leave with a hope that the company might change. Do we have a deal?"

"Well, Louis, this looks like the beginning of a mutually beneficial friendship. Lay it all out for me."

"You have to consider that Bill is no von Clausewitz, so his plan is pretty much à la Nathan Bedford Forest: show up 'firstest' with the 'mostest' and be sure that they'll be the meanest motherfuckers in the valley. He'll always try force before negotiation."

"Do you know where and when he'll make his move?"

"Yeah. He's accepted that Brooks is going to go through with giving the land to the tribe, and he intends to intimidate the Apaches into making a deal for the pitchblende."

Mary Jo asked Holland to hold for a minute, buzzed Amy, and asked for a map of the reservation. When Amy brought it in, Mary Jo pointed to an empty chair and mouthed, "Sit here." Then, Mary Jo said aloud, "Okay. I've found the reservation here on the map. How do they plan to get there?"

"Bill and his guys plan to ride their Harleys cross-country, coming into the reservation from the north."

"Okay, we know who and where. How about when?"

"They plan to show up just after midnight on Wednesday and hit the Indians just before dawn."

"What can we expect them to have in the way of weapons?"

"Just the usual personal stuff. Some of the guys prefer knives for close-in work, but all will have pistols, rifles, and shotguns. Nothing crew-served or fully automatic."

"How good are these guys?"

"Fearless. Most of them have some military experience, but they remind me of the Polish cavalry in WWII. Brave, but poorly led and totally disorganized. Don't make the mistake of pinning them down; always allow them an escape route. If they feel trapped, they'll fight to the death."

"I'd have thought you'd want that."

"No, in fact, I hope most of them decide to ride away. I just don't want Clark to be one of them."

"Will Clark lead the attack?"

"Not likely. He'll stay back and try to direct it, and I doubt if he'll take too many risks."

"Speaking of which, will they have a communications setup?"

"Just the CB system built into their helmets. They'll be on channel 8, if you want to listen in. Clark's supposed to keep me in the loop by cell phone."

"Okay. I think we can take it from here."

"I hope you can give the Apaches warning of what's coming their way."

"Louis, you needn't worry about the Apaches' ability to take care of Clark and his buddies."

"Good, I'm counting on that."

"Thanks, Louis. Like I said, we've got it from here. Is there anything else we can do for you?"

"Actually, there may be. I'd like to pull off a management buyout of my Chinese bosses. They're pushing New China close to the line where their interests and the interests of the United States conflict. I swore an oath to defend my country, and I'm getting really uncomfortable."

"That's interesting. Let me give it a little thought, and I'll be back to you ASAP."

"Please do. I'd like to keep the company intact if I can."

"You'll hear from me shortly if I think I can help."

Holland hung up, and Mary Jo looked around the table. "Now I understand how Nimitz felt before the Battle of Midway. We know what's coming and when it's coming, and we've got two days to get ready."

The group heard Alan come in the back door, and Amy got up to get him. She brought him back to the conference room, and Mary Jo said, "You're going to need a cup of coffee; we've just received a good news/bad news call from New China."

Alan poured a cup, took a seat, and said, "Okay, let's have the bad news."

"Bill Clark is planning an attack on the Jicarilla reservation," Mary Jo replied.

"And the good news?"

"We know all of his plans, and how he's going to do it."

"That should come in handy. What'd you guys do in Los Angeles...break their code?"

"No, but close. It seems that Louis Holland wants to dump the Chinese and clean up New China."

Mary Jo spent the next 15 minutes bringing Alan up to speed. When she finished, he thought for a moment and said, "What do you recommend?"

Mary Jo looked around the table and replied, "There are only two viable options, now that we know they're coming. You can alert the tribe and let them handle it, or we can take them down ourselves. Personally, I think it would be better to let the Apaches handle it. If the U.S. Army never tamed them, then it's unlikely that a bunch of thugs from L.A. will pose much of a problem."

"Yeah, why don't we wait until everyone else gets here," Alan said. He looked at his watch and continued, "I asked Pete and Carson to be here by 5:30, and it's 5:00 now."

Mary Jo said, "Okay. How'd it go with Ellen?"

"Not all that well. She's got a pretty good understanding of how securities trading works, and my explanations aren't passing her smell test. Sooner or later, I'm going to have to level with her, but I'd like to have a little more time."

Mary Jo asked, "Think she'll agree?"

"She promised to hold off until the first of September, but I doubt she'll go any further."

Mary Jo asked, "Would you like me to talk to her, girl to girl?"

"Maybe, as a last resort. I may just come clean and trust her sense of journalistic ethics."

"Did I hear you say 'trust' and 'journalistic ethics' in the same sentence?"

"Yeah. Kinda like 'military intelligence,' isn't it?"

"Watch your mouth, Commander," Amy retorted.

Alan smiled and said, "Sorry, Captain Wilson. Present company excepted. Well, I'll have to deal with Ellen after this thing with New China is done."

They all chatted for a few minutes, when Pete came bursting in the back door and yelled, "Alan!"

Amy found Pete and brought him into the conference room, where he sputtered, "Damn it, Brooks! Just what in the hell did you say to set Ellen off?"

Alan looked a little puzzled and answered, "I'm not sure, but it's been my experience that it doesn't take much to set her off."

"Well, she called me up and ate my ass out. Tells me that we have till September 1 to level with her, or all hell's gonna break loose."

"Damn, Pete. I hate to see a man who can't handle his woman. I think you need to lay the law down."

"Lay the law down, my ass. I'll just throw you and your money machine under the bus, and Ellen will be driving it."

"If we're still around come the first, then we'll deal with her then. In the meantime, we need to talk about how to deal with an imminent attack by a bunch of hoods."

"I'll face the hoods, if you'll handle Ellen," Pete replied.

Carson Black rang the back doorbell, and Amy let him in. He joined the group and took a cup of coffee and a seat. Alan stood and said, "Thanks, everyone, for coming."

Alan then motioned to Maurice, introduced him around the table, and continued: "Mary Jo and Maurice visited New China this morning, so I'll let her fill you in on that meeting and subsequent events."

Alan returned to his seat, and Mary Jo walked to the corkboard mounted beside the chalkboard. She pinned a topo map to it and walked everyone through the meeting in L.A. and her later conversation with Louis Holland. When she was done, Mary Jo paused and said, "Any questions so far?"

Carson raised his hand and asked, "Are we certain that Holland's giving us the straight poop?"

Mary Jo considered this and said, "Certain? No. But it makes logical sense that he'd be willing to let Clark be taken off the board. Maurice and I have been unable to see how he benefits from compromising Clark's plans and then selling us out. Still, we'll have to assume that he might know something we don't and be prepared for any eventuality. Alan, for what time did you make the dinner reservations?"

"I thought we'd work until about 7:00, so I made them for 8:00."

"Okay. I've been thinking about a plan that might give us the best of all outcomes, with a minimum of risk on our part. I want to run it by y'all." Mary Jo laid out her idea in broad strokes and then asked, "Well, what do y'all think?"

Amy was the first to speak up. "Mary Jo, I think it's brilliant. If we can pull this off, then all of our problems will be solved, and we'll have dodged any direct involvement."

Alan said, "Yeah, and I particularly like the fact that none of the action will be on my land. What do you think, Carson?"

"I like it. If you can make the first part work, then I believe the tribe can handle Clark and his goons — in fact, the tribe will relish the chance to put on the war paint, and, Alan, don't forget you have an extended family now."

"I don't know, Carson; I'd hate to drag the tribe into my personal problems."

"That's what family's for, and I'll bet convincing a bunch of Apache warriors to take on some L.A. thugs will be the easiest sale you ever made."

"I'll keep it in mind, but, right now, let's get to work on the logistics; we've only got two days to get it all ready."

The group worked until a little after 7:00; then, everyone headed to Lester's for steaks. Mary Jo and Maurice rode with Alan, and, on the way, she filled him in on the plan for a permanent security office and the hiring of Daniel Cannon. Alan suggested that they include

Cannon in on the New China plan, and Maurice said he'd give him a call and alert him.

After dinner, they all sat around and talked about what needed to happen to make Mary Jo's plan work. She said, "Okay, there's nothing we need that'll be all that hard to come by. First, I'll need to talk with Emile and see if he agrees that it will work."

Amy asked, "Can he do it on such short notice?"

"Two days shouldn't pose a problem."

"Maybe we should try to postpone Clark for a week, and you and I could do the whole job. Of course, the last time you tried that, you got shot down," Alan quipped.

"I went to school the last time I had to save your ass, so I'll do it my way this time," Mary Jo replied.

Soon the evening wound down, and everyone headed for home. The next day would be a busy one, and everybody agreed that a good night's sleep seemed like the ticket. On the way to the truck, Alan pulled Mary Jo aside and asked, "Do you want to share a bedroom with Maurice?"

"Want to? Yeah. But it might be better for us to have two, at least at this time. Is it that obvious?"

"Only to those of us with a certain level of sensitivity. In other words, everybody but Pete."

"Oh shit. I guess they'll just have to get over it. Hope it doesn't cause you any problem."

"No problem...just a little envy."

TWENTY-FIVE

AT BREAKFAST ON TUESDAY MORNING, Maurice asked Alan to give him a complete ride-around of the Circle B. Alan offered to do it on horseback, but Maurice asked if they had a Jeep or a Land Rover, and they agreed to use two Yamaha four-wheelers. Mary Jo dialed Emile's office in Mobile and, when Emile came on the line, she said, "Maurice and I met with Louis Holland, the CEO of New China Industries yesterday, and I want to bring you up to date."

Mary Jo walked Emile through the meeting, and, when she was done, there was a silence on the line. Finally, Emile replied, "Very interesting...are you sure the Apaches can deal with Clark and his goons?"

"Yeah. In fact, I suspect it will be a totally one-sided affair."

"Will you and Maurice be a part of it?"

"No, we'll be working on the New China end of things, which brings me to the point of this call. Do you think we can help Holland pull off an MBO?"

"There's no question that we can, but do we really want to be involved?"

"You've seen his file; he looks like a first-rate executive to me. What do you think?"

"I'd want to meet him in person before I decide."

"Let's assume he passes muster and proves to be someone we want to be in business with. Do you think we can make a deal?"

"That depends on a whole list of things. First, we'd have to do a world of due diligence to be sure we'd want to invest in New China, and then his shareholders would have to agree to sell. We don't want to get entangled in a hostile takeover."

"I see. Let me have another talk with Holland to get a little more info, and I'll get back to you after I speak with him. In the meantime, I'd like to get Dan Cannon out here as soon as possible."

"That won't be a problem; I'll send him out on the Lear later today. I'll have Melissa give Amy a call with the flight information. Call me back after you've talked with Holland."

"I'll call as soon as I know something. Thank you, Emile."

Maurice and Alan completed their survey of the Circle B just before lunch. Maria laid out sandwich makings, and everyone fixed his or her own. When they finished, Maurice said, "This is one big and beautiful spread. Alan gave me the grand tour today, and I can see why he's not interested in selling it."

Mary Jo smiled and said, "Sounds like you're falling under the Circle B's magic spell."

"It wouldn't take much to make you love it. It's a shame there is so little water because it could be a paradise with a little rain."

Alan nodded in agreement and said, "If everything works out, then we may be changing the water situation." He turned to Mary Jo and asked, "Did you have a chance to talk to Emile?"

Mary Jo replied, "The Dalhousie plane will be delivering Dan Cannon from New Orleans this afternoon. In fact, they'll be landing in a little over an hour from now, and we'll need the pickup to meet them."

Alan said, "No problem. I'll take one of the farm cars into the office. I want to check with Amy to see if we need to turn the system on for a while. Don't want to run out of cash."

Mary Jo said, "We'll bring Dan to the office and meet you."

"Okay, I'll see you when you get to the office."

Mary Jo and Maurice stood on the observation deck and watched the Lear make a graceful landing and taxi to the terminal. They were waiting as the stairway descended, and Dan Cannon came bouncing down. He was a sandy-haired guy in his mid-thirties, and he had a wide grin on his face. He stepped onto the tarmac, shook hands with Maurice, and then greeted Mary Jo. "Hello, Miss Thibodaux. It's good to see you again."

Mary Jo shook his hand and replied, "Good to see you too. We always seem to be meeting just before a fight."

"Yeah. Maurice gave me a heads-up. I suppose we need to get cracking on the Chinese deal."

By the time they had turned out of the airport, the Lear was clearing the end of the runway, heading east, and the group headed back to the office. On the way, Maurice briefed Dan on the latest developments. They parked behind the building and came in the back door. Mary Jo asked Maurice to show Dan to the security office, and she tapped on Amy's door. Amy looked up from her computer screen and said, "Hi, Mary Jo. Come on in."

Mary Jo took one of the chairs facing Amy's desk. "Have you reviewed our plan thoroughly?"

"Yes, and I think we'll have an excellent chance of success. Is something bothering you?"

"Nothing I can put my finger on, but something's nagging in the back of my mind."

"I suspect that, like every commander in history, you're wondering what could happen to wreck your battle plan."

"Yeah, that's probably it. I know that, once the shooting starts, the plan is usually out the window."

"I agree. It's impossible to consider every consequence beforehand, and adjustments have to be made while the battle rages. Even the best plan requires strong leadership, but a bad plan will be a disaster no matter what you do. In this case, I believe we have a sound plan and that we can depend on the experience of our guys to react to any surprises. You've just got a case of pre-game butterflies. You'll be fine once the balloon goes up."

"Thanks, Amy. I suppose you're right. If I'm this uptight, think how Ike must have felt on June 5."

"Same questions, just a smaller arena. Remember, you're essentially an operational soldier. If all you had to worry about was playing your part, then you'd sleep like a baby tonight."

Mary Jo thought for a moment and then asked, "Is Alan in his office?"

"As far as I know, he is. Want me to buzz him?"

"No, I'll just walk over. Thanks for the pep talk. I feel better."

"No problem. Been there myself."

Mary Jo found Alan in his office, talking on the phone. She tapped on the glass, and he motioned for her to come in. She closed the door behind her and sat in one of the wing chairs by the fireplace. When Alan hung the phone up, he said, "That was Emile; he thinks we should run the system for several hours every business day. He thinks it will establish a regular pattern and call less attention to our trading system. I'll dial it back to yield a couple of hundred thousand a day, unless we need more."

Mary Jo said, "Great! Dan Cannon is here, and I'd like to introduce you to him."

"Okay, I'm anxious to meet him. I'll get Amy to send Maurice and him in."

The two of them came in shortly, and Alan shook hands with them and suggested that everyone grab a cup of coffee and take a seat at the small conference table. When they were settled, Alan said, "Dan, I'm looking forward to working with you. Maurice tells me you're his best man, and I'd say that's high praise."

"I'll do my best to live up to that," Dan said.

"Maurice also tells me that you're a Texan. Where are you from?"

"I grew up in Odessa, and then I went to Texas A&M on a baseball scholarship. I took my ROTC commission and did a couple of deployments in Iraq."

"You were Military Police, I believe."

"Yeah, but we were mainly involved in investigating looting and the antiquities traffic. Not much in the way of regular police duties."

"I did one tour in Iraq during Desert Storm as a marine company commander; there was a lot of money floating around over there."

"Yeah, and it got worse after the fall of Saddam, particularly among the civilian contractors. Millions disappeared and were never found."

"Well, I guess you know that, for now, we're concentrating on our immediate problem, but I'll be interested in your thoughts on day-to-day security issues after we resolve this."

"After we finish with the Chinese problem, I'd like to share some ideas with you. We have a complex security situation to deal with," Dan responded.

"Complex? Tell me what you mean."

"Normally, the focus would be on protecting the personnel, premises, and data. In this case, we have to be certain that our systems and methods are kept confidential. There will be multiple people trying to figure out what we're doing."

"Give me an example," Alan said.

"We'll be trading securities on a regular basis. This will automatically attract the attention of several federal agencies. The SEC will monitor us for trading irregularities, and the Commodity Futures Trading Commission will have an interest, along with a half-dozen other federal organizations. Then, there'll be foreign governments and global competitors."

"Do you have any idea how to deal with all of it?"

"I had an opportunity to visit with the Dalhousie traders, once Maurice recommended me, and we're crafting a comprehensive plan. The basis of our plan is to duplicate monitoring stations that use the same parameters of each of the agencies or entities that are monitoring us. Think about the sonobuoys that alert us to submarine activity. These monitors will allow us to know when we show up on someone's radar."

"Damn, I never realized all of this! 'Complex' certainly describes it. Let's get the Chinese out of our hair, and we'll give this our full attention. Thank you, man. It's good to have you on board."

"Glad to be here, and don't worry about the security issues."

After 5:00, the group closed the office and headed to the ranch. Maria had prepared a light dinner, which they ate on the back deck, and then everyone turned in for the night.

Early on Wednesday morning, Alan and Mary Jo went for a morning ride and then joined Maurice and Dan for breakfast on the veranda. Maria laid out eggs, ham, bacon, sausage, grits, and biscuits. Mary Jo looked at the spread and said, "Looks like Maria is carbo-loading us."

"First rule of thumb. Eat when you can because you might not be able to later," Alan responded.

Mary Jo said, "This ought to hold us for a couple of hours. Do you plan on going to the office this morning?"

"Yeah. I'm gonna go in until noon. I've got to run the system, and then Amy and I will grab lunch and come on out. What are your plans?"

Mary Jo said, "Maurice and Dan are going to check out the security layout here at the ranch, and I've got to call Holland to go over a couple of things. We'll meet everyone back here around 3:00 this afternoon."

"I'll be sure that Pete, Amy, and I are here by then, and Carson and some of his buddies should join us."

Maria came out of the kitchen and said, "I'll have sandwiches, cold drinks, and coffee available for the rest of the day. Let me know if you need anything else."

Alan thanked her and started for town. Dan and Maurice got in the pickup and began their tour of the Circle B. Mary Jo went into Alan's home office and dialed Louis Holland's private number.

"Good morning, Mary Jo. How can I help you?"

"I told you I'd call if we had an interest in your MBO plans, and it may be possible that we do."

"And 'we' are Brooks Capital?"

"I suspect Brooks would play a part, but others would be involved, as well."

"I see. What do you need from me?"

"The first step would be a meeting with my principals. Are you available?"

"I'll make myself available. When and where?"

"Here at Brooks Capital in Pecos Springs, and sometime after Wednesday night."

"Yes, I suspect we need to see how Clark's visit to the Apaches plays out before we take the next step."

"I don't anticipate a problem with Clark, so why don't we schedule something for Friday morning?"

"I can make that happen. I'll bring updated financials on New China with me."

"Okay…consider it a plan, unless you hear differently from me. Let us know when to meet your plane."

"I'll email that info as soon as the flight is planned. See you on Friday."

"I'll pick you up at the airport," Mary Jo said.

Dan and Maurice completed their tour of the ranch, and the three of them were sitting on the front veranda eating sandwiches when Alan and Amy drove up. Pete's car was just behind them. The newcomers grabbed some sandwiches too, along with a couple of cold beers, and sat down on the porch. Alan propped his feet on the railing and asked, "How'd your recon go?"

"Great," Cannon replied. "We can devise a security plan. We can't seal off 16,000 acres, but we can know if we have intruders."

Alan looked at his watch. "It's almost 3:00, and sunset will be just before 7:00, so it'll be pitch dark by 9:00. I think I'll meet Carson and head on up to the res. It's my mess, and I need to help clean it up. I'll be back by early mid-morning if all goes well."

Mary Jo smiled and said, "Alan, you may be a SEAL, but, remember, covert warfare is the natural condition of the Apaches. Try not to get in the way."

"Carson assures me that we will only be observers unless things go badly…then it becomes our fight."

"Be safe, and we'll see you in the morning," Mary Jo said.

Just then, Carson Black's dark-green Jeep drove up, and Carson climbed up on the porch. He embraced Alan, who then suggested that they get some sandwiches and drinks to take with them.

Mary Jo hugged Black and said, "Carson, take care of yourself, and keep an eye on Fighting Otter, as well."

"Yeah, we'll let the tribal 'swat squad' handle Mr. Clark, but we'll be ready to help if we're needed."

"Tell me about your squad," Mary Jo said.

"The tribal police have seven men who are the fiercest warriors in the tribe. They also have all been to the FBI academy for additional training, but, tonight, I suspect they'll rely on the proven Apache methods of warfare. I'll be there as an observer from the Rangers."

"Do you think seven men and one Ranger will be enough?"

"It better be. Remember, the governor of Texas once sent a single Ranger to break up a race riot."

"Okay. Just let us hear from you when you can," Mary Jo said.

Carson and Alan got in the green Jeep, and Alan said, "See you in the morning," as they drove away.

Mary Jo watched them until they were out of sight, and then she asked Amy and Maurice to join her in Alan's home office while she called Emile.

Everyone gathered around the speakerphone as Emile was connected. He said, "Mary Jo, were you able to get in touch with Louis Holland?"

"I was, and he plans to be in Brooks Capitals' office on Friday morning. Will that work for you?"

"Yeah, I cleared my calendar awaiting word from you. I meant to ask you to see that he brings fresh financials, but we can use those in the New China annual report and their latest 10-Q. My team will have reviewed them by the time of the meeting and be ready to talk to Holland. I'm bringing Earl and my mergers and acquisitions guys along."

"Holland said that he would bring the latest financials, so you'll at least have them to compare. When do you plan to get here?"

"We'll take the Lear and leave close to 7:00. We should touch down before 10:00."

"We'll have someone meet your plane, so give me a call when you're 30 minutes out. Look forward to seeing you."

"Until Friday morning," Emile replied, and the line went dead. Amy and Pete joined Mary Jo and Maurice on the front porch, and everyone polished off the remaining sandwiches and cold drinks. They watched the sun set until it was fully dark. Then, Amy and Pete left for town, and Mary Jo, Maurice, and Dan Cannon went to their rooms for the night.

TWENTY-SIX

BILL CLARK AND TWO OF HIS MEN sat around a table in dimly lit King of the Road, a biker bar in Carlsbad, New Mexico. There was a USGS topo map spread across the table, and Clark focused his penlight on the area just south of Carlsbad. He pointed to U.S. 180 leading southwest to the small village of White City and said, "The reservation straddles the Mexico-Texas state line. We'll have to cross-country from there. As best as I can tell, it's about 15 miles to the main settlement on the reservation. Here's an aerial photo of the settlement, and I've circled the chief's home." Bill passed a photo around. The bigger of the two men asserted that they should be able to ride right up to the chief's front door at two in the morning without being seen.

"Damn, Jocko, ain't you ever been on an Indian reservation? They ain't got much, and most of them will be drunk in bed, but they'll have a hundred stray dogs all over the place. We'll stop on this ridge just north of the town and scope it out before we go charging in," Clark growled.

The other guy agreed with Clark and said, "Bill's right. Cora and I rode out to the reservation between Albuquerque and Santa Fe to check it out. You ain't never seen as poor a place. It made Nam look like a regular country. Everybody we saw was either drunk or passed out. If it hadn't been for the dogs, you'd have thought it was deserted."

"If they'll all be drunk, why don't we just ride in and let the chief know what we want him to do? What makes these Indians different?"

"They're not. An Indian is an Indian, but we're still going to be careful. I don't want to have to kill any more than necessary."

"Well, like the old saying goes, 'the only good Indian is a dead Indian.' Let's do it the easy way and get the hell back to L.A.," Jocko answered.

Clark looked at his watch and said, "We better get going; I want to be on that ridge by midnight."

The three of them cranked their Harleys and pulled out of the bar. None of them noticed the man sitting in his pickup truck talking on his cell phone. They hit U.S. 180 on the edge of Carlsbad and roared into the night. They rode single file until they came to a sign that read:

STOP HERE!
YOU ARE ENTERING THE JICARILLA APACHE
RESERVATION.
NO TRESPASSING.
STOP HERE!

The three riders blew by the sign without slowing down, and, again, they failed to see the man sitting on a rock with a cell phone. They rode for five miles or so, and then Clark turned left off the road and started cross-country. This was duly reported by the man following them on a four-wheeler without lights.

The three riders slowed down to move across the open desert but didn't bother to turn off their headlights. Finally, they reached a dry creek bed with a ridge rising to the southwest. They parked their bikes in the creek bed and began to climb the ridge. When they reached the top, they dropped to their knees and saw the lights of the tribal center in the distance.

Clark pulled a pair of high-powered night binoculars from his pocket and began to sweep the area between the ridge and the town. He saw nothing. He turned to Jocko and said, "I want you to work your way down to the right of the town until you reach the first house. When you get there, give me a call on my cell. Blackie, you do the same to the left side. Both of you check your phones and make sure they're on vibrate."

Both men grunted and began to slip down the hillside, and Clark watched through the binoculars as they descended toward the glimmering lights. Soon, both men slipped below the shoulder of the ridge, and Clark put down the glasses and waited to hear from them.

Jocko Morgan had been an 18-year-old tunnel rat in the last days of Vietnam, and he could move like a phantom. He glided down the ridge, keeping low, until he heard the first dog bark. He dropped to the ground and started a low crawl toward his objective on the edge of the housing development. He finally reached the back corner of the house, when he bumped into something soft. He reached out and touched a leather-wrapped leg, and he looked up just in time to see the steel hatchet as it pierced his skull.

While Jocko was meeting the angels on the right side of town, Blackie Dolph had managed to reach his designated house, where he stood against the back wall in the shadows. He fumbled in his pocket for his cell phone, just as the arrow slapped into his chest and punctured his heart. He was dead before he hit the ground.

Bill Clark watched for signs of life. He could see both of the houses, and the dim lights of the town had little effect on his night vision. He could see the millions of stars gleaming overhead. Bill Clark was not one to dwell on the wonders of nature, but even he had to admit that you'd never be able to see this in a city like Los Angeles. There was a warm breeze coming from the north, carrying the sweet smell of wild desert flowers, and he took it all in.

Bill looked at his watch and saw that Jocko and Blackie had been gone for over 15 minutes, plenty of time to have reached the outskirts of the town. Bill swept the village with his glasses but couldn't see any movement. He dialed Jocko's cell phone, and there was no answer, so he tried Blackie and got the same result. Bill decided that they were unable to risk a cell conversation, so he texted both of them to come back and meet him in the creek bed near the bikes.

Clark put the glasses back in his pocket and began to work his way to the creek bed. He dropped down into the sand and tried to determine which direction the other two had parked the bikes. Bill decided to walk to his left and went about a hundred yards before turning around and retracing his steps. He could see his footprints in the moonlight, so he continued for another hundred yards before he stopped and thought, "How in the hell can I lose three Harley Davidsons in a creek bed?"

Clark was pondering the situation when he looked up and saw an Indian in full war paint, staring down from the top of the creek bank. The Indian stood motionless, holding a war lance. Clark quickly reached inside his jacket and pulled his Browning 9MM free of its holster. He was bringing it up when the lance pierced his chest and severed his spinal cord. Bill never felt it.

Alan and Carson were sitting in the tribal police headquarters watching the action on GoPro cameras, and, when it was over, Carson said, "Looks a lot like the tribal swat squad was able to detect and prevent an act of terrorism to me. I saw nothing to concern the Texas Rangers…did you?"

Alan grinned and replied, "Not a thing. I guess our work here is done. I think I'll head on back to the ranch."

***

Thursday morning, Mary Jo, Maurice, and Dan Cannon were sitting around the conference room at Brooks Capital discussing the security arrangements, when they heard Alan come in the back door. He stopped by Amy's office, and the two of them went into the conference room. Alan looked tired, but he had a big grin on his face. He poured a cup of coffee and then gave them the news they'd been anxious to hear. "I'm pleased to report that the threat to the reservation has been neutralized, and we can be assured that Clark will no longer pose a problem for anyone. The New Mexico State Police have located three Harley Davidsons in the parking lot of a Carlsbad biker bar. The motorcycles are registered to Clark and two other employees of New China Industries. It seems the three of them left the bar around midnight last night and haven't been seen since. I'm sure that New Mexico will investigate their disappearances, but it won't involve any of our friends. Mary Jo, when we meet with Holland in the morning, you'll be able to tell him that the quid pro quo has been satisfied."

As though the events of the previous evening were an everyday occurrence, Alan moved on to the next order of business. "So, now that this not only serious but also untimely threat has been dealt with, we can move on to more productive projects. Let me bring everyone up to speed on what's going on with the decimal harvesting. First, the system is running without a hitch. We're booking profits of several hundred-thousand dollars a day, and we have the capacity to do more, if needed."

Amy held up her hand, and Alan nodded to her. "I've checked with our friends at Dalhousie, and all of our trading activity is blending into the general market, so there's no trace of a problem."

"Since that was an obvious and huge potential problem, that is, of course, excellent news," Alan replied. "We've completed the handover of the pitchblende deposits to the Jicarilla, and all of the paperwork has been signed and the title passed. Now, we're in the process of negotiating a joint development agreement that will provide for Brooks Capital to supply the necessary capital for a 5% profit sharing. Our profits from the deal will be used to fund an educational trust for the tribe."

Alan paused for a moment and then said, "Pete, would you be willing to serve as our liaison with the Jicarilla? Now that I'm a member of the tribe, it might be a conflict of interest for me to do it."

Pete smiled and said, "I'd be honored, Fighting Otter."

Alan gave him the finger and continued: "We've signed the licensing agreement with Mississippi State University for the commercial rights to the atmospheric electrical generation system that Professor Vassily Volanov developed. We've also completed an agreement with Will Ransom, who's going to conduct the initial test of the technology on his Mississippi farm. Brooks Capital will be funding this project, e.g., the cost of the construction of the tower, and Will has an arrangement with the local REA to buy any excess energy we might produce."

Dan Cannon held up his hand and asked, "Do we have a timetable for these tests in Mississippi?"

Alan answered, "Not yet. You and I will have to meet with Will to see what we're looking at. We'll get on to that next week. While Dan has our attention, let me make those of you, who don't already know it, aware of what his part will be in our operation. Mary Jo and Maurice have recruited Dan as our permanent head of security. Dan was serving as Maurice's number-two guy at Dalhousie until he agreed to our offer. He'll be building a security system to protect not only our facilities and our people but also our trading system. It's a daunting challenge, particularly where the trading system is concerned, but one Maurice and Dan have convinced me he can handle with confidence."

Alan concluded, "So that's about it for now, but, in case you forget and in order to keep you all energized, I'd like to reiterate our principal purpose. We're seeking technologies that will provide clean and abundant water for the foreseeable future. We want to develop technology that can provide other clean, efficient, and renewable sources of energy, and, finally, we want to provide support for and cultivate a variety of health, educational, and enriching projects that will benefit the world at large. As overly ambitious as this may sound, we're about to generate enough available resources to easily make all of it happen, and I, for one, am pretty damned excited about it."

Friday morning, Mary Jo met Louis Holland at the airport, and the two of them sat in the coffee shop awaiting the arrival of the Dalhousie jet, which was still a half-hour out. While they waited, Mary Jo gave Holland a rundown of what had happened with Bill Clark. When she finished, he said, "That's it? They just disappeared from a biker bar in New Mexico?"

"So it seems. The New Mexico State Police will probably be calling to see if you know why they were in Carlsbad."

"Well, all I can tell them is that Bill and his buddies like to take road trips and that the world's a better place if we never hear from them again. I guess we can consider the deal done and move on to my MBO."

Mary Jo's cell rang, and Emile told her that they were making their final approach into Blister. Mary Jo and Holland met them in the lobby, and Emile introduced Earl Lipscomb and Harry Dunn, the Dalhousie head of Mergers and Acquisitions. They all loaded up and drove over to Brooks Capital, where they joined Alan, Pete, and Amy around the conference table.

Once all of the introductions were made around the table, Alan turned the meeting over to Emile, who thanked Alan and began: "Mr. Holland, it's my understanding that you wish to pursue a management buyout of your company. Is that correct?"

"Yes. I think the company has many opportunities to grow both internally and by acquiring smaller companies in need of capital and management skills."

Emile said, "I see. We've had the opportunity to study your annual report and your latest 10-Q. If we have it right, New China has 50,000,000 shares issued, and the current share price is $9.87, giving the corporation a capital value of $493,500,000. Your Chinese shareholders own 59% of the outstanding shares, leaving 41% in the hands of all other shareholders. You own 4.8% of the shares personally, at a value of $23,688,000. Are we accurate?"

"Yes, you're spot on so far."

"When we look at the balance sheet, we find assets valued at $876,566,000, liabilities of $534,566,000, and a net worth of $342,010,000. In the first half of this year, New China had a taxable profit of $43,688,000. On an annualized basis, that would be a little less than $.18 per share, for a P/E of nearly 55, and the company is trading at a premium to its book value of almost 50%. We feel that the company's market value is highly inflated, and an MBO makes no sense at these levels."

Louis Holland paused for a moment and then said, "I'm aware of these numbers, and I agree that a successful MBO would have to be done at a discount to market value. It's my plan to offer the Chinese book value for their 59%, or close to $200,000,000. I'm hoping to raise funds through a combination of debt and equity. I don't believe we would be sitting around this table if you didn't have an interest. Share that with me, if you're willing."

"Even at the discount to market value, I believe we have a better idea," Emile replied.

"We don't have much interest in taking over New China, but we do have a great deal of interest in doing business with Louis Holland. Rather than buy the Chinese out for $200,000,000, we suggest you sell your shares to them at market value and reinvest the proceeds with us in a new operating company. We will provide almost unlimited capital, and you will provide an experienced CEO. We would propose an ownership split of 25% for your investment of

$20,000,000, and we will put up $150,000,000 for the balance of ownership. Think you might be interested?"

"You're offering me 25% of a new company worth $170,000,000 for $20,000,000, and you ask if I'm interested? You bet I am. I'm not sure why you're doing it, but I'm all for it."

Emile looked at Holland and replied, "Louis, we invest in people, not concepts. We have done extensive research on you and your skills, and we feel like you're a sound investment."

"I'm very flattered. I've tried to build a company that's a good place to work, while building shareholder value. It's nice for someone to recognize it. The only problem we might have is convincing the Chinese to release me from my employment contract, and to buy my stock. As you know, it's restricted and cannot be sold on the open market without their approval."

"Louis, the Dalhousie firm has extensive interests in China and sound relations with the government. Let me worry about your stock. I'll be surprised if you don't get a premium to market value, as well as all of your exit package. Now, let's go to work on making all of this come about. Are you free to come to Mobile early next week?"

"I can be there on Monday morning. I'll fly commercial to avoid any suggestion of a conflict of interest."

"We can get a lot done today and then resume on Monday. We'll pick you up at the airport, and you can stay in our guest cottage while you're there."

When Emile finished, Alan stood and said, "Louis, glad to have you on board. Emile and the team from Dalhousie will hammer out the details, and, in the meantime, the rest of us have work to do, so we'll leave y'all to it."

Everyone spent the balance of the day working on his or her specific project. Finally, at close to 4:00, Emile announced that his team and Louis Holland had finished for the day and that both would be heading home. Dan Cannon drove them to the airport and joined everyone in the conference room when he returned.

TWENTY-SEVEN

WHEN THEY ALL REASSEMBLED, Alan addressed the group. "Because Mary Jo and Maurice will be returning to their day jobs tomorrow, I'm throwing a little farewell dinner tonight at the Circle B, and I hope all of you will be there. Cesar and Maria are roasting hogs and goats, so I can promise a real West Texas feast. Since tomorrow is Saturday, I want everyone to take the weekend to get caught up on some sleep, and we'll hit the ground running on Monday. Anyone have any questions?"

Pete Corelli raised his hand and said, "Could you find a moment to sit down with Ellen and bring her into our plans, so she'll get off my back?"

"Of course! She's begrudgingly allowed us the time to get set up, and I promised her a story, so I'll give her the whole ball of wax now. She can decide how to handle it. Be sure to invite her to tonight's dinner."

"Oh, she'll be there."

Alan asked, "Anyone else got a question? If not, let's get out of here, and I'll see everyone tonight."

Mary Jo and Maurice drove the pickup back to the ranch, and Dan rode with Alan. Once Mary Jo and Maurice were alone, Maurice said, "Having any regrets about Clark?"

"Yeah. I'd rather he hadn't come, but, when you think about it, that was never in the cards and deep down I knew it."

"Clark was one of those misfits who would never adapt to a civilized world. We're all better off now that he's gone," Maurice replied.

"Yeah, I agree. But then you and I are cut from the same bolt of cloth; we just disguise it better."

"I prefer to think we recognize the laws of human intercourse and try to acclimate. There's a big difference between you and me and your garden-variety psychopath."

"I hope you're right, but sometimes I wonder."

When the couple arrived at the ranch, Alan was standing near the creek talking to Cesar and Pablo. He waved and motioned for them to come on down. When Mary Jo and Maurice got nearer, they could see a mound of dirt with smoke venting through a pipe that was stuck in one end. The odor of roasting meat filled the creek bottom. Alan said, "Thought y'all might like to see tonight's dinner in the making."

Mary Jo sniffed the air and said, "Didn't realize how hungry I was until I caught that wonderful aroma."

"Well, you're in luck; Maria has a huge pot of her chili simmering for our lunch. Let's go grab a bowl and eat on the porch."

After consuming the delicious bowls of chili, Alan left to go over some ranch business, and Maurice and Mary Jo opted for an afternoon nap. Mary Jo was dead to the world when her mental alarm went off. She began to get ready for the evening, took a long, hot shower, and dressed in fresh jeans and a cotton button-down shirt. She threw a sweater over her shoulders in case the night air was cool. When Mary Jo stepped onto the porch, Maurice and Dan were sitting with beers in their hands. Mary Jo spotted the cooler and pulled the tab on a cold Coors. She took a sip and said, "If every swallow of beer tasted as good as the first one, I'd be a beer drinker."

"I can't see you giving up your bourbon," Maurice said.

"Probably not, but an occasional beer is pretty good. Where's Alan?"

Maurice pointed toward the creek and said, "He's down there helping get everything set up for dinner."

Mary Jo saw Alan and Cesar putting a table and chairs under a large tent near the firepit. She said, "I guess Alan doesn't need any help."

Maurice said, "We offered, and he told us to enjoy the sunset and relax."

"What time do we to eat?"

"Everyone is supposed to be here for cocktails by 6:00, so they should show up soon," Maurice answered.

A few minutes later, Pete and Ellen drove up with Amy. Mary Jo acted as hostess and made sure that they had drinks and some of Maria's party tacos. Carson Black's Jeep pulled up and parked, and he came bounding up the stairs with a broad smile on his face. Everyone was trading stories, when Alan walked up and said, "Let's move down to the tent! Cesar's about to open the pit and begin serving dinner."

The friends walked on down to the creek and found seats at a long table. Alan sat at the head. He stood, tapped his wine glass, and said, "Welcome to the Circle B, everybody! Tonight, we're celebrating the founding of Brooks Capital and the resolution of a major problem. Ellen, you'll hear some things tonight that won't make much sense, but bear with us. Tomorrow, I'll answer all the questions you have, but, for tonight, just try to roll with the punches."

Ellen raised her wine glass and said, "You might just be surprised at what I know already, but here's to Brooks Capital and to those intrepid souls who dealt with the Chinese."

Everyone raised their glasses and said, "Hear, hear."

"Okay," Alan said. "Let's all get up and serve our plates with some of Cesar's roast pig and goat, and the wonderful side dishes Maria's made. This is a genuine Texas BBQ. Enjoy it, y'all!"

The diners filled their plates with heaping mounds of roast pig, goat, and delicious side dishes, and soon sighs of satisfaction reverberated throughout the tent. When they'd all eaten as much as they could possibly hold, dessert and coffee were served. Alan stood. "Okay, let's get started with the fun part of the evening. My recent windfall has put me in a position to show some well-deserved appreciation. To that end, I've got some gifts I'd like to distribute."

Alan reached under the table, placed a large box in front of him, and continued: "First on my appreciation list are Cesar and his ranch hands, who give me the support I need to keep this place going. They work hard, and they don't have any recreational facilities close by."

Alan reached into the box, pulled out a rolled-up blueprint, and spread it on the table. "Here are the plans for a rec center to be built down here on the creek bank. The center will include a giant TV, a pool table, and a swimming pool for the kids."

Everybody clapped, and Alan went on. "Cesar and Maria have never had a honeymoon or a vacation trip, so here are three tickets for a two-week cruise in the Caribbean for them and Maria's mother, Inez."

Alan motioned for Cesar to come up, and Alan immediately gave him a bear hug. "Y'all have a wonderful time, and don't worry about what's going on here."

Cesar had tears in his eyes and said, "Muchas gracias, Señor Brooks. Muchas gracias."

Alan continued, "For the newest member of our team and native Texan, Dan Cannon, I picked something practical for him to use in his work."

Cesar came in, carrying a drone with a six-foot wingspan, and put it on a side table. Alan handed Dan a set of operating instructions. "The Circle B is big and empty. This may make your security job a little easier."

Maurice leaned over and whispered to Mary Jo. "Did you see Dan's eyes light up? Every boy wants his own radio-controlled model airplane, and Dan just got the best one available."

"He'll probably leave early to try it out," Mary Jo laughed.

Alan turned to Carson Black, smiled, and said, "We Apache have always envied the white man's guns. We had to steal from him to be able to fight. Well, Carson, your gun-stealing days are over."

Alan reached into the box, pulled out a Henry Golden Boy lever-action rifle, and handed it to Carson. Carson held the rifle and worked the lever. He then said, "You are wise, Fighting Otter. Very wise, indeed. Thank you."

Everyone laughed and clapped, and, when the applause died down, Alan said, "The next gift was almost impossible. What do you get for someone who has every toy known to man? Pete Corelli has been my friend, and my go-to guy, since I protected his scrawny ass on the high school football field, and I was determined to find something he didn't have."

About this time, Cesar came into the tent holding a black puppy and handed it to Pete, who looked utterly shocked. Alan laughed and said, "Otto, my German shepherd, sired a litter of puppies six weeks ago, and Corelli now owns the runt."

Ellen choked down a giggle and said, "Finally, Corelli has something to be responsible for. I hope he's not housebroken."

The puppy curled up in Pete's arms and promptly fell asleep. Pete rubbed the puppy's ears and said, "Don't forget the operating manual, and, by the way, what's his name?"

"According to the AKA, he's Otto Maximilian von Brandenburg, but we call him Max."

Pete looked at the little dog and said, "Thanks, man. I'll have to admit…you found something I'd never buy for myself, but I love it."

Alan then turned to Mary Jo and said, "I first met Mary Jo Thibodaux when the Taliban shot our helicopter down. Despite injuries that would later hospitalize her, she led a recon of the enemy's position that allowed us to completely rout them. I gave her the code name Shiva the Destroyer that night. When I started Brooks Capital, I called Shiva and asked for her help. She introduced me to Emile Dalhousie, and Mary Jo's skillfully set up our security system. Tomorrow, she returns to Mobile and her Civil Engineering firm, but we're indebted to her for finding Dan Cannon to take over security."

Alan continued: "I'd like to announce that Mary Jo's firm will design the pitchblende-extraction facility on the Jicarilla reservation, the energy-recovery project in Mississippi, and any other such projects that Brooks Capital might become involved with. I hope we're able to keep her busy for years to come. Let's give Shiva a hand!"

When the applause for Mary Jo died down, Alan said, "My great-grandfather served in the AEF during WWI, and, while he was in France, he managed to find a case of 1865 Chateau Boutelleau Cognac. It's been a Brooks family tradition to open a bottle for special occasions, and we're gonna try a snifter tonight."

Maria came in with a silver tray of crystal brandy snifters and passed them out, while Alan held a bottle and carefully opened it. He wiped the neck of the bottle and began serving everyone an inch of the amber liquid. When they all had warmed and swirled their glasses, Alan raised his and shouted:

"Here's to us,
and those like us.
Damn few, and *they're* probably dead.
Cheers!"

The friends raised their glasses and took sips, and a murmur of approval filled the tent. Alan continued, "Thank you all for your support. Let's try to make a difference. Now, the bar is open, so let's have a party."

TWENTY-EIGHT

ON FRIDAY MORNING, Mary Jo joined Alan, Dan, and Maurice for coffee on the veranda, followed by breakfast at the dining-room table. Maria had cooked a full ranch breakfast, including huevos rancheros, country ham, and hot biscuits. Everyone overate, and, when they were on their last cups of coffee, Mary Jo said, "Well, Alan, Maurice and I need to head for the airport, but I want to thank you again for including me in this little adventure."

Alan smiled and said, "Mary Jo, I'll never be able to thank you for what you've done. You'll be involved as we test the power source and build the pitchblende plant, so we'll be working together a lot. Is there anything you'd like to see Brooks Capital do?"

Mary Jo paused and then said, "As you alluded to last night, this is the type of thing that will make a huge difference, and it'll likely open up many similar opportunities."

After breakfast, Mary Jo and Maurice packed their bags, and Alan took them to the airport. Mary Jo and Maurice were airborne by 10:00. Once the little jet had reached cruising altitude, Mary Jo turned to Maurice, who was sitting in the co-pilot's seat, and said, "I thought last night went well."

"Yeah, so do I. That cognac was the best I've ever had, and the Don has some great stuff. I'd like to take him a bottle as a gift when we go to Corsica."

"You probably ought to come up with a plan B. I googled the label last night, and it's close to $6,000 per bottle."

"No shit! I guess it *was* good. Perhaps I can find something when we're in Paris that will be good at a tenth of the price. Alan should have bought a bottle of Remy Martin and saved the good stuff."

"Believe me…Alan can afford to buy it, by the case, if he wants to."

"Yeah, I guess he can at that. His system is idling in neutral and still dragging in $100,000 per day. That'll buy a bunch of brandy."

"And most anything else he wants."

The couple chatted about their trip to Paris and decided to go in December. They could be in Paris for a week and then spend Christmas in Corsica. The sunny Mediterranean would be a welcome relief after several winter days in Paris.

It was nearly 3:00 when the two landed in Mobile, and Mary Jo dropped Maurice off at the Dalhousie compound. Mary Jo parked in the visitor parking lot, leaned over, and gave Maurice a lingering kiss. He smiled and said, "Give me a day or two to catch up, and then let me take you to dinner."

"I'm going to New Orleans at the end of next week to see a client. Maybe you could come over on Friday, and we'll spend the weekend together."

"That sounds nice; I'll make some hotel reservations."

"No need. I own a house on Esplanade, just on the edge of the Quarter…we can stay there."

"Okay. Do you own any restaurants? If not, I'll make us some reservations."

"No, no restaurants, but, if you have a problem, I have a contact at most of the top ones. Remember, this is my part of the world. I'll leave Paris up to you."

"That's a deal. My family owns a flat just off Avenue St. Germaine on the Left Bank, and I'll reserve it for us…and restaurant reservations will be no problem. The children of Mafia Dons can usually get in."

"Okay! You handle Paris, and leave New Orleans to me," Mary Jo replied and drove away.

When Mary Jo pulled up to her town house, she opened the gate and parked in the garage. After she unloaded her bags, she entered through the kitchen door and found Laurie puttering around the stove top, stirring something with a wooden spoon. Laurie broke into a huge grin when Mary Jo came in. "Lawdy me! It's good to see you! I hope you're home for a while."

Mary Jo said, "It's good to see you too, and, other than a weekend in New Orleans, I don't have any travel plans anytime soon. What's on the stove?"

"I'm making oyster soup for dinner," Laurie replied.

"When will it be ready? I haven't had time for lunch, and I'm starving."

"Give me 10 minutes, and it'll be on the table."

"Great. I'll just take my bag upstairs and be right back down."

"Some flowers came for you this morning. They're on the table in the dining room."

Mary Jo took her bag up to her room and came back down to Allie's office on the second floor. Allie was on the phone and waved her in. When Allie finished her call, she smiled at Mary Jo and said, "That was Emile alerting me to a rather large addition to our account. I guess your trip was a success."

"I believe it was, and we'll be getting a lot of engineering work in the near future. I think you and I need to talk about hiring some help."

"I've been thinking about that and want to suggest we outsource, rather than hire additional personnel. The somewhat delicate nature of our secondary work requires total discretion, and the more people who are here, the greater the risk."

Mary Jo thought for a moment and then said, "Okay. I think you're dead on. I suspect we'll continue to take on alternate projects, and I agree that the fewer folks around here, the better. See if you can make arrangements to outsource our overflow."

"I'll get on it. We're set up to hand over the Ono Island project on Tuesday, and, by the way, you've been receiving flowers all morning."

"Yeah. Laurie said there were some in the dining room. Guess I better go check them out. See you after lunch."

Mary Jo took the elevator down and walked into the dining room. The table was covered with vase after vase of flowers. The closest arrangement was a couple of dozen yellow roses from which she pulled a card.

Just a taste of what's waiting for you in Paris…Maurice

"He must have called these in before we left Texas. They're lovely," Mary Jo thought and moved to the second arrangement, which included a dozen red roses. She read the card.

Mary Jo,
Don't forget our dinner date when you hand over the project. I've made all of the arrangements. Call for details. Bill Thornton

Mary Jo paused for a minute, trying to remember just who the hell Bill Thornton was and then it came her. He was the owner of the Ono Island project, and she had sort of agreed to go to dinner with him.

The last flower arrangement was at least three dozen black roses. Mary Jo reached for the card.

Shiva,
Thanks for keeping your promise. I'd like to take you to dinner the next time you're in L.A.
Louis

Mary Jo smiled and thought, "Two dinners and a trip to Paris. You wait ages for a bus and then three come along all at once."

ABOUT THE AUTHOR
THOMAS RAINER LAWRENCE
September 6, 1939 – March 22, 2017

Photograph: Tim Patton

A son of the Mississippi Delta, Thomas R. Lawrence was a retired venture capitalist and self-proclaimed serial entrepreneur. He was a graduate of Mississippi State University, and he remained an avid Mississippi State University Bulldog fan throughout his life. Tom founded *Front Porch Press, LLC* (to provide an outlet for new Southern writers) and *Porchscene: Exploring Southern Culture*, www.porchscene.com, an online blog. Tom was residing in Opelika, Alabama, at the time of his death in March of 2017.

Other books by Tom Lawrence are available at www.amazon.com, www.barnesandnoble.com, and www.frontporchpressllc.com.

www.ingramcontent.com/pod-product-compliance
Lightning Source LLC
Chambersburg PA
CBHW050511260626
47157CB00004B/1279